Sticky Fingers

Jodie's nerves were wound so tight they hummed, as did that most private part between her legs. Years had passed but she'd never forgotten the pleasure, the heart-pounding feeling of when she first got away with that beautiful silver lighter. She remembered every step of the theft: putting the lighter in her purse; leaving the party with it; feeling her heart race and the thought someone might have seen her – might have guessed what she'd done and punished her. She loved behaving in a manner that was completely unexpected – a bad girl in good girl's clothing.

In Jodie's world, stealing had become entwined with sex. The more expensive an item, the more aroused she became at the prospect of taking it. Of owning it. After a successful night, she could hardly contain her libido.

Sticky Fingers

Alison Tyler

In real life, always practise safe sex.

This edition published in 2004 by
Cheek
Thames Wharf Studios
Rainville Road
London W6 9HA

Originally published in 2003

Printed and bound by Mackays of Chatham PLC

ISBN 0 352 33901 2

For SAM.

Prologue

www.yoursforthetaking.com

It's a rush. Flat out. Plain and simple.

You hear people talk about taking risks – jumping out of planes, bungeeing off bridges, engaging in seductive sex with total strangers. But stealing is what does it for me. Foreplay is the surveillance. Checking the scene. Making sure the possibility of escaping undetected is higher than the risk of getting caught. The odds don't have to be perfect. For me, danger equals arousal. But luck has to be on my side. It's all about the senses. A feeling that the timing is right.

Sometimes you might scope out the location with every intention of going forwards, but your plans will occasionally go awry. A cop might stroll by. A store detective will appear overly attentive. A shopclerk decides to make pointed eye-contact and simply will not look away. But usually, none of those things happen. Not to me, anyway, because I don't look like a suspect. I possess the appearance of someone who not only has plenty of money, but who takes great pleasure in spending.

And sure I do. When that sort of situation arises. Dropping crisp bills on to a counter and purchasing what I want does hold a semi-thrill. Especially when the bills are hundreds and the item I'm buying is of the more frivolous variety. Thousand-dollar bottles of perfume made from flowers hand-picked in the valleys of France. Face creams created by astrophysicists. But, in general, playing the role of the consumer is not what

I'm all about. The art of taking excites me. Slipping something into my pocket or up my sleeve without any hesitation. No sideways glances. No flushed cheeks or rapid breathing to give me away.

Just palming the item and walking out undetected.

Trust me, nothing beats it. Not drinking. Not smoking. Not sex.

Well, maybe sex . . .

From the notes of Detective Nicholas Hudson:
Case File: 582
File Description: Protect Ancient Black Sapphire Ring
Employer: Confidential
Facts: Scattered/vague (see clippings below)
From *The Associated Press*:

The black sapphire ring, nicknamed *The Unforgiving Heart*, is known as the most often stolen gem in history. The piece can be traced back to ancient times, and references appear quite often in poetry – Fierce light which burns within, unyielding stone and unforgiving heart – and in masterpieces dating pre-Renaissance . . .

From the *Transformed Treasures* catalogue copy:

This grouping of jewels may seem haphazard to some, but each piece shares a historical similarity with the rest. All have been stolen, redesigned, and hidden for long periods of their existence. The jewel in the crown of this exhibit is *The Unforgiving Heart*, a piece which has been duplicated many times, sometimes by master jewelers. The true stone is said to hold a red light within, but carefully crafted replicas have fooled even the most schooled experts . . .

From an article in *Jewelry Today*:

There is much to be said for the possibility that the black sapphire ring currently traveling with the

Transformed Treasures exhibit is yet another one of the fakes that has circulated for centuries. This doesn't make the exhibition any less interesting, of course. Good forgeries are difficult to come by. But don't hold your breath in anticipation of seeing the opal-like fire burning within the midnight blackness ...

A press release from the ARTone museum:

Several security companies have been hired to guard the gems on display. Mixed in with the throngs of curious customers expected to view the artistic creations will be many private investigators. Nothing will be stolen from this exhibit, ending the curse that many have felt tainted these pieces for centuries, if not millennia ...

From an Internet posting on www.yoursforthetaking.com:

Makes you want to go out and get it, doesn't it?

Scrawled in Detective Nick Hudson's own handwriting below the scattering of notes on the case:
What the hell? It's just a ring.

Chapter One

- Diamond clip, circa 1920s, estimated value $3500
- Pearl-and-emerald brooch, white-gold setting, engraved, $4200
- Pink tourmaline-and-diamond engagement ring, Tiffany's, $12,000
- Red opal ring, platinum setting, $56,000
- Ruby necklace, worn by silent screen star Emma Vogue, $89,000
- Black pearls, double-strand, one-of-a-kind, $160,000

The last entry was circled twice in bold red ink. This necklace was the sole reason that Jodie had come to the auction. Not to buy it herself, of course. Where was the fun in that? Her job for the afternoon was to see which bidder walked off with the jewels. Based on her extensive research, she had a strong idea who the buyer would be. Now, all she had to do was wait and see whether or not her guess was correct.

As she scanned the room, she saw several acquaintances in the field: appraisers, bidders, and other middlemen who made their fortune on the resale. She nodded to a competitor from a different firm, and he tilted his head at her and raised his eyebrows in a silent query. She understood the look immediately. He wanted to know which item she was after. She smiled at him, then shook her head.

'Tell,' he mouthed to her.

'Not going to happen,' she whispered back, enunciating carefully so that he could read her lips. He shrugged impishly, as if he couldn't be faulted for trying. All of the people in the room knew how to keep their desires under cover. Sharing information too early was rarely beneficial.

Casually, Jodie took her seat at the back of the room, choosing a spot near the exit. As soon as she found the information she needed, she would leave; make a quick phone call and put the rest of the plan into action. There was no need to wait out the remainder of the show. Maybe she'd place a few bids while she waited, simply to take part in the excitement of a live auction, but none of the other items on display caught her eye.

As she flipped through the glossy pages of the auction catalogue, she found herself staring once again at the picture of the pearls. There they were, glistening divinely on a rippled sheet of pale blue silk. The auction catalogue's art director had been creative, draping the pearls over several splayed oyster shells. Mother of pearl insides gleamed with an opalescent lustre. Jodie's fingertips traced over the one-dimensional rounded baubles, and she felt as if she could almost touch them through the heavy paper. When the vibrant blonde auctioneer in the severe black suit started speaking, her striking voice pulled Jodie from her daydreams with a jolt.

'Starting with lot number 347. Do I have $60,000?'

Blinking quickly, Jodie looked up as the games began.

Strong hands moved along the delicate line of Jodie's spine, palms expertly rotating on either side. Slowly, the knowledgeable fingers traced lower, making smooth, circular motions as they worked their way towards the prize of her rounded ass. Cupping her gently here, the hands spread her heart-shaped bottom cheeks. For a moment, there was nothing but a long, tremulous beat of silence. Then Jodie felt a rush of air tickling against her, and a delicious shudder ran through her entire body.

'You like that?' the man whispered, moving aside slightly as he waited for her answer. Jodie responded without words, sighing as she rolled over on to her back and stretched her arms over her head. Although she was being intimately attended to by a well-built blond youth, her deep-set grey eyes were now locked on her own reflection in the gilt-edged mirror on the opposite wall. She saw herself spread out on the ruby satin sheets, and Lucas watching her patiently. Then she stared into her own eyes as the different expressions flickered over her face: yearning, lust, submission.

Her lover gazed up at her fondly, not the slightest bit put out by the change in positions. Jodie knew from experience that he would always follow her lead. 'You look like a movie star, don't you, baby?' he asked her now.

She didn't have to say a word. Lucas liked to keep up a steady conversation while they were fucking. Talking about what they were doing made him harder than simply doing it, while listening was a pleasure to Jodie. Now, she ran her fingers through her long dark hair, fanning the length over her bare shoulders. That chestnut-hued curtain nearly covered the curve of her breasts. Only nearly, because her bedmate reached up quickly to brush her hair out of the way, instantly gaining an unhindered view of her body. Complementing her dark hair, Jodie had pale skin, eyes the ever-changing colour of the surf, and full, kissable lips. Leaning against the mattress, her body looked firm and compact, like that of an expensive automobile, something that would handle easily on dangerous turns.

'You like to watch?' Lucas murmured next, his voice soft.

Jodie still said nothing. It was obvious what she liked from the way she moved and the way she shifted her supple body on the mattress. Slowly, she spread her slender legs wider apart so that she would be able to see each little action as it unfolded. She was so ready. She could see the dampness coating her. Her lover responded exactly as she had hoped. As soon as she opened herself up to him, Lucas made himself comfortable between her legs, his mouth a sliver of space away from her skin. It was as if he belonged between her thighs; his curly blond hair tousled slightly from their exertions made him look dishevelled in a sexy, sleepy way. Even with his tanned skin, he showed a deep flush along the strong rise of his cheekbones. Excitement in his amber eyes let Jodie know that her handsome partner didn't mind his questions being ignored.

Lucas never did.

Without waiting another second, he got busy working between her legs, licking in long, wet strokes up and down the sweet curves of her inner thighs before teasing her most sensitive flesh with the very tip of his tongue. He knew when to move forward, going in deeper, like a diver after a precious pearl – a perfect analogy of his current task. Each time he kissed her there, he tugged on the expensive necklace tucked up inside her. And each time he tugged, Jodie's muscles contracted fiercely on the irreplaceable baubles, as if she might be able to keep them within her. But she didn't really want that. The pleasure of being emptied one pearl at a time was far preferable and almost too much to bear.

With his lips alone, her lover carefully withdrew the hidden strand of pearls. The necklace slid slowly into view, bringing a new flood of heady juices with them. Beneath her body, the crimson satin sheet grew more damp, and Jodie shimmied her hips against the shiny surface, moving even closer to her mate. She leaned back against her locked arms, feeling the tension of anticipation pulse through her body.

Between tugs on the rope of pearls, her lover nuzzled at her sensitive spot, using his tongue, his lips, even the sharp angle of his chin against her. His mission was easy to guess. He wanted to bring Jodie all the way to the point of climax, expertly timing her orgasm to arrive as the last link of the necklace was pulled from her body. Coming as the necklace was freed would be the ultimate ending to the events of the afternoon. The detailed planning. The actual theft. The ultimate success.

'Harder,' she finally moaned, her first sign that she was nearing her peak. 'Do it harder, Lucas.'

Obeying immediately, the man tugged more purposefully. The pearls easily slipped free, making soft popping sounds as they appeared one at a time. When Lucas had removed the last black pearl from her, Jodie looked down and gave a harsh sigh of pleasure. Each bead shone in the light, polished with a sheen from within her body. In style, the necklace looked similar to the strands of sexual-enhancement beads available from any X-rated mail-order catalogue. But this was the most expensive erotic toy in the world. That thought made Jodie more excited than any other.

'Oh, God, yes,' she sighed, and her lover paused at the sound of her voice. Then, urgently, he resumed his previous actions. With a hypnotic rhythm, he lapped between her legs, then thrust his tongue deep inside her. Finally, he resumed the circles that would always bring her to orgasm. Lucas pressed hard, and when his tongue flicked back and forth, making true contact, she grabbed his shoulders and groaned.

As she came, Jodie let go of her partner and slid one hand slowly down her body and between her legs. Grasping hold of the slippery beads, she brought the necklace back up to where she could see it in the light and purred, 'Oh, Lucas, aren't they beautiful?'

Chapter Two

Nick Hudson was hard at work on a case ... a case of good scotch. Although, at this point, the quality of what he chose to imbibe no longer mattered. He'd progressed well beyond slowly savouring each sip to appreciate the woodiness of the flavour. Now, he was drinking steadily, as if to satisfy a thirst but, even in his wavering state of mind, he knew that this was a thirst that could never fully be quenched.

He'd been given the expensive liquor as a gift for completing a difficult job successfully, but that didn't mean he felt good about himself. Drinking alone was never a positive activity for his psyche. He should have gone down to Sammy's this evening. There, he would have spent the night in the affable atmosphere of the neighbourhood bar, listening to the cool sounds of Sinatra crooning from the jukebox in the corner and talking with the owner, who was also his best friend. But he hadn't been in the mood for company tonight. That's what he'd told himself anyway, and he'd bought the lie because he hadn't wanted to search out the truth.

A private detective unwilling to mine the depths of his own soul. Now, *that* was a sad situation, but it wasn't a rare one. Just like psychiatrists who won't face their own mental problems, Nick understood that most detectives were probably adverse to looking at the secrets they kept inside themselves. Knowing a fact didn't make facing it any easier. That was the cold, hard truth he'd learned when confronted with the end of his most recent relationship. This evening, he was also working on a case of the lonelies, and that's what made him pour the drink right after the drink he should have ended the evening with. When the phone rang, he knocked the receiver over with his foot, listening intently for a moment before ignoring the male voice on the other end.

'You there, Nick? What the fuck –'

There was not one person in the world who he wanted to talk to right now.

Another lie.

Hey, Nick, his mental voice chided him. *This is me you're talking to. Don't pull my chain. If I want the truth, I'll beat it out of you.*

Aha. That was an idea. Beating off was never a total waste of time, right? The end result always justified the means. Pleasure, even fleeting, would be a welcome sensation, no matter how pathetic the circumstances. A quick climax might shake him out of this dismal mood. Right his wrongs. Clear his fog.

Standing, he made his way unsteadily down the hall to the bathroom. With a graceless jerk, he released his penis from his tan slacks. He was hard already, but before he could get a solid grip around himself, he glanced straight at his reflection in the polished silver mirror above the sink. Captivated, he stared at himself, not as if he was seeing his face for the first time, but as if he were looking at a client. He saw the short blond hair, rock-hard jawline, bay-blue eyes. He knew where to look to find the slim line of scar that cut through his right eyebrow, and could easily pinpoint the flaws that others might not have so quickly found out.

'Come clean,' he said aloud in the echoing tiled bathroom. 'It'll make you feel better. It always does.'

Yet another lie. The truth will set you free? Not likely. Not when you've been left by the girl you thought was actually the one. When you'd moronically opened yourself up to actually believing there was something like 'the one'.

The truth will set you free? The truth that she was shagging your goddamn partner? Christ, here we go. Right out of a classic black-and-white Bogart movie. Except Nick had always thought *he'd* be the one to play Bogie, not Hunter. In all the mental movies that he'd ever starred in, he was Sam Spade, right down to the gruff way of talking, the sneer in his voice and the method of remaining cool-headed in dangerous situations. If his ex-partner Hunter got to be Bogie, did that mean that he was the other asshole? Archer? The one who got shot in the chest by Mary . . .? Mary Astor. No, that was the actress. Who did she play? What the hell was her name? That wasn't the way this plot was supposed to go down.

Suddenly, he had an idea. The first one to give him a true feeling of peace in the eight days since he'd discovered his girlfriend's actual desire. He knew just what he'd do with the rest of his evening. He stumbled back down the hall, then slid in the DVD for *The Maltese Falcon*. After pouring another drink, he parked himself in front of his high-tech media centre.

As the opening of his all-time favourite movie started to play, he reached down and replaced the phone receiver. He did it almost casually, as if he were simply fixing a piece of prop scenery on the stage of his life. Still, he shook his head at the pull of optimism that charged this small action.

What if she called? That's why he did it. What if?

He'd have gone up the river for Bailey. That wasn't a lie. But she hadn't wanted him to paddle along at her side.

Chapter Three

The black velvet string of silver bells tied to the front door of Belle's Beauty Box tinkled musically. The sound alerted the shopkeeper to an entering customer and brought an end to Isabelle's work-hour tryst with Cameron Sweeney in the back room.

'I thought you put the closed sign out,' she sighed unhappily.

'My mistake,' he said. 'I was too busy peeling that naughty skirt off you. When you dress like that, you make me forget things. And that skirt just had to come down.' He groaned, watching as she lifted the item in question off the floor. 'I needed to see that beautiful ass of yours underneath.'

'This ass?' Isabelle teased, 'and this skirt?' she continued. She pulled the zipper back up the side, then cocked a hip in Cameron's direction. Isabelle didn't have to glance in a mirror to know how good she looked in the zebra-print leather, but she loved seeing the expression of sadness on Cameron's face as her momentarily-naked body disappeared beneath the fine fabric.

'That sweet, sweet skirt. Take it off again. Don't leave me like this.' He gestured with one hand to his hard-on, exposed in the opening of his black gabardine slacks. 'Come on, Izzy. Baby. I need you. *This* needs you. You're not being fair.'

He was so pitiful in his begging that Isabelle gave in to him for a moment, bending to suck just the head of his penis in a little goodbye kiss. Her mouth closed around it and she swallowed hard, hearing him sigh at how good that felt.

'That's right,' he said softly. 'That's my baby.'

She swirled her tongue in a tickling massage, then dragged the point of her tongue up and down the length. Really, how could she resist something that so obviously craved the mystical ministrations of her mouth? But after a quick bob, she backed away from her man.

'Don't do it,' Cameron begged. 'Just say no –'

'That's about drugs, not sex. Or customers.' Now, she darted her tongue along her top lip, savouring the taste of him. 'Besides, what we just did was only a warm-up,' she said. 'A little glimmer of what you'll get when I finish my business. Right now, you'll have to wait. Exercise a little self-control.'

'I'm not a patient man. You know that.'

Isabelle grinned. Yes, she did. She knew all about Cameron's amazing sexual appetite. He was ready all the time, and he didn't like to postpone pleasure for even a moment. Cameron couldn't understand the concept of hunger as an aphrodisiac. 'Why don't you meet me around the corner at Sammy's? After I help whoever's out there.' She turned to point to the monitor on her desk that was focused on the front room of her lingerie store. 'I'll close up for the day and we can have a drink.'

'What I want you to drink, they don't serve at Sammy's.'

'Patience,' she repeated. 'It's a virtue.'

'Not one that I possess,' he sighed. 'Never have. Never saw the point in it.' Spoken, Isabelle thought, like someone who had everything. In general, Cameron did have everything he could ever want, but maybe not right this moment.

'Be a good boy,' she said.

Pouting, Cameron stared at the monitor, too, and then he turned to look at Isabelle. Exhilaration from a new idea shone in his green eyes. 'Why don't I wait?'

'You can't watch ladies change. That's illegal.'

'A
eyebr
'I'll ↕
'But t↕
heart?' H
slacks, the
strong arm
seductive sa
was very goo
he was a multi
extreme standa↕
to get people to ↕
I'm back here doi↕
there, helping to sli↕
of tight-fitting silver ↕rim.'

'You like those pant↕

He nodded. It was c↕ ↕ook on his face that he knew he'd won ↕e before they'd even started. He knew becau↕ isabelle had a customer waiting. Ever the professional, she couldn't hang back here and engage in an erotic dispute. Isabelle understood that even though this sole sale might not make her day, good customer service always accounted for repeat clients. And when it came right down to it, she didn't mind Cameron getting his kinky turn-ons from his voyeuristic fetish. Cheap thrills for the man with the big bank account. Of course, she understood just how much he liked to watch. That was how they'd met, Cameron watching her model a new designer's lingerie at a trunk show. Afterwards, he had come back behind the changing curtain and offered her ten thousand dollars for a private showing. She'd taken him up on the offer of a show for his eyes only, but she'd refused the money because she wasn't on the game.

No time for tantalising trips down memory lane now. She pointed to the white-washed wooden stool where he could gaze at the trio of monitors, and then she put her finger to her shiny cherry-hued lips. 'All

ALISON TYLER

right,' she said. 'Just this once. Wait↕ be a good boy.' 'Aren't I always?' She refused to answer ↕ would probably ↕ she knew him ↕ sucking he↕ down h↕ long↕

for me here, and

the loaded question because
ead to a series of others, which
ead to her mouth opening again and
down. Instead, she brushed her hands
smooth black-and-white skirt, shook out her
blonde hair, and put on her best professional
expression. No time to think about it right now. It was
time to work.

With her blue eyes narrowed into dangerous slits, Isabelle watched the dark-haired beauty rifle through the racks of new arrivals. The girl discarded each one with a half-sneer, then pushed on to the next with a combined look of little interest and obvious disdain. She'd left a fun frisky scene with Cameron for this caustic customer? What was the point? The woman clearly was not interested in anything she had on display. Isabelle stared at her for a moment, recognising the shopper from the neighbourhood. She'd seen her around, but had never spoken to her before.

'Are you sure that I can't help you?' Isabelle said, putting as much good cheer as she could into her voice.

The girl just shook her head. 'Browsing,' she said tersely.

Picky patrons like this one stepped all over Isabelle's nerves. She knew that her lingerie was by far the best locally. In fact, for three years running, Belle's Beauty Box had been voted the number one lingerie store in the region in the *Wicked Weekly*'s Conscientious Consumer Report. There was no way to find anything more exquisite in the department stores downtown. You had to go to Europe and look through the manufacturers' supplies, search out the very best creations, and train your eye to spot the dreamiest silks, softest satins, delicate and fragile hand-woven, hand-stitched designs. The unusual is what she sold: the intricate and elegant. This was why Isabelle ventured to Europe twice a year on her foreign buying binges. Nothing compared to the items she found in France and Italy.

So exactly what did this ritzy-looking bitch want?

Nothing. Wrinkling her brow, the girl tipped several transparent bras off a tiny silver display, and Isabelle hurried to catch the rack before the rest tumbled and created chaos. While she was leaning down to pick up the crushed items, she saw the girl steal a thong. No way! Isabelle thought. All that for nothing. She'd done her best to help, offered her capable assistance, oohed and ahhed at every item handled, and it turned out the customer wasn't a customer at all. She was a common thief. Or maybe not so common. The girl looked well-heeled, plenty refined. Someone she'd seen often enough strolling through this high-end district, down at the bar around the corner, and occasionally in her store, as well. So not common, perhaps, but a thief nonetheless.

Without considering the consequences, Isabelle allowed her hand to dive forcefully into the woman's pocket after the stolen thong. There, she reached around, and came up ... empty-handed. Confusion rather than anger now marred the shopkeeper's pretty features.

'You're looking for what precisely?' the customer said indignantly. 'My thigh?'

'I saw you –'

'Saw me what?' the woman asked, testing Isabelle with her icy gaze.

The struggle played out in Isabelle's eyes: confront the girl and demand she hand over the purloined panties immediately before the police were involved? Or err on the side of caution? As a shop owner, Isabelle

knew that old clichéd saying well enough: the customer was always right on some level. But this afternoon Isabelle was too upset to be rational.

'I saw you,' Isabelle said again, through clenched
teeth. Anger had fuelled the intensity of the connection, but although her hand was still deep in the
customer's pocket, suddenly a different set of emotions
ran through her.

'You saw me what?' the dark-haired beauty repeated,
her dusky tone of voice altered slightly. She wasn't
asking the same question at all, this time, was she?
Isabelle squinted her light blue eyes and tried her best
to read the thief's face. Exactly what was going on
here? This was her store, her territory, yet she felt
completely lost and out of place, as if she'd entered the
translucent world of a wet dream.

The two women were standing next to each other.
So close. Finally, Isabelle started to withdraw her hand,
admitting failure with her actions. Now, the customer
grabbed on to her wrist firmly and slid it back into the
pocket, where Isabelle could feel the tiny opening cut
through the bottom, and could also feel the customer's
smooth naked thigh.

'Secret pocket,' the woman said, 'high up on the
inside.'

Isabelle's fingers probed further, finding the lacy red
ribbon of thong tucked in there like some sort of prop
in a magic trick and finding something else, as well.
Something that both surprised and excited her. She
hadn't fully recovered from her carnal connection with
Cameron in the back room. Sex was in the air, all
around her, and she felt herself moving with the
palpably sensual force of the situation.

'What's going on?' Isabelle asked, her voice low.
'What are you doing?'

'You're the owner, right?'

Isabelle nodded. She could feel a heat in her cheeks
as she continued to trace her fingers up and down the

lace-edged panties of this most curious customer she'd ever had.

'I'm Jodie Silver,' the girl said. 'I work around the corner, at 770 Chestnut.' She indicated with a nod of her head towards a building somewhere down the street. 'The truth is that I've been watching you.' Her voice remained calm and even. There was nothing from her expression to give away any sort of emotion. Was she scared? Pleased? Excited? The only evidence Isabelle had for any of these possibilities was the slick wetness on her own fingertips.

'Watching?' Isabelle murmured, and as she spoke the words, she drove her fingers further inside, probing beneath the satiny panties and into Jodie's ready sex. Still, the girl didn't flinch. Didn't give up anything.

'Every day, walking by on my way to work, I see you. See you watching me back. Staring through the windows. Or into the mirror to see my reflection as I pass by. I know all about you.'

'What do you know?'

'I know that you try on the clothes at night. Without the special liners the customers are required by law to use. I know that this thong, this exact scarlet thong, has caressed your own beautiful naked body.' There was a pause then, and Isabelle felt her cheeks heat up further, but she didn't say a word. 'And I know you want me to do that for you,' Jodie finally continued.

'Do what?'

'Caress the very same spot –'

Isabelle, her fingers slippery now, pulled her hand from Jodie's slit pocket. While Jodie watched, she slowly licked her fingertips clean. Then she turned and walked to the front door of the store and flipped the lock, put the closed sign out, which Cameron had failed to do a half hour earlier, and leaned back against the cool glass plate. There was a moment when she worked out in her mind what she was going to do next. She saw the scene unfold as if it were a movie and she owned the master reel. As she approached Jodie, she pointed to a metal-framed sign hanging on the back wall.

'You can read, right?'

Jodie nodded, but a smile changed her stone-like features. It was clear from her expression that she knew where Isabelle was heading with this question, yet she didn't say a word to stop the inevitable.

'So read it to me.'

'Shoplifters will be prosecuted –'

'Keep reading,' Isabelle demanded, and now she stepped even closer to Jodie, waiting to hear each word. 'Prosecuted to the full extent –' As Jodie said the words, Isabelle pushed her forcefully towards the dressing room at the rear of the store. Jodie's high-heeled spectators made a click-clack on the polished floor as she worked to match Isabelle's long stride. The blonde store owner thrust aside the creamy velvet curtain, then dragged Jodie in after her.

Inside the dressing room, Isabelle pressed Jodie against the rose-printed wall, knowing that they were now out of sight from any passers-by on the street. But Jodie could still see the sign from where she stood, and Isabelle said, 'Keep reading,' before she dropped on to her knees in front of her and undid the zippered fly of Jodie's pin-striped slacks. This was one of her all-time favourite positions. In front of a lover for the very first time, about to learn the most intimate secrets a new partner had to offer. Would Jodie be shaved bare? Would there be a drag-strip of dark curly fur waiting or was she the type to go in for one of those wild wax jobs, where colour was applied and shapes were etched in?

'Prosecuted to the full extent of the law.'

'You know what that means?' Isabelle murmured, slipping Jodie's slacks down her lean thighs to the rounded curves of her calves. Oh, the girl was shaved. Isabelle loved the feel of purely bare skin against her lips. When Jodie didn't answer, Isabelle kept talking. 'You look educated enough. You do know what the word "prosecuted" means, don't you?'

'We don't need the law here, do we?' Jodie asked, now digging her fingers through Isabelle's silky gold-streaked mane.

'No,' Isabelle agreed, shaking her head back and forth, revelling in the feeling of being caressed like that. 'I can always mete out the punishment myself.'

'But not yet,' Jodie sighed, arching her back and pressing herself hard against Isabelle's ready, willing mouth. Finally, she seemed to be melting into the situation. 'Please, not yet –'

The camera poised innocently above the women caught everything that happened between them, although this wasn't the video's official purpose. Cameron knew that the lens was highly focused with the intention of recording some naughty customer slipping Isabelle's expensive merchandise into a purse or a pocket. Generally, the high-tech machine did the job commendably. More than once, Isabelle had told Cameron about the benefits of using the monitor system. She'd said that she probably didn't even need to have film in the thing. She would simply point to the discreet video camera, and a guilty look would flash across some woman's face. Then that woman would undoubtedly pull an incredibly confused act. 'Oh, my gosh! How did this pair of panties wind up in my purse? I'll pay for them immediately. Just to smooth things over. And, um, let me take a few extra bras, as well. Would that be okay, Miss?'

But this afternoon, the lens of the camera recorded two women making love for the first time, and Cameron Sweeney couldn't believe his luck. There was nothing like the cheesiness of porn movies about the situation; yet here were two totally gorgeous girls getting to know each other in a very personal way only moments after having met. Perhaps that part was like an X-rated movie, he thought. The plot. Or what wasn't actually a real plot, just a 'cute meet'. You know, cut to the chase. Whatever you called it, the scene turned him on. He stared at the screen, hand wrapped tightly around himself, and he pulled hard as he watched his favourite girlfriend lick another woman's pussy. How sweet that was, the way Isabelle's hands caressed the girl's thighs, then moved back, obviously cradling her ass.

From the women's positioning, he couldn't see Isabelle's face clearly. That was because his blonde nymphet had pressed her mouth against the new girl's sex. He thought about Isabelle's knowledgeable tongue as he watched the brunette sigh in true pleasure. He had a wealth of personal experience with Izzy's mouth, knew just how amazing it could feel when she decided to really treat a lover. She did things with her tongue that few girls had done to him before because of his size. It wasn't only that she could truly suck him, but that she seemed to like the act. She got into the action forcefully, and every time he boned her after she'd gone down on him, she was really moist. To Cameron's way of thinking, this was a real-life sign that she was as turned-on by treating him as he was at receiving the oral wonders of her amazing mouth.

But now he was on the watching end, which was something Cameron could never get enough of. Didn't matter to him that she was with a woman instead of a man. In fact, that turned him on even more. How beautiful the two women looked together: Isabelle all tall and blonde and golden; and the other one, dark and sweet and pale. What he would have paid to have seen them in a sixty-nine, body sealed to body.

If he'd been downtown at one of the dirty 'Live Nude Girls' theatres, he could have done just that. He'd just slide his twenty-dollar bills through the slot in the black-painted wall and whisper what he wanted the 'actresses' to do. They would reach for the money and turn his fantasies into realities. But this was different, because it truly was live. Even if he couldn't choreograph the scene, he got pleasure watching the brunette's expressions change as Isabelle worked forcefully between the girl's spread thighs.

This new girl had the most intense lips. They were full and dark in the black-and-white image on the screen. Her soft white skin seemed radiant, as if he could almost feel the heat coming off her. Isabelle was definitely doing some fabulous things to this girl. Her hands were moving now, sliding behind the dark-haired woman's hips, cradling her there. Was she touching the woman's ass? Was she sliding one wet fingertip between the girl's rear cheeks? Oh, wouldn't he have liked to know that? Wouldn't he have liked to have been right there with Isabelle, standing behind the girl, spreading those cheeks himself?

Yes, was the quick answer to those queries. Cameron loved to be with two girls at once. Two, at least. Playing multiple bedmates was one of his favourite night time games. Getting sticky and wet and confused by who was with who never failed to turn him on. He liked to roll around in his big California king-sized bed with his eyes closed, reaching out one hand and grabbing on to whoever was closest to him. He would thrust in fast and tight, then reach out for the other one to join in; to help out. But watching was almost sexier. He was so stealthy, tugging on his cock, staring at the screen. Dreaming of turning their twosome into a threesome.

How long would they go at it? Would Isabelle make the girl come? Would he have time to come, himself? Sadly, no. He watched Isabelle stand, and then he shuddered when she looked at him directly though the monitor. Her chin was upraised and defiant. I know you, her expression said. I know all about you, Cameron. I know what you like and what you want. And look at this. I'm giving it to you. Without a word.

Without you needing to beg. I'm giving you everything you crave.

Her eyes told him so many things. Separated as they were by the scope of the camera, her gaze was still able to penetrate him. To make him squirm. Then she winked one shadowy lid, and he found himself smiling back at her even though he knew she couldn't see him.

Time to move, he realised, watching her hand on the curtain. Time to find what he seriously hoped would be a spanking new location.

Isabelle gave Cameron a moment to get himself together before ushering Jodie into the small back room of the store where she kept the special gear: the high-priced fetish items. This part of the store housed a whole separate business – called Understatements – an area that few of the women and men who browsed her racks up front even knew about. The products in the back room were imported for clients with a specific bent; those who weren't intrigued by the normal array of frilly lingerie, but who preferred a darker, more obscure selection of goods: black leather bra and panty sets; dresses made of PVC and shimmering vinyl; chokers lined with fur. Aside from the racy get-ups, she also had an antique wood wardrobe filled with high-end sex toys: bone-handled crops, five-hundred-dollar silver cuffs, heavy velvet blindfolds.

Yes, there were plenty of stores in the Castro and the Haight filled solely with this sort of merchandise, as well as Internet sites devoted to the fetish consumer. But Isabelle didn't attempt to compete with either. She purchased the upscale kinky outfits for a clientele who lived in Pacific Palisades and who didn't want to get their hands dirty in the search for naughty costumes. Just because you were rich didn't mean you didn't have your own filthy fantasies. In fact, Isabelle had learned that the kinkiest customers she had were the ones who appeared the least likely to play dirty, based on their day-to-day activities: bankers, business executives, owners of electronics corporations. These were the people who called on Isabelle when they wanted to let their inner beasts out of their million-dollar closets. But the rest of the world would never have guessed that Isabelle's clients had secret sex lives.

'Oh, my,' Jodie sighed when she saw all of the different outfits. 'These are magnificent.'

'I know,' Isabelle said, proudly, looking around the room for a different reason entirely. Cameron was hiding here somewhere. But where? She caught sight of the white-painted leg of the wooden stool behind a far curtain on a tiny dressing room, and she realised he'd moved over to that region of the back room. If he stayed truly quiet, she could give him a great show. That would turn Isabelle on almost as much as her man.

'Why don't you have this out in front?' Jodie asked, touching one of the most exquisite pieces. Isabelle was impressed with her good eye. There were levels of quality. She understood that some players went in for the cheaper stuff, knowing that an outfit could get torn or destroyed in the act of misbehaving. But Isabelle's clients didn't care about cost. They wanted the best. Even if a dress might get whipped to shreds on its debut in the bedroom, the piece had to be made of the finest quality to start with. Isabelle enjoyed buying for these clients, because they were such a different set from her normal day-to-day customers. Even more important, these were the types of outfits that she favoured herself. She was never satisfied with the girlish products; she preferred black leather to white lace for her own trousseau.

'Don't want to scare off the regular clients,' Isabelle finally said.

'Regular?'

'Normal,' Isabelle said next, laughing at how silly that sounded. Because what exactly was normal? She wasn't, in her own estimation. Wasn't vanilla, anyway, if that's what normal equalled. No, you wouldn't be able to tell it from looking at her – but that was part of the fun, wasn't it? Isabelle had grown up in the type of Bible-thumping town that bred milk-fed girls with peaches-and-cream complexions. She had the innocent quality of a milkmaid herself, but she could wield a crop with more ease than most dress-up dominatrices. No matter that her exterior made one think of an angel. Inside, her soul flamed with the hot fire of one who metes out pain to reach pleasure.

She thought again about Cameron hiding in his little corner, watching excitedly. He got turned on simply by gazing in a monitor as women chose their panties, bras and garter belts. And he got even more excited when Isabelle punished him for his devious ways. He'd ask for what he wanted, knowing exactly which position would bring him to the level he craved. 'Spank me, tonight, Izzy,' he'd whisper, his voice urgent, or, 'Use the belt. Please.' Someone as successful as Cameron Sweeney knew how to get what he wanted on every score. From the way he lived his life during the day to the way he came at night, he managed to exude the same power, even when that power was bent in submission. Isabelle loved him for his openness with his desires. But sometimes she felt that she wasn't equally open with him because, while she played fair with Cameron, she never could go as far as she liked. Now, he would be able to witness her work in action – not directed at himself, but at this stunning, silver-eyed minx. She was sure this would be a show that both would remember.

'I love it,' Jodie said, turning around. 'I love how secret it is, and I love the décor. The gold and the black. The fierceness of everything. It's such a different quality from the way you decorated the main room. All pink and frilly and feminine.'

'I'm so glad you approve,' Isabelle said coolly. 'And I

know you said out there that you were only looking. But I think that's enough browsing for the moment. You and I have business to deal with.'

Even as she spoke, she was secretly pleased that Jodie had noticed the difference between the main store and this separate world. The back room of her store was decorated in her true style, and it was here, surrounded by high-end X-rated attire, that Isabelle took care of her problem thief. 'We're going to make a little editorial change,' she said, 'from "prosecuted" to "punished". I have a special way that I take care of all the naughty little girls who find themselves in my back room.'

Jodie waited, her eyes locked on Isabelle's. She didn't say a word, which was fine with Isabelle. Right now, the shopkeeper was the one in charge. On the lip of her desk sat an antique vanity set on a gleaming silver tray. While Jodie watched, Isabelle reached for the polished wooden hair brush situated next to a comb and silver-backed mirror. This was what she felt like using tonight. She liked the feel of the brush in her hand, and she liked the heft of the handle, a good solid weight. Isabelle knew from experience that the piece would definitely withstand the trial she was about to put it through. But would Jodie?

'I'm guessing that you know the drill,' Isabelle said, looking Jodie over. 'You have that quality.'

'What quality?'

'You look to me like someone who needs a lot of spankings to keep her in line.'

There was a smirk on Jodie's face as she nodded at Isabelle's words. Then, at a single gesture from the blonde dom, Jodie took a step closer. With ease, Isabelle bent the girl over her lap. Jodie's slacks were still unbuttoned from their dressing room session, and Isabelle immediately slid them down the backs of Jodie's thighs.

How she knew that Jodie wanted to be spanked

wasn't an easy question to answer. It was the same way she sensed the instant that Jodie had stolen something. An inner feeling. Now, she placed the flat back of the brush against Jodie's upturned ass and just held the weapon there for a moment. She gave the naughty thief the chance to tell her 'no', to tell her that this was all just a farce, she hadn't meant that she wanted to be punished at all. She'd simply been playing a game. But the girl was silent, and from the way her hips slid in a shudder against Isabelle's lap, the shopkeeper knew that she'd guessed correctly. Jodie wanted this.

Without a word of warning, she brought the brush up and back down, landing it hard on Jodie's panty-clad bottom, and the thief let out a soft sigh in response to the impact. Not a groan of pain, but a moan of pleasure. Isabelle was instantly wet at the sound, and she brought the brush up and down again quickly, wanting to hear Jodie moan again. She was pleased with the way the girl seemed to have given herself completely over to the situation. There was no hesitation about her body language. A willingness to experience both pain and pleasure was required for these sorts of bedroom theatrics. Jodie seemed perfectly in tune with the concept, and this fuelled Isabelle's own passion, her own need to keep spanking.

She raised her hand up a third time, catching sight of her reflection in the second before she landed the next blow. She looked tough, didn't she? In control, as always, and firm in the set of her mouth, the gossamer-glow in her eyes. When she hesitated another moment, she saw the curtain in the rear pushed aside. She saw Cameron staring at her, then lowered her gaze to see his hand around his penis. He was still dressed, but he'd released his hard-on and was taking care of it with his hand. With a nod from her man, she began the action again. The brush connected against Jodie's hindquarters, and Isabelle found herself lost in a slight tremor of pleasure. She loved the sound that the brush made against the satin, and she adored the way Jodie squirmed her body forcefully against her own.

Spanking had always been exciting to Isabelle. Meting out punishment to a wayward lover turned her on like nothing else. It didn't matter to her whether she was with a man or a women. Different people brought out different aspects of her desires. She loved all parts of the erotic situation: the foreplay of a down-and-dirty discussion, the power of being in charge, the electricity that flowed through her when she really connected with another player. She liked bending a naughty lover over her lap. Liked the heat that whispered in the air before the first whack landed. As she did tonight, she adored the sounds that her partner made – cries, moans, even whimpers. The anticipation pulsed through her like the most delicate aphrodisiac.

This evening, she was even more excited because Jodie was a stranger. And Jodie didn't know the best part; there was an audience. People watching always made an event seem more real to Isabelle. Tonight, she was living out a total fantasy, and doing so with the most beautiful woman she'd ever seen.

Lucas knew that there was no excuse. If caught with his dick out, he'd have nothing to say in his defence. He'd stand there, palms upwards, an expression of total shame shining in his gold-brown eyes. 'Guilty, your honour,' he'd murmur under his breath, hoping desperately for leniency just like any other criminal would if found in his situation. He could easily see the picture in his mind – Jodie wearing the deep black robes of a judge, staring down at him with her stern, unforgiving eyes. (Of course, knowing Jodie, she wouldn't be wearing panties underneath that robe. But that wouldn't help him out in the least.)

Trembling before her, Lucas would beg for understanding. But would he find it? That was the true question. How would Jodie act if all the facts were presented neatly before her? Sometimes, he was certain that she'd leave him if she discovered his secret. She'd shake her head sadly and ask him how could she continue to be with him if she couldn't even trust him? That was the thought that always made him reconsider whether this activity was truly something he couldn't deny. But see? There was always the possibility that she *wouldn't* leave him. That she'd understand and be supportive. That the whole situation might even work to excite her.

Ultimately, none of those thoughts carried any real weight. Catch him and dump him? Forgive and forget? Didn't matter. Flat out, plain and simple, Lucas couldn't help himself. Like an addict, he had a craving that he just couldn't shake. Even though he told himself to get the hell out of her bedroom, to walk out the front door of her apartment and lock it behind himself, he couldn't. The bounty was too divine to him, although he knew the prizes were not normally accepted as treasures. Lucas wasn't interested in gems, jewels, furs or art masterpieces. None of those appealed to him. What Lucas wanted was Jodie's panties.

Neon red ones, high-cut on the hips, so soft and silky that he had to bring them up to his face and inhale the delicious scent that lingered there. He knew exactly what she looked like when she was wearing these panties and nothing else. The last time she'd had them on, she had posed for him in the doorway before they made love, playing the role of a screen goddess from the 1940s. He'd sprawled on the bed watching her, taking in her performance, growing hard as she made her way to the bed. She was always on, wasn't she? Blowing him kisses, or smoke rings, or simply mouthing the filthy words that told him exactly what she was going to do to him ... or what she wanted him to do to her.

Oh, or these green ones, coloured like a highly polished emerald, with a ridge of lace in dark orchid on the edges. These were from France, he recalled. Not imported to some fancy shop, but pilfered on a trip to Paris. Jodie had no fear; she stole even when abroad, not caring or worrying about the possible repercussions. Winding up in a foreign police station wasn't even a possibility in her mind. She was too good. Taking things as small as panties came as second nature to Jodie by now. She hardly thought about slipping a thong into a pocket or a bracelet down her sleeve. Sparkling rings wound up on her fingers as she walked by sidewalk vendors.

She was like magic in motion.

Lucas plunged his hands deep into the white net lingerie bag filled with dainty items waiting for the wash. His fingers stirred through the fine fabric, creating a rustling turmoil of silk and lace. For several moments, he let his hands delve into the world of her luxurious undergarments. Then he caught sight of the dreamy slippers lined up on the low shelf in her closet. Swallowing hard, he pushed the laundry aside and went on his hands and knees in the closet. There. The white ones. God, she'd looked amazing in these the previous weekend, hadn't she? Dressed in a gold negligée that was totally sheer in the candlelight. Shoes dangling from her feet as she'd wrapped her legs around his waist. He'd turned so he could watch in the mirror as he'd slammed into her, for some reason needing to do it harder when she was dressed in the most feminine attire.

Now, he brought the soft slide up to his face and caressed his cheeks with the feather-fluff on the tips. Heaven. Nothing was softer than that. Nothing except her skin, her hair, her lips. He thought about the different slippers she owned. High-heeled ones with steel tips. Imported Italian confections lined in leopard-print velvet. Each had their own appeal, but these were by far his favourites.

She wouldn't know, would she? There were too

many different items in this closet for her to miss one pair of shoes. Two pairs of panties. A single stocking. A garter. If she did realise that the items had vanished, what could she possibly say? She had no reason to suspect him. What use would he have for her panties?

A simple one.

Lying down dead in the centre of her bed, Lucas split open his faded blue jeans and began to rub the pretty panties up and down his rigid cock. The red ones were perfect for this erotic exercise – silky soft, satiny smooth against his skin. He touched his balls with the fabric and shuddered at how intense that simple gesture felt on his body. As he stroked himself, he thought of Jodie rubbing her panty-clad pussy against him so that he could feel both the fabric of her underclothes and the wetness seeping through the whisper-soft panties. Sometimes when they were together, she stayed dressed until the very last moment. He'd be naked on the bed, and she'd move her body up and down his until he could no longer stand it. Either he'd have to strip her clothes off her in a heated rush, or he would simply push the garments aside briskly with his fingers and drive into the willing wetness of her.

Now, he used the entire pair of lipstick-red panties to wrap around himself. With his free hand, he dropped the green set on his face, and breathed in harshly. The fabric fluttered with his exhalation. He could smell her scent, which was why he always went for the briefs from the laundry bag rather than the clean ones folded so carefully in her top drawer. Those were pretty, too, lightly perfumed from the rose petal sachet she kept tucked in one corner. But these made him delirious. Her private, secret smell surrounded him.

He imagined Jodie walking in right then, catching him in the middle of what he considered his most depraved act. Although this was one of his deepest fears, the vision also made him harder than anything else. What would she do if she caught him? In his mind, the penance she made him perform only worked to turn him on even more. She'd have him wear the panties for her while she spanked his satin-clad ass. That was one fantasy. He'd work to stretch the fabric over his muscular thighs, trying hard to get the panties to stay in place without letting them ride up between the cheeks. She'd tease him as she spanked him, which would only make him grow larger still. Or maybe she would ball the lingerie up and gag him while she punished him. He'd bite down on the fabric and taste her. Really taste her.

But she didn't find him. Not tonight. He was safe with his own filthy fantasies, drinking in her scent, pleasing himself with her underwear. Crazy, right? Wrong, or bad, or something –

No, that wasn't it at all. It was good. Being here, surrounded by her most personal items, that's what brought him all the way up to the brink. He was in ecstasy. Or almost. He reached for the slipper and pressed it against his cheek again, moaning. How quickly he could get to the end when he played with her stuff. It didn't really make sense. He could have the real thing, the lady in the flesh, almost whenever he craved her. But occasionally, simply screwing her belongings took him even higher.

Tonight, he'd come by to find her, and he'd actually been more excited when he'd realised she wasn't home. Quietly, he'd used his key to get in, hurrying to shut the door behind him, keeping the lights off so as not to alert any neighbour to his presence. From the moment he'd entered the apartment, he had throbbed violently in his jeans. It had seemed to know long before he did that he was going to lose control of himself once again. He'd done this often enough before but he simply couldn't help himself.

Jodie wouldn't mind, he decided, even if she knew. She had enough of her own fetishes that she'd accept his own. One of the very best things about her was the fact that she never judged anyone based on a sexual desire. Need a little kink to push you over the edge? That was fine with Jodie, as long as the fantasy clicked with her own. Yeah, deep down, Lucas was sure she'd accept his, certain of it, even if he never dared to ask her. Never honestly considered confessing.

'I've wanted that for a long time,' Jodie sighed, looking up at Isabelle from the soft, lambskin rug in the tiny back room. 'Too long –'

'Which part?' Isabelle asked, staring back at the raven-haired beauty. How innocent Jodie looked on the rug. How small and fine, and completely comfortable. It was almost as if this were *her* store, the way she spread out and claimed her space. There was no shyness about her. No first-time jitters. No nervousness about being naked with a new lover. Jodie appeared relaxed and at ease, lying back on her crossed arms and gazing at the sky-blue painted ceiling, the skylight framed in gold and the white clouds that Isabelle had printed on with a sponge.

'Oh, all of it,' Jodie said, spreading her arms dramatically.

'But how did you know?'

Now, Jodie smiled, as if she perfectly understood the query but was unwilling to give away trade secrets so soon. 'How did I know . . .?' she teased.

'About me watching you. About me trying on the special lingerie. About every single thing you said.'

'I didn't. Not for a fact.'

'Come on. You nailed me. It was as if you were here with me when I know I was all by myself. That was amazing.'

'I just made an educated guess. Who wouldn't try on this stuff late at night? If you owned a car dealership, wouldn't you take your fastest sportster out for a spin in the sunset? If you had a bar, you'd pour an extra-good shot at the end of the evening, right? The one from the hundred-dollar bottle.'

'But the panties. You chose the exact same ones –'

'I just knew,' Jodie said. She stood and reached for the underwear in question, then slid the silk back up her toned thighs. She admired herself in the mirror over Isabelle's marble-topped desk before glancing over her shoulder at the shopkeeper. 'Sometimes you know.'

But she didn't know about the watcher. That part remained a secret. Even though Isabelle thought about pulling open the black satin curtain and revealing Cameron to Jodie, in a broad gesture like the big scene in *The Wizard of Oz*, she didn't. She'd considered telling Jodie that they were being filmed while they'd rutted against each other in the dressing room, but had remained silent. At least, on that angle.

Maybe someday in the future, they'd all gather around a roaring fire and laugh about the time Cameron had sneaked a peak at Jodie's personal punishment. Isabelle could easily visualise the scene – the three of them naked, everything out in the open. The thought turned her on intimately. She could imagine Jodie astride Cameron's body, pushing up on her thighs, riding him. And then she could imagine bending down between Cameron's legs and licking the place where his body met Jodie's and joined hers.

But not yet.

Isabelle had to protect Cameron's identity, and she also had to protect what were strange feelings inside of herself. She liked Jodie. Liked her more than a casual fling would suggest. So she'd wait, and deal with each of her lovers separately, and see where that got her in the end.

By the time Jodie left, Cameron had worked himself into a frenzy. He'd already come twice, he told Isabelle, once during the spanking, and once immediately afterwards, just from watching the women have their conversation. He'd been forced to come silently, which was torture for him – Cameron liked to be loud – but making himself be quiet and watch had been worth it, he said.

'It was insane,' he sighed. 'The way she could just talk to you while she was naked like that. Her ass must have been on fire, yet she was able to just talk to you normally right after you'd spanked her so goddamn hard.'

'How hard?' Isabelle smiled at him, running her hands through his soft, dark brown hair, then staring into his grey-green eyes. Sometimes she got lost in how good-looking he was. It didn't seem entirely fair that someone so young – he was only forty-three – could be handsome and rich and suit her personal desires so cleanly.

'Harder than you spank me.'

That was probably true. Cameron liked a glimmer of pain, but he got off more from the thought of being bad than from truly experiencing any sort of real solid pain. In his daily life, he was in charge of so much. Giving up was what he needed to do at night. Giving up was what he needed to do tonight, as well.

'So you were watching,' Isabelle said, and the smile left her face as she spoke.

'Yes,' he said, and he looked down at his feet, becoming that wayward schoolboy in an instant. Isabelle hadn't climaxed when spanking Jodie, and the feelings of impending pleasure were alive within her.

'And what did you see?'

'You know –'

'Tell me.'

'I saw you and that girl.'

'Were you supposed to be back here?'

He shook his head.

'Answer me. You know better than that. This isn't Day One, Cameron.'

His eyes remained downcast, but he said in a rush, 'No, Izzy. You told me to go. I should have.'

'But you couldn't. Is that right?'

Again he shook his head. Isabelle lifted his strong chin with one hand so that he was staring at her. Oh, he was fine. Inside herself, she melted. Outwardly, she remained the cool ice princess that Cameron required for this sort of game. 'I said I wanted a response. You shouldn't test me tonight. You saw the kind of mood I'm in.'

'Sorry,' he said immediately. 'I couldn't help myself.'

What precisely did she need to top the evening? She glanced around her back room at the various accoutrements most favoured by those who dabbled in S/M and b/d. What tool was she looking for? What weapon? After a moment, she realised that she really didn't need anything but her hand when it came to taming this lover. And that's what she chose for the evening's next event. Her firm and steady hand and his naked, humble backside.

Cameron didn't look at her as he lowered his slacks and bent over the polished white-veined black marble counter top of her desk. He waited, trembling slightly, for her to take care of him. Because that's what it was all about. Taking care of his needs by exercising her own. It couldn't get any better than that, could it?

No, Isabelle thought, answering her own question. Really, it couldn't.

She punished him with an intensity that had been building all evening long. If Jodie hadn't ever come into the store, she and Cameron still would have ended up in this position because it was one of their favourites. But now that she'd been yearning for release, the fire consumed her. The way her hand felt against his raised ass was unreal. For a moment, she felt almost as if she were outside her body, watching players put on a show for her pleasure. The whole exchange was a blur, a fast-paced interaction that was deeply necessary to both of the lovers. Necessary before they got down to the main act of the night: the sex that would fulfil each one of their darkest needs.

As Jodie made her way back to her apartment, she couldn't help but be deeply pleased with herself. She'd wanted to pursue a relationship with Isabelle Monroe for months now, but she'd been waiting for just the right time to approach the statuesque store owner. In fact, she'd been waiting until she had figured out Isabelle's routine. Did Cameron Sweeney really visit the blonde bombshell late every Wednesday afternoon? It seemed that he did.

Jodie made it her business to know more about the people around her than they knew about her. So yes, she knew that Cameron's expensive automobile was the one parked behind Belle's Beauty Box, his deep red Jaguar parked up alongside Isabelle's sleek racing green Saab. And she also knew that Mr Sweeney had a thing for watching. Her sources had let her know he was a regular at one of the more upscale gentleman's clubs in the city.

By meeting Isabelle in such a dramatic way, she had ultimately fulfilled two jobs at once. She'd gotten an itch scratched while making the first connection in her latest plan. Jodie's mind was rich with plans. She knew that they changed sometimes, regardless of how much effort she put into the preparations. But this evening, everything had gone exactly as she had hoped – even better than she could have dreamed.

Even though she was happy with how the whole evening had unfolded, she took the time to review her technique. Her butt was still sore, but it was a pleasurable type of soreness. The best type. She'd enjoyed every breath she'd shared with Isabelle, and she was pleased that she had left without crossing any barriers. It wasn't that she didn't want to move too fast – Jodie was never the type to play those false waiting games, as witnessed by her willingness to move from dressing room to back room to spank session with a stranger – it was that she needed time alone to think about what had transpired.

She wouldn't have been caught if she hadn't wanted to be. That was the truth, and while Isabelle might not understand that, it was important to Jodie to be mentally clear on that fact. If she'd wanted to steal an item undetected from Belle's Beauty Box, she would have. Easily, without even a half-thought. Truthfully, she'd done so in the past without detection. This afternoon, she could have had that thong, and several others, in her private pocket without Isabelle being any the wiser. At least, not before she'd made her way out on to the street. Perhaps in a few days, the woman would notice something amiss, but not while Jodie was present. So the shopkeeper was eagle-eyed. That didn't matter. Jodie had outsmarted far more intense scrutinisers before.

No, she had wanted something else this evening – aside from putting on a show for Cameron Sweeney and creating a connection with Ms Monroe. There were other simpler ways she could have forged the same results. But this evening she'd had an urge to experience the different, much sexier type of rush only found in getting caught.

And she'd chosen correctly, hadn't she? Because right away, Isabelle had read that desire in her. Every so often, more than anything else, Jodie liked the penance that came afterwards. Paying for something with her pain, yes, but also with her will.

For Jodie, taking it was something that never got old.

Chapter Four

www.yoursforthetaking.com

You slip in – through a door left discreetly ajar by one of the staff who has been previously paid off; a person on the interior who knows how to supplement his or her generally meagre income by engaging in the seedier side of life. Or you scurry through an open window, or up a fire escape. The goal is to slide in with the grace of a shadow – stealthy, undetected and unexpected. Move in quick. Press up flat against the wall. Check out your location to make sure everything is clear, that everything is going according to the plan you've worked so hard to formulate. Planning is the foreplay of the encounter. It's the most important part. Most people forget that, going for the big climax without properly researching the event. That's the equivalent of sex with no lubrication.

You have to know exactly what you're doing down to the last tiny detail. Because once you take that first step into a place where you don't belong, your mind goes numb. Hot waves of energy wash through you. A low buzzing fills your head.

Adrenaline is magical. Like some super drug, it makes you move quickly. Makes you feel as if you have super powers. But don't get too complacent. It also can make you stupid. Jumping at any unexpected sound. Tensing like an animal when the wind blows outside. Or when the howl of a car alarm flares up from the street. Even when a phone rings. Jesus, try not to get panicky from silly noises. Only if you hear someone answer the phone. That's the time to freeze.

Everything has to be researched, to the point where you know how many steps it takes to snatch the object of your desire. How many paces when walking, tiptoeing, or running. The whole experience takes work. So much preplanning that a less-organised or less-motivated person would go crazy from the constant attention to minuscule details. Where will the car be parked? How many employees live in the mansion? What is the secret code for the security alarm? Pulling off a successful heist requires partnerships and trust. But, most importantly, it takes balls: the strong inner core lacking in so many people these days. In the men who can't commit. In the women who are constantly on the lookout for something better to come along. Always shopping for a sweeter deal.

Create a circle, a sanctum, and stick with it. Build your bonds from the inside out. Then learn your style. You don't have to be old-school. Find something new. A new shtick, a new tick, and make it your own. Even better, never solidify your style. Be fluid and confuse the masses. Be ever-changing and always prepared. You need more than two escape plans, and you need to know what to do in an emergency. What do you do when the light flicks on and you find yourself standing in a room with your hand on the prize?

What do you do if you get caught?

Don't let your mind get worked up about that one. Focus on the wild ride of success. For me, it's all about the feeling of escaping. Of getting away with something. Pulling the scam once again. And the rush, the intense rush that starts inside and radiates outward, that's the part that's better than coming. The only thing more intense is when the two sensations are entwined.

Stealing and fucking. I know of no better aphrodisiac.

Nick spent several days watching the Bogie movies in his personal library. Watching them endlessly. On repeat. Slipping another disc into the machine as soon as the words 'The End' appeared on the screen. He didn't even pay much attention to the actual movie any more. He simply listened, letting the dialogue flow over him, until he could actually mouth the words with the characters. Pathetic, perhaps, but oddly reassuring. Like knowing the lyrics to a favourite song. The dialogue was rhythmic, and the way Bogart delivered his lines held an infinite attraction. Bogie chewed the words up and spat them out, even the tender ones.

When Nick slept, he dreamed in hard-boiled detective talk. When he was awake, which didn't feel an awful lot different from sleeping because he was almost constantly drunk, he talked to himself in a harsh undertone. 'Pick it up, Hudson. Pour it neat, man. Don't spill the good stuff, for God's sake.'

What he honestly wanted to do was to go and watch Bailey and Hunter. He knew where the two would most likely be. Out on Hunter's houseboat in Sausalito. Just like a postcard. The golden water shimmering as if dusted with a scattering of sequins. The sky alive with deep yellows and candy-coloured pinks at sunset. As he paced in his small, dark apartment, he could see the image clearly. Too clearly. He'd tipped back enough brews on the deck to know just how lovely a picture that was.

Were they laughing at him, or didn't they even have the time to be bothered with what he was thinking and how he was feeling? Too fucking busy – too busy fucking. He recalled that old bumper sticker from the seventies – 'If this van's a rocking, don't come a knocking' – and he guessed that the boat would be rocking a'plenty.

Bailey was a number one sex fiend. It was one reason they'd been so good together. The way she moved her lithe body underneath his had made him come like no one else ever had. The way she slid up and down when they did it with girl-on-top drove him crazy. Sometimes she'd push up on her thighs until he was almost completely exposed, and she'd grip onto him, grip firmly and squeeze, her blue eyes focused on him, reading the need she saw there. Other times she'd simply straddle him until she came, riding him like a cowgirl. The girl was game for anything: going out to his favourite erotic night club and engaging in a sex act on stage in front of strangers; letting him blindfold her. 'No' wasn't in her vocabulary. She refused to give a safe word, took anything he had to give. That's what he'd liked best about Bailey – she knew how to take what she wanted. Which is why she'd taken off from him and gone to his partner.

Hunter. What was it about Hunter? What did Hunter have to offer that Nick didn't? This was his least favourite question of all time. The one he would have happily obliterated with the stroke of an 'erase' key if such a thing existed in his mental realm. Instead, he tried to knock the question out to left field with a steady stream of alcohol. But that didn't work. Sometimes alcohol made him calmer when he felt like shit. This time, the pain simply spiralled around in his mind, creating an endless circle that left him breathless and just as depressed as when he'd started.

When he finally collapsed on to his smooth chocolate-brown leather sofa and tried to figure it out again, all he could think was that Hunter was the seedier of the two of them. The one without morals. Without a conscience. Christ, without a soul. He wasn't even single, a dark horse bachelor who moved from girl to girl without thinking of a lover's feelings. No, he was married to an actressy type who travelled extensively and had too much faith in her own beauty to believe that Hunter would ever cheat. And he wouldn't; not while she was in town. But when she was off on a shoot, the gold wedding band came off, and his true personality came out. Hunter was the type of lucky bastard who constantly drew the girls to him. If he'd been born in a different era, Nick thought

Hunter would have been a guy who actually notched the lash of his leather belt with his scores. Were women that easy to fake out? Did even the ones who pretended to be above the 'bad boy' hype still have that raunchy urge within themselves to play on the wrong side of the line?

He hadn't thought Bailey would be mentally soft enough to fall for that sort of style. Hunter, coming in snake-like, making his greasy little promises to her, wooing her away. He could just picture it. He'd been in enough bars with the man to hear his come-on lines, and he'd seen enough women go down for the count. But, if she *had* been going to slide out of his embrace and into Hunter's, why did she have to do it like all the others? The ones he tailed for a living, that is. Why hadn't she had the guts to say it to his face? That's what hurt the most. The way he'd found out. At least, that's what he told himself. And he believed himself. At least, he did when he was drunk.

So when was Nick going to learn? Nice guys don't ever finish first. Bogie would understand that. Bogie would sit at his side and pour him a stiff drink and shake his head sadly at the state Nick was in. His dark eyes would look Nick up and down, and then he'd growl an insult in Nick's direction. 'You call yourself a dick, Hud,' Bogie would say. 'You're giving the rest of us a bad name.'

The redhead in Lucas's arms pressed her body against his and then rotated her hips in a smooth gentle swivel. He stared into her green eyes and felt his dick expand to mammoth proportions as her wetness surrounded him. She was cool, this lady. Lucas was already melting away, yet his lover remained calm and collected, as if she had all the time in the world. As if he should be working harder than he was in order to turn her on.

Her eyes were striking, a pure and perfect emerald

colour that cleanly matched the colour of the choker-style necklace around her long, delicate neck. When the woman moved, her razor-cut bob swung with her, the edges of her hair brushing against Lucas's cheeks, tickling him. He nuzzled against the hollow of her throat. The scent of her skin was delicious; the fragrance of her perfume mixed with a heat and depth. As he kissed her, she squeezed him tight. Squeezed and released, sending instant waves of pure pleasure crashing through him.

'Oh, Christ. Do that –' he hissed. 'I mean, do that *again*. That is so good.'

She responded immediately to his request, wrapping her legs even more tightly around Lucas's muscular waist and holding on firmly. Her muscles pulled him deeper inside her.

'Like this?' she murmured, eyes on him.

'Yeah.' His voice was hardly a whisper. 'Oh, yeah –'

'Give me one reason,' she taunted, and now she pressed her body upwards, riding him. 'Can you do that, Luke?'

The dare made Lucas even harder, and he immediately embraced the girl's waist, sealing her body to his. He wanted to take that smug look off her face, wanted to make her feel exactly what he was feeling. He plunged into her, and when he slid her body up and back, he couldn't help but sigh. Inside, she was juicy wet, so ready for him. Even more important to his pleasure, she was there. Right there. When he looked at her beautiful face, he saw the heat alive in her almond-shaped eyes. From her intent expression, he could see how much she was in the moment, and that thrilled him even more.

Sometimes he lost her.

Occasionally, when they did this, she was off in her own world. No matter what he did, or how hard he tried, he couldn't bring her back to him. Talking to her. Stroking her just the right way, the way she liked best.

He could do everything exactly right, and still know that she was far away from him, somewhere impenetrable. Maybe she was receiving a surface thrill from his tantalising tricks, but she wasn't present. Those times, he felt as if he were fucking a synthetic doll – pleasing on the surface but without a necessary soul. Sure, he knew there was nothing wrong with using toys to enhance sex but, when she reverted into herself, it was different. Afterwards he always felt dirty.

'Oh, God, Jodie,' he groaned. 'You feel so good.'

But now, she was all his. In tune and turned on. That made him even hotter than before. Pressing forward against the cool painted metal wall, he sped up the pace. Thrusting his body against hers, he took her with the force of the moment. Quickies like this could be more potent than lengthy lovemaking sessions. Especially when there was the risk of getting caught.

Shimmering lilac ball gown up and out of the way, tuxedo slacks slit open and pushed down. He understood that Jodie had dressed for the possibility of a public encounter. She had no panties on beneath the gown, and her stockings were secured by the innocent pink rosettes on her garters. She and Lucas went at it fiercely, even as the sound of the orchestra flared up in the hall. Even as the rest of the dawdling concert-goers rushed to their seats so as not to miss too many notes of the second half of the night's performance.

Lucas was almost there. He could almost taste the pre-pleasure of it. A rush filled his head, that rumbling white noise, alerting him to the fact that he was on the very verge of coming. Lifting Jodie in his arms, he pushed out of the stall and set her on the marbled edge of the men's room sink. Mirrors behind her. Gilded globe lights all around. They'd lucked out this evening. The man meant to staff this rest room had been an easy buy-off. Twenty bucks had won them privacy, as long as no security guard got wise and pushed through the swing doors. In Lucas's opinion, that was money well spent. Now, he watched in the mirror behind Jodie's head as he took her. Watched his own expression as he dissolved within her.

Coming, finally coming.

Back in the lobby of San Francisco's decadent Opera House, Jodie and Lucas put their pre-planned scam into motion. Lucas had checked his three-quarter-length trench-style jacket earlier in the evening. Purposefully, he had stood behind a grey-haired woman in an ankle-length mink, and he knew precisely what her twenty-thousand-dollar coat looked like and which number it had been checked under. His tag came one number after: 723.

He and Jodie had been coming to the Opera for several seasons. They knew from experience when the girls switched off at the cloak room. One went outside on her break to the parking lot downstairs to smoke a joint with her boyfriend and maybe embark on a quickie in the back seat; the other took over the counter with a bored expression and a gossip magazine to read surreptitiously between customers. Now, Jodie came forward, Lucas's ticket in hand, and prepared to collect her merchandise.

'Here you go, miss,' the check-girl said, immediately handing over the coat Lucas had dropped off. She put her hand out, waiting automatically for the expected dollar tip.

'There must be some mistake,' Jodie said. 'This is a man's coat. Mine's a black mink.' She described it almost casually. 'Ankle-length, lined in red silk.'

The girl shook her head. Looked at the number, looked back at Jodie again.

'Look,' Jodie said, 'it's a Vivian George. Made in London. It has to be there –'

The girl was flushed now and confused, and as Jodie's voice grew more heated, the girl tried to move faster. 'I don't know what happened,' she was saying, 'that's the coat that matches your number –'

'Please look again,' Jodie insisted, the sound of impending tears in her voice. When she saw the girl retreat to the back room, she knew she'd won. How else would the check-girl be able to explain it? The number was one over. The jacket was precisely how she described it. She couldn't go and get the management – that would mean ratting out her friend, who probably had her mouth all full of her boyfriend at the moment.

What else could the girl do but give Jodie her coat?

'Don't you feel even a little bit guilty?' Lucas asked as he spread Jodie out on the beautiful black mink.

'About what? Fucking on fur? You know I'm not one of those PETA people. I love leather!'

'You probably cost the poor girl her job.'

'I didn't. Max did.'

'Meaning?'

'They'll most likely go into that coat left there at the end of the evening, and they'll search for the man who checked it. If they work really hard, they might trace the jacket back to the store in New York City where Max bought it. But I doubt the police will ever get that far.'

'And if they do,' Lucas said, taking over her line of defence, 'what will they have? A coat that Max forgot to pick up at the end of the evening.'

'I have to admit, though. I was sure the management would be called in. That's the only thing that surprised me.'

'She didn't want to get that involved. You know – point out that her friend had cut out early and was getting stoned downstairs –'

'That's what I was banking on.'

'But she will have your description.'

'As a redhead,' Jodie reminded him, 'with deep green eyes and full cleavage thanks to the wonders of a fantastically created push-up bra,' she continued, shaking off the wig and blinking hard as she removed the coloured contacts. 'But don't worry. I'll put in a call from the woman who had her coat stolen. I'll make sure the girl isn't permanently out of a job. Just transferred to some different department. Does that make you feel better?'

Lucas grinned at her. 'Come on, baby. You know what will make me feel better.'

'You're easy to please.'

'No,' he said, shaking his head. 'Not easy. Just ready.'

'And what are you ready for?'

'Do I need to say it? Put the wig back on, Jodie.'

'Oh, I get it,' Jodie said snidely, reaching for the discarded wig and tucking her long hair back up beneath it. 'You want to do it with another woman.'

'Nope,' he told her, shaking his head as he watched her check out her reflection in the mirror. 'Not ever.'

'Then what?'

'Lie down on that coat, Jodie.'

She did as he said, gazing up at him still. 'What do you want, Lucas? You need more pussy?'

He pinned her wrists together and then spread her lips with two fingers. 'Not yet. I need something else first.'

'So what is that you need?' she murmured, her voice suddenly hoarse.

'Need to punish you first, baby doll. Been such a bad girl, haven't you?' He grinned at her, a knowing look in his eyes. 'You don't even have to try to answer that one. We both know all about you –'

Jodie shivered, unable to answer as Lucas pinched her hot spot tightly between his thumb and forefinger, then rubbed over it firmly. 'You know the position,' he said, 'don't let me down.' Sighing, Jodie pulled free from his grip and rolled over. Her body pressed firmly against the soft fur, her ass lifted in the air. Lucas reached for one of Jodie's own leather belts, which hung from a hook on the back of the closet door. He ran the leather against her naked back, then traced it down her lean legs, letting her feel the kiss of the leather on her skin before doubling the belt with a snap.

She shuddered at the sound, then waited, totally still, for the first blow.

'Higher,' Lucas ordered, and she lifted her hips off the bed in an automatic gesture to please him. He would make her work for this. That was fine. Because if she did exactly as he said, the rewards would be overwhelming.

There was a moment when the heat pulsed between them even though they weren't touching in any way. This connection was what made Jodie grind her hips against the soft fur as Lucas traced the belt against her naked skin once again. Their quick session at the Opera had brought her a sweet flush of pleasure. But she'd known that Lucas would truly take care of her when they got back to her apartment, and that's what really brought the wetness on.

She slid one hand under her body, pressing her fingers against herself as she waited for Lucas to start the punishment session of the evening. He took his time, walking around the bed, looking at her from all angles. Jodie closed her eyes tightly, tense with antici-pation, and then she tried to make herself relax and give up the power to Lucas. Give up everything.

'Higher,' Lucas insisted, and Jodie lifted her hips even higher off the bed.

A battle of wills ensued between them. It always did. Jodie was too strong to let her power be taken away. Yet all she wanted to do was submit. Making her wait, making her wonder, was one way for Lucas to get on top. She was pleased with him for taking control of the situation. He knew exactly what he was doing, knew exactly what she needed. When the first strike of leather finally landed, she turned her head and opened her eyes, staring at him. When the second blow landed, she was his.

Chapter Five

Jodie's small fist closed tightly around the ring of keys. The whole set disappeared into the palm of her hand. Only three dangling keys tinkled off the heart-shaped ring, but Jodie didn't need a lot of keys. She only needed one.

Sometimes opportunities arose unexpectedly. When they did, you had to have the nerve to take a chance. For weeks, she'd been watching this woman, one of the members of her gym. That was a little too close for comfort, wasn't it? But the lady lived in Pacific Heights in a house that interested Jodie. She'd tried lots of different ways to figure out how she was going to get in, not revealing her plans yet to Lucas because she wasn't sure if she would actually take the risk. So far, her main plan had been to steal the woman's keys while the lady was working out. Then she would copy the house key and replace the set before the lady ever noticed.

As it turned out, she hadn't even needed to go to that trouble. She'd seen the keys slip out of the bag at the gym and fall on to the grey rubber mat under the bench, and she'd waited, holding her breath to see if the woman would notice.

No.

But, surely, the woman would return right away. How could she get home without her car keys? If she did come back, Jodie would simply hand over the key ring with a smile. 'Found these,' she'd say. 'I was just about to bring them to the front desk.' But that didn't happen.

Slowly, Jodie dressed herself. She took several extra minutes with her hair and make-up, giving the woman plenty of time to realise her keys were missing. When five minutes had passed, Jodie trailed out of the dressing room and into the lobby. There, she waited, checking out the situation. Was the woman at the desk, asking if anyone had seen her key ring? No.

Silently, Jodie stood in the lobby and stared through the plate glass windows as the woman climbed into a waiting car. Luck was on her side. It could be hours before the woman knew that her keys were missing. Breathless at what this meant, she hurried down the street to the nearest key-copying store. She waited, feet tapping on the floor, for the boy behind the counter to make one copy of the house key. Then she sprinted back to the gym and left the keys on the counter for the lost and found.

'Saw these,' she said. 'Someone's sure to miss them.'

'Thanks so much, miss,' the receptionist had said, bored with her job, dropping the keys into a pile of miscellaneous items in the large plastic barrel under her desk. She began flipping through her magazine again without another glance up towards Jodie. That's it, Jodie thought. I'm free. The world was a blur as she exited the gym for the second time of the morning. All she could think of was one simple fact: Now, she had an easy way in.

One important part of Jodie's 'job' was to know people. When she'd lived in Los Angeles, she could pick out the winners on sight. Not only the celebrities that every star-eyed tourist could recognise, but the people behind the scenes. Real money doesn't always come in a sparkling package, Jodie had learned. Often, the people who she needed to get right next to were the ones dressed in subdued clothes, driving unassuming vehicles. Yes, their outfits might be specially made by hand in Italy, but they possessed none of the glitzy and gilded edges you'd expect.

Now her job was specifically to know her neighbours in Pacific Heights. She knew this woman well on sight, had been in her house on several occasions for parties. Open houses. Always as a guest of a friend. Now, knowing that the lady was off somewhere, she made her way quickly to her own car. Drove to the house. Parked. Then waited.

Her mind reeled with possibilities. Could she get in today or would she have to come back another time? Now that she had an entry way she could put some planning into the situation. But why not go for it?

Light filtered through her windshield. The spring breeze showered her car with tiny white petals from the plum tree above. Jodie hardly saw them. What would she take? It had to be something small and something quick. What would she do if the staff found her? She sat in her car until she saw a lady in a stark white uniform leave through the front door and walk down the street towards the bus stop. Then, heart racing, Jodie went for it. If she ran into someone unexpectedly in the house, she'd simply say that she was there to do an appraisal – that the door was open and she'd let herself in. People generally believed what they wanted to hear, and there was no reason for anyone to think she was lying.

The key slid in cleanly. She'd done it. With careful steps she walked inside the hall. The air here was cooler than outside. The light was dim. She looked around, remembering. That's right. The bathroom off the frescoed entryway. That's where she wanted to go. A glass case on one wall held a collection of tiny erotic figurines. The sensuality of the small statues was unexpected in an environment like this. Jodie found the out-of-place items to be extremely fetching in that sense. Once in the bathroom, Jodie hurried. She scanned the grouping of erotic art, found the one she liked the best, and slid it into her pocket. Taking a breath, she dropped a simple golden cufflink, watching as it slid almost silently to the floor behind the sink. That done, she left as she'd entered, walking right out the front door.

It couldn't get any better than that. There was no way for anyone to guess she'd been there. No way for the woman to think that someone had broken in with her own set of keys. Crazy laughter bubbled up inside Jodie as she made her way back to her car. She had to hurry to meet Isabelle.

They had a lunch date.

'So, what do you think?' Isabelle turned around twice in front of Jodie, showing off her body, clad in a pair of fine-boned corduroys the innocent colour of a first blush. Jodie admired the back of the slacks without speaking for a moment, as Isabelle scrutinised her figure in the full-length mirror taking up the rear wall of the eclectic boutique. 'Your honest opinion,' she urged, prompting her new friend.

'Honestly,' Jodie began, 'I think you look good in everything.'

Isabelle spun again, then stopped, looking over her shoulder at her tight rear view. 'Sometimes I wish I bothered to wear panties,' she said in a low voice, so the snooty-looking woman behind the counter couldn't hear her. But, although Isabelle had spoken softly, the woman didn't have to strain in order to hear Jodie's immediate response.

'You're kidding,' Jodie said, then quickly lowered her voice to match Isabelle's hushed tone. 'I mean, you are kidding, right? You're just toying with me for my reaction.'

'I wear them when I'm in the mood. But mostly I go bare. I think it's sexier.'

'You sell lingerie for a living,' Jodie continued, incredulous.

'Don't judge a girl by her bra and panties –' Isabelle laughed. 'Seriously. I'm surrounded by the stuff all day.

It's nice to take a break. Look at you. You buy jewellery for a living, and all you wear is that oversized man's wristwatch and the platinum signet ring. It's not like you're ever draped in pearls.'

At her words, Jodie experienced a brief flashback to her pearl escapade with Lucas, and she smiled at the memory before locking back in on what Isabelle was saying. 'I totally understand the fantasy of frilly items. But I prefer the feeling of really good fabric against my naked skin. And it gives me this extra-naughty charge. Generally, I'm the only one who knows the secret. I get to choose who I share it with. You know what I mean?'

Jodie did know. Staring at Isabelle again, she focused on her friend's ass, packed perfectly in the gorgeous slacks. 'You look good enough to eat,' Jodie murmured. Isabelle took a step closer, and then she pressed her lips against Jodie's ear. 'I like the sound of that,' she whispered. 'Just let me buy these, and I'll take you up on the offer.'

The girls didn't make it all the way back to Jodie's apartment. They hadn't even fully settled on the ripped blue vinyl seat of the taxi before Jodie reached for Isabelle, pulling her tightly into an embrace.

'We can't do it in a cab.'

'Why not?' Jodie asked, her hand up under Isabelle's tight, white T-shirt, stroking her friend's pert breasts. She hadn't lied on that point. No bra in sight. Or touch.

'Because he's watching,' Isabelle hissed, nodding her head towards the dark-haired driver.

'So what? You'll never see him again.'

'It's too clichéd.'

'Have you ever done it before?' Jodie asked, grazing her mouth against the side of Isabelle's neck. She was just kissing here when she felt Isabelle's will begin to break. The blonde beauty leaned back against the steel-blue seat and sighed.

'No,' Isabelle answered.

'No, meaning that you want me to stop.'

'No, I've never done it in a cab before.'

'Oh,' Jodie said happily. 'That is good news. And even if you think it's clichéd, it's new to you.'

The ride took ten minutes. Up and down San Francisco's famous hills. Usually, it would only take five minutes maximum to get from Union Square to the Marina, but Jodie paid the driver extra for a scenic tour. 'As long as you keep your eyes on the scenery out the window,' she told him, pushing a folded fifty through the slit in the plastic divider. The man nodded, but Jodie could tell from his eyes looking at her in the rear view mirror that he was lying. And that made her even more aroused. Performing in front of an audience was one of her favourite sports. She liked to do it with either sex. Didn't really matter to her, as long as there was a watcher. Despite her friend's hesitation, she knew that Isabelle felt the same way.

Isabelle closed her eyes and let Jodie stroke her through her T-shirt and new slacks. When Jodie unzipped the corduroys, Isabelle groaned loudly. Jodie looked up into the mirror, meeting the driver's eyes again, and she gave him a quick, encouraging smile before bringing her lips to the split of Isabelle's body. Hungrily, she licked up and down over the bud, then pressed her tongue deeper. A satiny liquid coated those pretty bare lips, adding a subtle sheen to them.

'Talk to me,' Jodie said, speaking into the split between Isabelle's thighs.

'I can't.' It was a rush of air more than a statement.

'Then I'll stop.'

'No, no. Don't stop. What do you want me to say?'

'Say how it feels.'

Jodie had a reason for wanting Isabelle to be relaxed. She was going to come out to her. Not out sexually. But out criminally. Yes, Isabelle knew full well that she was good with sleight of hand, but she didn't know as much as Jodie wanted her to. Tonight, Jodie was going to turn Isabelle into an accomplice, and she believed that would take some doing. If the girl couldn't even be sure about screwing in a cab, then she'd need extra incentive to abscond with something that wasn't hers. Isabelle was tough. A powerhouse. But she was a good girl at heart. Jodie could tell. She liked rules, because she liked order. It didn't matter that most of the time other people obeyed the ones that she laid out. A love for rules was a love for rules, plain and simple. Jodie was about to make her break some. Chaos could be so sexy.

'Oh, God,' Jodie said suddenly.

'Yes,' Isabelle echoed. 'Oh, my God –'

'No.' Jodie pulled away, looking through the clear plastic divider and speaking to the driver. 'We have a change of plans.'

Isabelle, rumpled and confused, tried to regain her composure as Jodie gave the driver directions.

'Why are we going to the Haight?' Isabelle whispered.

'It's a surprise.'

The Haight was a completely different part of the city from the high-class crush of billion-dollar real estate at Union Square. The centre of the Summer of Love back in the 1960s, the region was still known for its bendable rules of society. There were runaways and street people, musicians and hippies. Still. As if they'd come to a party decades before and forgotten to go home. Even now they resembled the hippies from 35 years in the past, wearing a rainbow of tie-dye and sporting long ponytails and round sherbet-coloured sunglasses. The original ones had gone grey and wrinkled, but many remained dedicated to their causes – even if their causes had long been abandoned by most. The youth tried their best to emulate pictures they'd seen in *Rolling Stone* magazine – but there was something a little too clean about them, as if they didn't tie-dye the shirts themselves, but bought them at some high-end store at the mall.

Many things had stayed the same during the decades since the original hippies had lived there. The Victorian buildings remained with their brightly coloured trim and stained-glass inlaid windows. The thrift stores thrived en masse, along with organic groceries, vinyl record shops, and even the old-fashioned movie theatre attached to one of the most famous hotels in the city. This theatre played vintage movies and artsy documentaries. The organically grown popcorn came in a wooden bowl and you were able to bring a real glass of organic apple juice to your seat with you. No Styrofoam or plastic packaging found in the place.

But the region *was* changing. The Gap had arrived on the once sacred corner of Haight and Ashbury, along with some higher-end clothing stores catering to the young hipsters rather than the old hippies. While progress encroached, the core of the Haight worked to retain its values. What the relaxed social codes of the region really meant was the feeling of being transported to a faraway place when walking down the street: a Mecca, such as Amsterdam, where there was a plethora of easily available drugs and the freewheeling attitude that went with them.

Jodie and Isabelle exited their cab and walked along Haight Street. Isabelle was still giddy from the erotic cab ride experience, but Jodie had a focused expression on her face. They passed the Dreams Come True Head Shop, where you could buy incense, tie-dye, chess sets with lava-lamp-shaped pieces, and any sort of bong that you wanted. It was here that Jodie had once overheard a young preppy-looking boy begging for information about giving a good drug test. 'Isn't there anything you can eat?' he was asking, desperate. 'Parsley, or mint, or something? Come on, man. I've got a job interview tomorrow. Mandatory testing.' Then, more to himself than to any of the people around him, 'Jesus, I'm ruined.'

As they got closer to the grassy strip of park at the end of the street, Jodie started listening more closely to the scruffy youths on the sidewalk. They weren't just muttering to themselves. They were offering commodities. 'Green bud. Weed. Red hairs.' The dealers spoke in harsh undertones, talking after the women had passed them. If the girls were interested, they could turn around and walk back a few paces. Jodie knew the concept of this sort of street-hawking had something to do with the law, but she couldn't remember all of the rules. Was it illegal for a cop to backtrack in order to make an arrest? That seemed too ridiculous to be true. But the kids hawked their wares in that style for a reason. She knew that.

To her way of thinking, this was all a silly game. People should be allowed to buy marijuana if they wanted to. Sure, it was a mind-altering substance, but so was alcohol.

When she saw the dealer she was looking for, she nodded and kept walking. The pink-haired street urchin followed after her and Isabelle, and the three women kept walking towards the park. Once in a comfortable location out of sight from the traffic on the street, Jodie handed over three twenties, folded cleanly into a packet that could easily be palmed. The girl slid the money into the pocket of her faded green cargo pants, then turned and hurried away.

'You paid her for nothing?'

'She'll be back,' Jodie explained, grinning at Isabelle's naivete. 'They don't carry the product on them. The street kids are just the delivery mechanism. She'll take the cash to her higher-up, who will give her the product to bring to me.'

'Product,' Isabelle repeated, obviously liking the word.

'Don't you ever just want to kick back and get stoned?'

At her question, Isabelle locked on to Jodie's expression. 'Do I?' she repeated. 'Oh, yeah –'

'You're talking about an apple.'

'I *know* I'm talking about an apple.'

'You're not hungry and you're not poor. Why would you want to steal a piece of fruit?'

'I don't,' Jodie said, matter-of-factly. 'You do.'

'Oh, come on.' Isabelle smiled. The marijuana had made her feel relaxed and easy-going. She was enjoying this conversation with Jodie, as if they were simply discussing theft at an intellectual level; the artistic concept of thievery as an illusive rush. 'I don't want to steal anything.'

'Yes, you do,' Jodie said, exhaling a silver-grey cloud of smoke. 'You want to. Deep down inside, you want to. It's making you wet just thinking about it. You want to palm that ripe ruby-red fruit, slip it into your pocket, and walk out the door without anyone being the wiser.' As she spoke, she toyed with a small ivory-coloured object in one hand. Isabelle couldn't see exactly what the item was, but she moved closer, trying to figure it out.

'And then what?'

'And then nothing. Then you're done.'

'But why would I ever do that?' Even though Jodie had been explaining the idea for some time, Isabelle couldn't wrap her drug-hazed mind around the concept.

Jodie sighed. 'For the thrill.'

'I'll get caught.'

'No. Thinking that you'll get caught is what makes it fun and exciting. But you won't. You'll get away with it, and your heart will be pounding. Pounding hard. And you'll find it difficult to breathe for a minute or two. And then you'll want to do it again.'

'Screw?'

'No, baby. Steal.'

'I'd rather screw.' Isabelle grinned, spreading her thighs wide beneath the Oriental jade-green sheets and gazing at Jodie with her best do-me expression.

'Then do it,' Jodie agreed with a shrug. 'But it won't be the same.'

'Tell me why.'

'Do it just this once, and you won't have to ask.'

Isabelle was silent for a moment, waiting to see if this whole conversation was all just a game. Yes, stealing had been intimately involved in how she met Jodie, but now she couldn't tell whether or not the girl was provoking her for a reaction or whether she was downright serious. When Jodie didn't say anything else, Isabelle suddenly understood that this was more than a dare. It was a test.

Slowly, she rolled over and pushed herself off the mattress. Her legs felt weak. After all that sex, she didn't know how she found the energy to slip into her new corduroys, put her white T-shirt back on, and slide on her favourite black mules. But with Jodie watching her like that, she couldn't help herself. Do what she was told and come back to the bed to get boned like that again. She'd do a lot of unexpected things in order to have sex that good, wouldn't she?

'An apple,' Jodie instructed. 'From the store on the corner. Bring it back and then we'll talk.'

'Talk?'

'Whatever. We'll do whatever. I promise. But wait one second.'

Isabelle walked closer.

'Take down your pants again.'

'Why?'

'Just do it.'

Isabelle slid them down her thighs, then shot Jodie a curious look.

'Now turn around and bend over.'

'Come on –'

'Just do it,' Jodie repeated.

Isabelle bent over, offering her bottom to Jodie, who wet the ivory-colored toy that she'd been playing with and slowly began to slide it between Isabelle's rear cheeks. Immediately, Isabelle pulled away. 'What are you doing?' she started to say. She heard the next words in her head: I'm the one on top. But when she looked over her shoulder at Jodie, she saw something in the girl's eyes that made her back down. Why not experience everything that Jodie was offering? Taking a deep breath, Isabelle bent over again.

'Now, spread yourself open for me,' Jodie said, and the sound of humour in her voice let Isabelle know how much she was enjoying this entire interaction. Still, Isabelle followed the instructions, reaching around to part the cheeks of her ass for Jodie. The brunette thief quickly slid the butt plug inside, then tugged on the base to make sure the toy stayed put. The sensation of being filled was instantaneous, and Isabelle found herself automatically clenching down on the toy.

'That's something to take your mind off what you're going to be doing. You'll think about how that feels inside of you, and you'll forget even to be nervous.'

'I can't walk with this –'

'So many can'ts,' Jodie laughed. 'Why don't you just give it a try and see how everything goes.'

Isabelle stood and walked slowly across the room, wriggling her ass as she moved. Would the toy fall out? Apparently not. She felt filled by the toy, and she felt deeply confused by her racing heart. Usually, she was the one issuing commands. What was Jodie doing to her? Rather than try to answer, she fastened an elastic band around her long straight hair and blew Jodie a kiss. It felt natural to do so, staring at her new plaything as she reclined in bed beneath the rumpled sheets and velvety bedcover. And she knew that under the sheets Jodie was wearing the thong that had started this all. That turned her on even more.

'Hurry up, baby,' Jodie called out as she lit another joint. 'I miss you already.'

Isabelle was going to do this by herself, just to prove she could. Silly, wasn't it? The things one would do on a dare? Not solely on a dare, she admonished herself as she walked the three flights of stairs down to the street. On a wave of lust that she couldn't deny. She strolled the twenty feet to the corner grocery store housed in the bottom floor of a converted Victorian. Casually, she glanced at the racks of produce as if she weren't even interested in the apples, oranges or the clusters of yellow bananas. A wide assortment of shining fruits and vegetables were piled into intricate pyramids. If she took the wrong one, all would tumble down.

The sleepy-eyed boy behind the counter didn't look up from his comic book as Isabelle made her way around the aisle until she saw what she truly wanted: grapes. Round purple grapes. Maybe she should teach Jodie something about stealing. An apple would be easy, wouldn't it? But a handful of grapes would be far more difficult to hide. Jodie was right about one thing. Just thinking about taking something made Isabelle's heart pound. Why was she doing this? She could simply pay for the grapes and be on her way. Back in Jodie's apartment, she'd lie to her newfound bedmate. Yeah, she took 'em.

But, as strange as it was to think this – *that* would be cheating.

As she walked around the tiny store, she had a personal Q & A session with herself. When had she last stolen something for real? Now, that was easy enough. At three years old she'd taken a candy bar from the rack of a grocery store while her mother wasn't looking. Upon discovery of the theft, she had been forced to confess her misdeed to the manager of the local store. The horror of embarrassment stayed with her after all these years and she'd never pilfered anything again. Not as a teenager. Not even as a giggly co-ed in college, when all of her sorority sisters had swiped food after hours from the cafeteria for late-night snacks while watching *Twilight Zone*. So why was she going to start now?

Because the sex was too good. She could hear Jodie telling her about the rush of stealing. Could hear each word in her head above the crackling white noise that buzzed beneath. Hands palming the fruits, squeezing, releasing. Not that apple. Not that one, either. No, back to the grapes. Green-haired punk boy at the counter glancing up, but not at her. A mohawked buddy coming to talk to him. Keep him company during the midnight hour.

When did punk come back in? she wondered. Did these kids know that they were being retro? That people old enough to be their parents had sported similar hairstyles way back in the late 1970s? That the original punk rockers were now grey-haired and paunchy.

The kid looked up at her, as if feeling her eyes on his hair, sensing when her gaze moved to the multiple piercings in his ear, his forehead, his chin. But Isabelle was seeing now without seeing. Jodie was waiting.

Do it, Isabelle, that voice told her. Do it and be done.

A handful of round purple grapes disappeared into the deep recesses of her jacket pocket. She held an apple tightly in the other hand.

'Got any figs?' she asked the boy behind the counter. This request won her a strange look and a shake of his head. The circular piercing in his eyebrow glinted beneath the fluorescent lights. 'Out of season,' he told her, brow furrowed, as if any true fig-lover would know that. She shrugged, self-consciously. 'Got a craving.'

'Would fig newtons work?' he offered. 'Back there against the wall.' He seemed to suddenly realise that there was a seriously pretty girl in his store, and that maybe if he chatted her up something might happen. It was clear in his eyes that he was already visualising fantasy number 641. The one in which he pushed a lithe customer against the frozen food case, pressing her body firmly against the cold wall of glass as he warmed her up inside. His buddy disappeared from the scene, slinking off to the corner to look at the assortment of skate rat magazines. But Isabelle wasn't interested.

Another nearly helpless shrug and she was free, bursting through the glass doors and down the street. The road was empty of cars and pedestrians, but Isabelle still felt as if millions of eyes were on her. After pressing the buzzer, and hearing the catch on the lock release, she raced up the stairs to Jodie's apartment, so aware of the stolen produce in her pocket and so aware of her ragged heartbeat and that other beat between her legs. Needing.

'Back so soon?' called Jodie from the threshold, joint still in her fingers, ashtray at her side. 'Empty handed?' she asked next, legs crossed at the ankle, hand propped behind her head.

And Isabelle, bringing out the polished red apple, opened her mouth wide to take a bite.

In reality, it was Jodie who liked to bite. Leaving marks to show that she'd been to a region before thrilled her. Claiming her place on the map of Isabelle's luscious body – or on the body of any lover – gave her an instant flush of pleasure. Coming upon those marks afterwards turned her on even more, the next time, than the actual bite. She started with kisses, fiery against Isabelle's soft skin. Then worked a little harder. Nipping. Nibbling. Until she parted her legs and bit for real.

'Oohh,' Isabelle sighed, moving away at the startling sensation.

'Stay there,' Jodie said. 'Take it.'

Body tense, Isabelle held herself in check. But she squirmed away again when the heat of Jodie's open mouth caressed her skin once again. When the teeth pressed in, Isabelle moved.

'Don't think,' Jodie instructed. 'Don't worry.'

Continuing down her chosen route, Jodie took her time. She licked and lapped, spending long minutes at each of her favourite areas. The nape of Isabelle's neck. The lobes of her ears. The delicate line of her spine. She moved all the way down Isabelle's naked body to the place where the plug remained. Gently, she rocked the base of the sex toy, and Isabelle moaned at the feel. Without warning, Jodie bit again, choosing a ripe, round part of Isabelle's ass to leave her next lovebite. It was easy to tell from the way Isabelle trembled that she was doing her very best not to jump off the mattress. This pleased Jodie. Nothing was as sexy to her as when a lover took what she had to offer.

She could take, herself; oh yes, she was very good at taking, but she could also give. The two aspects of her personality seemed at odds at first, but they weren't. They were simply two parts to the whole, two sides of the same story.

So Nick couldn't help himself – so what? If he was going to sneak a peek at what the two lovebirds were doing, at least he had the skill to do so. He wasn't some bumbling moron who made noise as he walked along the dock, disturbing the peace of all the innocent slumbering house-owners.

Innocent. Right.

When he approached Hunter's pad, he became even more aware of his surrounding environment. His skin prickled, and he found that he was holding his breath for long stretches of time, then releasing the air between his taut lips in a whispering hiss. His chest shook with each exhalation, and he clenched and unclenched both his fists and his jaw in a repetitive rhythm.

No, this wasn't the best idea he'd ever had. But was it more or less productive then just kicking back in his apartment getting drunk? That was the main question. One that he didn't have the ability to answer. Not now. Maybe not ever. He walked right up to the windows, moving slowly. He knew the layout of the houseboat intimately, as intimately as he knew the personal layout of the comely blonde woman on Hunter's bed. He could see her through the parted curtains. There she was – belly-down on the mattress, her ripe wheat golden hair spread out on the pillow, her hips raised up in an indecent position as if she was offering her body up for clinical observation. What was she doing?

Oh, that was easy enough to detect. She was touching herself; a hand under her long lean body, her fingers rubbing and circling her clit. Nick knew all about how Bailey liked to touch herself. One of her favourite methods of foreplay had been to ask him to wait while she stroked herself. Up and down. Round and round. Whenever he would try to come towards the bed, she'd hold him off with a look, and finally with words. 'Not yet, baby. Don't make me stop –'

What power she'd had over him. Why had he let her ever take charge? Because he'd seen what she was able to do. While watching her on her husband's dime, he'd fallen for the way she had moved her body, the way she could hold a man still with one single look. Were those the same reasons that Hunter had gone for her? Had he followed her when she was with Nick? Had he seen the sultry queen of slutdom in action with his partner?

Where was Hunter anyway? Nick peered in further, losing what remained of his inhibitions now that he'd got this close. Ah, Hunter was seated in a canvas director's chair across the way, video poised to capture Bailey in motion, casually reclining in the comfortable position of erotic film cameraman. The video caught everything – Bailey touching, stroking, moaning. Wasn't that kinky? Apparently, not kinky enough, because as Bailey thrust her fingers even deeper into herself, arching her ass up off the bed, Hunter set the camera on a waiting tripod and joined her on the mattress. With his clothes off, Hunter looked like a rodeo star, all sinews and tightly coiled muscles. He gripped on to Bailey's waist and locked into her, and even that wasn't enough for the duo. Nick caught sight of the big-screen TV across the way. They were simultaneously screwing and filming and filming and watching.

Was this why she'd left him? Jesus, he had filmed her, as well, hadn't he? Filmed rolls of 35 mm snapshots of her and her medley of lovers getting it on in the master suite of her mansion while her husband was at work. He'd lost his mind for her while watching her cheat. And now she was cheating on him while he was watching again. Maybe that was fate, because here he was, continuing in the perpetual loop that seemed to make up their relationship.

Carefully, he withdrew his own camera from his inner jacket pocket and started taking pictures through the windows. One after another. He might not have access to the woman any more. But at least he'd have the evidence. Of what, he wasn't precisely sure.

Nick didn't know what he would do with the film once he'd developed the roll. He wasn't thinking that far ahead. Yet he knew what he'd like to do: blow up the pictures and send them to Bailey's office. Or rent a billboard and put them up there for the amusement of the early morning commuters – that was a thought. But he couldn't truly fault her for her actions. All she'd done was behave exactly as she had from the moment he'd first seen her. Characters act characteristically.

That was something you learned on the first day of being a private dick. So when was Nick going to master the basic lesson of human behaviour?

'The first time? Very first time?'

'Yes,' insisted Isabelle, moving her mouth in a sticky line down the centre of Jodie's stomach. She used her hands to part Jodie's legs, then held them wide apart and breathed against the jewel within.

'Come on,' Isabelle begged. 'I know you remember. You *have* to remember.'

Of course she remembered and, as she grew ever closer to climax, the history of her double life unfolded itself in her mind. In truth, Jodie M. Silver didn't need to steal. In fact, she didn't even think of herself as a thief. To her, thieves were dirty, low-class and low-valued people who needed cash quickly. They behaved in erratic, uncontrollable manners, and generally had addictions – or simply mouths – to feed. Most importantly, they couldn't discern between art and artifact. Jodie knew the difference. She'd been to college and had gone on to get a PhD in art history.

Jodie didn't lift things for money. She stole only for the rush that came with taking things that weren't hers. A powerful pleasure, part excitement at the prospect, part thrill of success, pulsed through her with every heist. She'd been doing this for years, but not so long that she couldn't immediately remember the first thing she'd stolen. Her addiction to danger had started as a dare. Innocent, almost. A tease, a taunt. 'Take that one. The pretty glass ashtray. Put it in your purse.' A pause. A silky hesitation in the air between her and her boyfriend. 'You can't, can you? Such a good girl, can't ever break the rules.'

Jodie, young – so young that she'd do almost anything if someone thought she couldn't – passed on the clear crystal Lalique ashtray that her boyfriend was pointing to, then moved on to something far more

73

expensive and interesting. When she and Joshua had
left the party, they were no longer a couple. He'd tried
to kiss her, to back her up against the brick wall
surrounding the Bel Air chateau, to make out with her
beneath the heady blossoms of the honeysuckle vines.
She'd said 'no', moving out of his reach, strolling solo
down the twisting road towards Sunset Boulevard,
where she had caught a bus ride home to her tiny
apartment in Santa Monica.

And in her purse? The most beautiful sterling silver
lighter she'd ever seen in her life. She remembered
every step of the theft: putting the lighter in her purse;
leaving the party with it; feeling her heart race at the
thought that someone might have seen her, might
have guessed what she'd done and punished her for it.
Her nerves were wound so tight that they hummed, as
did that most private part of her between her legs.
Years had passed, but she'd never forgotten the
pleasure of the moment. That heart-pounding feeling
of getting away with something. Behaving in a manner that was completely unexpected. A bad girl in good
girl's clothing. That's what she was.

In Jodie's world, stealing had become entwined with
sex. The more expensive, or hard to get, an item, the
more aroused she became at the prospect of taking it.
Of owning it. Fantasies of possessing the desired object
became detailed masturbatory stories that she'd retell
herself again and again. Finally, after a successful
night out, she could hardly contain herself.

'Come on,' Isabelle insisted. 'Tell me.'

'First time I got caught?'

'First time it made you come.'

'Ah,' sighed Jodie as she came ecstatically. 'That's
different. That would be telling, now wouldn't it?'

Yet telling was exactly what Jodie did. On her website,
she was shrouded in the privacy afforded her on the
Internet. This ether-like existence was a fantasy world

to her. You could be anyone you wanted online. Not only in the chatrooms, where men were women, housewives were teenagers, teenagers were of the legal age of consent. No, you could be far more clever than that, creating a whole persona for yourself if you had the inclination.

And Jodie did.

Because while stealing was her passion, revealing wasn't something she was often able to do. She couldn't come flat out and tell most people. A select few knew about her side-games, her hobby. Basically, on a need-to-know basis. Occasionally, she slipped and let down her guard, as she had with Isabelle, but she rarely let herself enjoy that much freedom. Even with Isabelle, she hadn't exposed herself entirely. Not all the way. Never all the way. Don't be weak, that was her motto. Never tell everything at once.

Online, however, it was a whole different set of rules. On her website, she'd created an entire universe dedicated solely to the art of thievery. She featured sidebars of movies with thieves as the heroes: *To Catch a Thief*, *Object of Desire*, *The Thomas Crown Affair*, *Thief of Hearts*. She posted facts about average shoplifters. The most commonly stolen item? A tube of lipstick. Most often stolen book? Brace yourself: The Bible. Guess most people haven't read the Ten Commandments before they take that book, right? She posted articles that claimed most thieves didn't want to be caught, which Jodie wasn't sure that she fully believed. Didn't everyone want to share their darkest secrets at some level? Wasn't that what confessionals were all about? And therapists? And even diaries, journals, letters. What was the point of doing something if other people didn't find out?

What Jodie loved most about her site was the cat-and-mouse aspect of it. Maybe the police checked her out occasionally, but she was far more clever than they were. Her identity was so well buried that it would take an insane amount of time to unravel the clues and find her out. And then what would that even prove? She never kept tabs on her actual jobs. She only chronicled the delight in stealing – the art of the take. Her website was a homage to thievery, an altar to an evil occupation. Sure, she started with the codicil at the top to protect herself; it stated that the space wasn't intended to urge anyone to actually shoplift. But those were just words on a page.

Late at night, she did the upkeep. She could post a new column in less than five minutes. Sometimes, she featured histories of famous thefts, such as master-piece artworks taken right under the eyes of museum security. Other times, she rambled in her first-person columns, usually waxing poetic right before or right after she made a successful heist. When she was flying high from a job well done, she could write for hours. Now, on the verge of her most intricate and difficult job ever, she found herself putting more time on the web. It helped her to think, helped her to sort out all of the different parts. Pre-planning for a situation made her calm, and possessing a calm mind was exactly what she needed right now.

Chapter Six

Jodie was late, but she couldn't help herself. Usually, she arrived at the office by eight, making calls to the east coast or following up on European leads that had been emailed to her computer during the night. But today, one of those postcard-perfect San Francisco mornings, she felt like playing hooky. The salt-tinged air from the Bay seemed scented with the fragrance of the eucalyptus trees decorating Golden Gate Park. Lazily, the sun peeked from behind a ribbon of clouds, creating a pink-gold halo of light on Jodie's favourite neighbourhood.

She took her time walking to work along comely Chestnut Avenue, stopping at the Jones Cafe on the corner of Fifteenth Street, where she was a regular. 'Jonesing for a coffee?' was the slogan above the espresso-maker.

The scruffy kid behind the counter poured a double-shot of espresso into a small paper cup before Jodie could even open her mouth to place the order. Jodie slid an extra dollar into the tip jar on the counter, casually accepting the boy's admiring glance before she left. Turning thirty several weeks before hadn't slowed down those appreciative looks from strangers. If anything, she found that she was growing into a new confidence. One that she felt like a warm fire within her chest, radiating outward.

Jodie drank the first sip of coffee while standing in front of a new gallery next door and observing the art within. Nothing good. Nothing worth fantasising about. Not like Isabelle's store on the other side. This window here was filled with fancy, featherlight confections made of lace and satin, some trimmed with decadent marabou fluff, others slick and dramatic in black leather. Here, Jodie paused again, and the nymphet draped in a leopard-print nightie waved at her from inside.

'New arrivals,' Isabelle beckoned, holding up a peignoir set made of a pale ice-blue silk. 'Just your size.'

Jodie could read her friend's lips through the glass, and she smiled. Already, Isabelle knew her style, but Jodie didn't stop this morning to chat. Later, after business hours, they'd meet at a jazz bar by the bridge for a drink. Now, work beckoned.

Several paces down the street, a modern, two-storey building housed Jodie's office. Careful not to spill her coffee, she hurried up the Spanish-tiled stairs and pulled out her key ring. The glass door opened into a sun-filled atrium, and Jodie glided through the empty lobby and waiting area, then through the smoked glass door that served as the entrance to Max's private office. She could already hear the phone ringing, and she put on an extra burst of speed, entering the office and lifting the receiver on the third ring.

'Max Sterling, Fine Imports and Exports,' she said in her smooth accentless voice. 'How can I help you?' The phrases were lyrical, almost a melody. Jodie had uttered the words so often over the past four years that sometimes she found herself saying them for no reason at all, repeating the sentence to herself like a mantra when in the shower or working out at her gym in North Beach. 'So sorry, Max isn't available,' she told the caller, 'is there a question that I might be able to answer for you?'

'Perhaps you could,' the woman agreed.

While waiting for the request, Jodie sat on the edge of the antique mahogany desk and lit her first cigarette of the day. It was the best cigarette, in her opinion. The one that gave her the most pleasure. She didn't possess a bad smoking habit, indulged in only a few cigarettes a day, but she enjoyed the entire ritual of the pastime. Now, she cradled her silver lighter in one hand, savouring the gentle weight of it while running one finger along the engraved initials, JMS, before slipping the antique back into her side pocket. Her grey eyes were focused on a spot on the far wall as she listened to the caller offer an invitation to a gala silent auction.

'Yes, Max would love to attend,' Jodie said, sounding pleased. 'Put down one plus guest,' she added. 'And thank you so much for thinking of us.'

After replacing the heavy black receiver, she moved to recline in the berry-hued leather chair and put her feet up on the desk, legs crossed at the ankle. Another Pacific Heights black tie event to be attended by the bright human stars who lit the Northern California scene. In order to blend in properly, she'd have to book herself a manicure and pedicure at Celine's Day Spa on Main Street, choose a vibrant new gown, and give Lucas a call to see if he would be available that night.

What else would she have to do to get ready? Read about the wares scheduled to be on display. Thorough in her pre-auction research, she always worked hard in advance to find out which items on the block might be of interest to her wealthy clients. Would she need to bid for anyone specifically, or could she buy anything that caught her fancy, knowing her clients' desires and tastes so well that they were ingrained in her mind?

Blowing perfectly executed rings of smoke towards the old-fashioned ceiling fan, Jodie contemplated her life. After several moments lost in deep thought, she decided that it wasn't lacking. Not in any tangible way. But if that were the case, then why did she always have this urgency within her? The yearning feeling deep within her core that made her take?

Across town, in the Sunset district, Nick Hudson was having a far less pleasant morning. And, as usual on mornings such as these, he had no one except himself to blame. But that knowledge didn't make the pain any easier to deal with. It hurt to move his head. Hurt to move his feet. Hurt to move his eyelashes, which really wasn't fair at all, now, was it? Exactly what sort of poison had he been drinking the night before? With great trepidation, he opened one blood-shot green eye and stared weakly at the neon numbers on the digital clock on the nightstand.

Jesus, it was already ten. How long had he been out of it?

Not long enough, he discovered, gingerly pushing himself up from the sheet-strewn mattress. Peering over the lip of his bed, he looked down to see the wreckage of the previous night's party. Sprawled on the floor were the so-called friends who had contributed to his lousy attitude this morning. The names were innocent-sounding enough: Jack and Jim. But Jack Daniels and Jim Beam had a bite to them, didn't they? And Nick was old enough to know better, wasn't he? Yes, after thirty-four years on this planet, he most definitely was. Still, that was a thought to contemplate later, once he had regained his equilibrium, pried his tongue from the roof of his mouth, and imbibed a cup or four of strong coffee.

Stretching cautiously, he put both feet over the edge of the bed and hoisted himself into a standing position, which would have put him a bit over six feet tall if he could have managed to remain upright without slouching. There, that wasn't so bad. Walking was a little more difficult, but the thought of coffee, black and bitter, kept him moving all the way to the bare, 1950s-style kitchen down the hall. Once in the brightly painted room, a strange ringing filled his head, and it took him several seconds to realise that the sound was coming from outside of his personal hell – emanating instead from the cream-coloured telephone mounted on the canary-yellow wall.

'Hudson,' he murmured despondently into the receiver.

'Mr Hudson,' the woman repeated severely, as if telling him who he was rather than asking. 'I'm calling to request your attendance at a private party in two weeks.' Although this was the same invitation that Jodie had received only an hour earlier, the effect on Nick's psyche didn't come close to matching Jodie's excitement. Frantically, his eyes searched the kitchen cabinets for a sign of coffee and found to his dismay that there was none.

'Two hundred and fifty dollars an hour,' he said in response, 'and I need to know exactly what I'm supposed to be keeping my eyes on.'

'Of course,' the woman told him, her voice lowering slightly in volume as she added, 'but it's not a what, Mr Hudson. It's a who.'

Everyone has secrets. Desires that keep them awake at night. Old wounds that won't ever permanently heal, even after years of therapy. (And it is *so* chic – still – to rack up years of therapy in California.) It was Nick Hudson's job to search out those secrets. For a reasonable price, he could find out almost anything about anyone. Rich or poor. Celebrity or street person.

Usually, the search wasn't as difficult as one might think. Burying secrets was a skill that the majority of the population lacked. Clues generally remained visible to someone who knew where to look. Early on, Nick had learned as part of his on-the-job training that secrets have legs. Most people find the need to share, at least with some trusted friend, their darkest, most private thoughts. Crack open a newspaper, log on to the Internet, or peruse the gossip rags, and you'll find thousands of secrets that people hoped would never worm their way out into the light. Headlines scream about politicians losing their minds over risqué love affairs, or educators teaching our precious children while equipped only with false credentials. Or girl-friends who leave their men for darker, rougher players.

No, that wasn't really a secret, was it?

Once a secret is out in the open, it gets passed and spread from one person to the next. Gossip is too seductive to deny. But the best part about secrets, to Nick, was the way they changed as they spread. Like that old kids' game called Chinese Whispers, the facts would become altered, distorted as time went on. Unravelling the pieces and polishing them to find the truth – that was his main job.

Even in his hungover state, he was thrilled to be working again, because sorting out the truth from the garbage always captured his mind. More than any-thing else, he needed something to think about right now. Sure he had cases in play, but nothing like this. Most were long-term assignments. No urgency. No excitement. Here was the type of case that he lived for.

He spent the morning recovering. He spent the after-noon doing his best to gather information about his new subject: Max Sterling. What he discovered, almost immediately, was that Mr Sterling was abroad, run-ning his business from a small but expensive London office. While he was out of the country, his assistant, Jodie Silver, kept watch over the American branch of the company. So Jodie was the one to get close to if he wanted to find out about Max. She'd have the answers he needed. Yet it only took him several hours to learn that Ms Silver was different from the majority of the people he'd investigated in the past. She kept her secrets better than most.

As always, he tried to remain aloof as he searched for the seeds that would start him on the trail. You never knew exactly where one lead would send you. Nothing was disposable. Every fact was recorded, first in a notebook in handwriting that only he could decipher. (It wasn't code – it was just messy.) Later, when he needed to carefully sort through what he'd found out, he transferred all of the information to his computer. Reserving judgment was the only way to play this game. That, and not getting involved with the people he followed. He'd broken that rule only one time – and look where it had gotten him. That was a trick question: nowhere. Bailey had been the subject of a previous detective job. Her beau had wanted to know what she did when he wasn't around. And what she did turned out to be Nick.

Come on, he urged himself. Not the time. Not the place.

When Nick had something to keep his mind on, his whole body relaxed. He spent the afternoon learning where Jodie Silver lived. Where she worked. What type of car she drove: a sweet little black MG. Nice. It was a car he'd drive himself, except that it was too small for his large frame. Ah, but there was an opinion slithering its way into his assessment. Back off, boy, he told himself. Just because she's got a nice ass doesn't mean you get to ogle it.

He found out which gym she belonged to, which bank she kept her accounts in, and how many credit cards she possessed. None of these were difficult jobs for Nick. What was harder was learning about her social circle. He couldn't just go up and ask her questions, or ask any neighbours, people who might alert her to the fact that she was being watched. Never a good thing.

Instead, he followed her around for a day. Watched her get a midday cup of coffee, taking in the way she greeted the workers at the cafe, the way she was dressed, so clean and proper. He grabbed a cup of joe to go, then trailed slowly after her down the block. Saw her enter her office, and followed up the stairs to see if there was a place where he could sit undetected. No such luck. So he parked himself at a bookstore across the street, then at a record store, then back in his car.

He followed her again to see that she spent late lunch with a girlfriend out on the Marina watching boats go by. And then, when evening came, he watched her get that cute little tail of hers spanked.

San Francisco has its mystique built right in. An eclectic history gives the city a little push over the rest of the famous urban creations. There's the earthquake factor – both past and present. With no true stability beneath your feet, how can you build a permanent lifestyle? Maybe that's why the Summer of Love took place in a corner of the city, why the beat poets found their freedom of expression in North Beach, and why the Castro calls out to just about every gay and lesbian who was ever put down or picked on. Nowhere else has the Bada Bingo game run by the Sisters of Perpetual Indulgence. No other city seems so deeply confused about its inner psyche – about how to deal compassionately with the down-and-out so that the homeless find havens in the corners of the upstanding society – and nobody does anything about it.

But at first, San Francisco at night looks like any other big city. Sparkling sky line like a string of diamonds dangling against a velvet backdrop. Dramatic towers reaching for infinity. Rows of apartment buildings that are so noticeably painted a rainbow of pastel in daylight but fade to muted tones after dark. And then there's the bridge. The Golden Gate shoots across the dark dreamy waters of the Bay. Take the time to stare at that awesome structure and the city takes on a magic of its own.

Get a little closer, step one foot on the bridge itself, and San Francisco seems like the luckiest place in the world. The GGB spans the distance between the city and the County of Marin. Majestic red spikes tower into the fog above while tour vessels and freighters create glistening wakes in the Bay. Tourists throng to the pedestrian walkways during the day, hoping that the fog will part long enough to allow for a photograph – proof that they were really standing on such an important monument.

On this autumn evening, however, Jodie could see none of the beauty. Firmly blindfolded, her wrists locked to one of the red-painted railings, she waited in a state of tense anticipation for what would happen next. Her heart raced, and she worried her lower lip between her teeth, creating a hot spark of pain that added to her already mounting arousal. It was time to play. To play the way she most enjoyed. Outdoors. With the possible potential of exposure, and the probable potential of coming fiercely at Lucas's command and with his dominant help.

Aside from the two lovers, the tourist sidewalk was completely vacant at this late hour, and anyone driving along the nearly empty bridge would have only noticed the backs of what appeared to be two pedestrians staring innocently out at the view. Yet even this knowledge didn't soothe Jodie's vibrating nerves. She felt a wash of high-powered excitement flare through her body, concentrating on the pulsing spot between her legs.

Lucas could do anything he wanted. Now, he stood behind her, bringing his hands around her waist. She felt his hard-on pressed into her bottom from behind as he ran his fingers up under her white blouse, pinching her nipples between thumb and pointer. Her black-and-brown checked silk shirt lifted up in front from the movement, and the chilly breeze rushed against her warm naked skin making her nipples even harder. Lucas moved aside and let his firm hand come down flat against her still-clothed ass. Jodie lowered her head and arched her hips back towards him, lifting up. Her body spoke volumes while her lips remained locked together. Lucas landed another blow on top of her skirt-clad ass, and then he brought his lips right to her ear and whispered his plans for the evening.

'I'm going to spank you until you come,' he said sternly. 'It doesn't matter if people can see us. And it doesn't matter if you cry.'

Oh, God. She loved it when he talked to her like that. The strength in his voice made her melt. In their daily lives, Jodie was always in charge. That's just the way it was. She knew her business well, and she used Lucas as it suited her. The arrangement had never been spelled out formally, but they both understood why their relationship worked as well as it did. Yet every once in a while, Lucas got an idea into his head of how to take back a little of the power. Like now, as he slid her luxurious deep forest green skirt up to her waist, in preparation for spanking her panty-clad ass. Instantly, he uncovered the racy cornflower-blue thong that neatly separated her ripe round ass into two distinct regions. This was a thong she'd stolen from Isabelle's long before she'd had her first tryst with the Nordic beauty.

'Just look at that,' Lucas murmured, sliding his fingers under the waistband and tugging up, so that Jodie could feel the fabric pressing hard against her bush and between her bottom cheeks. 'What a naughty pair of panties you've got on, baby.' His fingers entwined with the elastic on the waistband, and when he pulled up gently, the lace separated her rear cheeks even further. She sucked in her breath at the feeling of being so intimately exposed. 'Don't tell me that you knew you were going to get a spanking today, baby doll?'

Without waiting for Jodie to respond, he started to spank her, really spank her, bringing his hand down hard on her left cheek and then her right in rapid succession. She pictured the prints he was leaving on her pale skin, pretty raspberry coloured handprints that she might admire later in her bathroom mirror. She'd stand with her back to the oval-shaped mirror and look over her shoulder, remembering what it had felt like to receive each breathless blow. Jodie loved those aftermarks of pleasure, plummy smudges that echoed an evening spent in one of her favourite ways. Sometimes, Lucas would stand next to her, watching her admire herself, grinning at the hot flush of excitement that remained in her eyes. A look that indicated their evening session was far from over.

'Such a bad girl,' Lucas said. 'These tiny little panties you've got on are positively indecent. Look at the way they divide your gorgeous ass cheeks.' He tugged again on the thong and her pussy spasmed as the ribbon of fabric pressed even tighter against it. The contact on her throbbing sex was entirely unique. She was getting off on the way he rubbed that little fluff of an undergarment against her. She liked the floss of lace against her skin and the way that she was opened up wider each time he pulled on the waistband. Lucas started to slide the blue fabric aside, as he continued talking to her. 'But I think that what you really need – what you really deserve, I should say – is a bare bottom spanking. Nothing on your ass at all. Nothing except my hand, that is.'

He was right. This was exactly what Jodie wanted, and she lifted her hips to help as he slid the thong down her thighs, then waited for her to step out of the panties. To complete her outfit, Jodie was wearing woollen stockings with garters and the tall, black leather boots that were so popular this season. But she felt intensely exposed to the night air and to the curious gazes of any passing traffic as he continued to discipline her haughty rear.

They only had several minutes to play like this, risking the possibility of catching the attention of the traffic cops who casually patrolled the bridge. They were risking arrest for indecent exposure, or obscene behaviour, or blocking a sidewalk. Some such charge. She was sure that their minutes were ticking away. One of the drivers would rat them out at the toll booth – 'Did you know that two people are being unacceptably kinky out there?' – and security would swarm towards them. By that point, Lucas would have been able to undo the cuffs and she would pull off the blindfold, turning them once again into a simple love-struck couple out to take in the sights of San Francisco at night. Her well-warmed ass would remain a secret that only she and Lucas would know about.

Their team efforts in this arena were well-honed. Exhibitionists always know how to make the most of every moment, just as Lucas now made the most of spanking her. Using the whole of his flat hand against her rounded bottom, he worked her hard and fast, so that soon her entire rear felt warm all over, an explosion of heat spanning both cheeks. Being spanked, especially in public, always made Jodie excited, and it made her want more, made her want him to fulfil the next dirty fantasy that bloomed in her mind.

To let Lucas know what she craved, Jodie spread her legs slightly and instantly her lover used his fingers against her pussy, spanking her there. Lighter, but shocking smacks raining down against that most sensitive area between her legs. Jodie groaned and spread her legs even wider, giving him better access. Those pat-a-cake spanks sent thrilling jolts of pleasure throughout her entire body. She wouldn't last much longer. Soon, she'd be coming, pulling uselessly on the cuffs, collapsing with her weight on them so that Lucas would have to grab her around the waist and support her as the climax rushed through her.

'Quickly,' her lover urged. 'Not much time.'

'Please,' she said. The only thing that made any sense. 'Please –'

He knew exactly what that word meant, and he gave her just what she wanted. She shuddered as his hand concentrated on her hot spot, now rubbing more than patting. Fingers splayed, he caught her clit on either side, stroking and caressing, sliding up and down, up and around. He understood her needs, didn't he? He was going to be able to make her climax from the combination of all that they were doing together. Playing in public. Being cuffed and blindfolded. And most importantly being punished. That's what did it every time for her. Even if Lucas couldn't fully understand the importance of giving in, how it wrenched her from the inside out, he was able to play the role she needed. And that, at least for the moment, was enough.

Suddenly, Lucas pulled at the bow beneath her heavy hair, and the blindfold was removed. In the steel-white light of the moon and the glazed glow from the sulphur-yellow bridge lamps, Jodie felt herself coming. Sensing exactly when it happened, Lucas stopped rubbing her and gave her a final series of startling spanks against her naked ass. Jodie moaned loudly and shivered all over as the flush of pleasure played through her body. Yet there was no time to bask in the afterglow.

Lucas said, 'Okay, baby. Time's up.' He indicated with one quick gesture a movement at the far edge of the bridge. Then he quickly unlocked her wrists from the span, straightened her skirt for her, and hustled her in the other direction, towards the visitor parking lot and their waiting car.

Everyone has a secret. That was Nick's mantra. It helped him to keep the concept in the forefront of his mind, especially when working on a difficult case. Just because he hadn't found out someone's secret was not a reason to believe that the information didn't exist. All it meant was that he'd have to work harder to uncover the hidden facts. The dark part. Nick got paid to spy, to pry, to peer into private worlds where nobody wanted his shining light.

'You can't tell,' he said to his best friend, trying to explain. 'You look at someone, and you think you know them, but you don't.'

'You have got to get over Bailey. That bitch isn't worth the time.'

'I'm not talking about Bailey.'

Sammy snorted. 'Right. You're just speaking about the world at large. Not the broad who broke your heart.' He poured a fresh shot for Nick. 'You knew what you were getting into, man. She was doing three different guys when you met her. It was like a bad joke: the cook, the gardener, and the delivery guy.'

Nick shrugged. 'I'm talking about everyone. You think you can judge somebody from the way they look, or talk, or act. But you can't. Trust me. You'll be fooled every turn. Just watch the politicians on the news. They act one way in front of the camera, and another behind closed doors.'

'Give me a fucking break,' Sammy sighed. 'People aren't that hard to read. And everyone knows politicians lie.'

'Spoken like a bartender.'

'I'm serious. Five minutes with someone and I have their whole life story. Why they hate their mother. Who they wish they could punch out at their office. What colour their secretary's panties were today.'

Nick hesitated. 'What colour?'

Sammy grinned. 'They were pale pink. Thanks for asking.'

Back on track, Nick continued. 'I'm not talking five minutes. I'm talking about looking at someone and judging them. Just from one look.'

'You'll lose if you bet against me,' Sammy said. 'Bartenders have a feeling about people. A sixth sense, if you will.'

'All right,' Nick said. 'You don't believe me. Fine. I'll give you an example. See those two girls over there?' He nodded casually with his chin towards a table in the far corner where Jodie and Isabelle sat drinking orange-pink mandarin Cosmopolitans.

'Yeah.'

'Which one of them doesn't have any panties on?'

'Like you'd know –'

'I do know. Wouldn't be a fair game if I didn't, would it?'

Sammy looked at Nick, then nodded. The one thing Nick always was – no matter what – was fair. You could trust him, right down to the wire. So if Nick said he knew, then he knew. Sammy glanced over at the blonde bombshell and the cool brunette with steel-grey eyes, then looked back at his buddy. 'I'm going with the blonde.'

'Why?'

'She looks ripe. Ready for action. Wouldn't I like to bend her over that table and slide her skirt up –'

'Sure, she looks ready. But she owns a lingerie store. She *loves* panties.'

'The other one seems too uptight.'

'You'd think so,' Nick said, 'wouldn't you? But you'd be wrong.'

'But how do *you* know?'

'Because I just watched her boyfriend take her slinky blue panties down and slide them into his pocket. So under that short green skirt of hers is nothing but pussy.'

'You're kidding!' Sammy looked around again, eyes wide open, but Nick pushed him with his elbow.

'Stop staring.'

'Where were they?'

'Out on the GGB.'

'Christ, that girl? You're sure? Where were you?'

'Driving by, at first. Twice, just to make sure. Try turning around and getting back on the bridge quickly. I'm lucky I didn't get pulled over. Then I parked the car and walked on the pedestrian sidewalk across from them.'

'You pervert –'

'That's not the only secret she's got.'

'I get it,' Sammy said, lifting his beer. 'You're on her tail.' He gave a low chuckle. 'Or you'd like to be.'

'Something like that.'

Sammy lowered his voice. 'But what did he do to her? What's the rest of it?'

Nick stretched it out, making his buddy wait. When he had really good information, he liked to spill the secrets slowly. Finally, he tilted his head and looked in the mirror over the bar. From this vantage point, he could see Jodie and Isabelle giggling together. Sharing some private joke.

'Come on, Nick,' Sammy urged.

'He spanked her.'

'No!'

'Oh, yeah.' Nick stretched it out, relishing the story, and enjoying the fact that he'd obviously shocked his buddy. As he spoke, he relived each image of the sensual scenario. 'He spanked that lovely, high-class tail of hers until she came. Right out there on the GGB. So you see what I mean?'

It was obvious from his expression that Sammy couldn't even remember what they were talking about, let alone follow Nick's point. His eyes were focused on the two lovely women, and his thoughts were most definitely on the hardening joint in his pants. Nick helped him out. 'You never can be sure. You think you know somebody, but you're almost always just waiting to be fooled.'

'But why are you telling me all this?'

Nick shrugged his broad shoulders and played with his empty glass on the counter. He spun the glass, then turned it upside down and tapped it against the wood until Sammy took the thing out of his hands, realising it would wind up on the floor or crushed to pieces. 'Sometimes I just need to tell somebody. Can't always keep it all in here.' He tapped his head. 'Gonna explode if I do.'

Case File: 583
Description: Fuck it
Client: An idiot

Back at home, Nick stared bleakly at the computer screen. Then he hit several key strokes to delete what was written before him. So he'd lied to Sammy about being over Bailey. Well, to be less than eloquent about it, so what? He knew he had to get over her, but knowing that didn't seem to make the situation any easier to handle. Maybe he thought if he looked at the facts clearly, put them into a case file just as if he'd been hired by someone else, then the pain wouldn't feel as strong. Christ, he never felt hurt for his clients when he learned that their loved ones were doing the nasty on the sly.

But this hit too close to home.

This was his heart.

He'd been the employer and employee on this case. When Bailey had begun growing distant, he'd tailed her himself. How pathetic was that? Couldn't trust his own girlfriend. Didn't have the balls to ask her what was up. Would it have gone down differently if he had? He'd never know the answer to that one, but he liked to think that at least he'd have escaped the situation without shredding his pride along the way. He could have sat her down in one of the rear booths at Sammy's. Bought each of them a stiff drink. Let her break up with him the way a girlfriend should. She might have gotten a little misty and choked out a lie or two in that actressy way of hers. 'It's not you, it's me.' That sort of shit. Instead, he'd tailed her.
Description: Find out why she's slipping away
Client: The loser

When it came right down to it, the temptation had been too great not to simply do what he was good at. Searching out facts. Finding secrets. Probing and prying, especially where he wasn't wanted. So when she called him one evening, saying she was too tired to get together – again – he'd staked out her apartment. It seemed like the natural thing to do. Emotions had been strained between them for several weeks, but every time he'd tried to broach the subject, she'd waved him away. Now, he planned on finding out for himself.

Deep down at his core, he'd wanted to be wrong, even though his gut instincts rarely lied. That's why he was so successful at his job. From the moment he met with a client, he generally got a feeling whether the person was coming clean with him or not. And from the moment he locked on to the subject of his search, he had a certain inner radar that let him know if he was going to find trash or treasure.

With Bailey, he'd wanted her to stay up there in her Victorian studio on Scott Street. More than anything, he'd wanted her to *really be* tired. Dog tired. It was fine with him if she needed to take the evening off. People went through phases. Everyone needed a break. Just look at him. There were long periods of time when he needed solitude. Needed it more than anything – more than sleep, food, or gin. If he was seeing someone, that person had to understand that Nick required time alone. Needed to hole out in his office, scanning his notes, smoking his smokes.

Maybe Bailey was the same way. Why shouldn't she be? She'd just gone through a separation from her husband, found her own apartment and decorated it with Nick's assistance. What did he really know about her personality for the long term? They hadn't been together enough time for him to learn her different moods. So now, he just had to find out what was going on. As crazy as it was, he wanted to be able to climb up the side of the fire escape, peer in her room, and see her crashed out on the bed, long birch-blonde hair spreading out on her pillow like a halo. Chest rising and falling gently in sleep.

But after only an hour waiting, there she was. God, it was almost too easy. He blinked at the sight of her, watching as she pushed open the door and then stood out on the stoop with her gorgeous long hair swept off her face and her cheeks flushed from the brisk weather.

She was wearing a halter-style red dress that was made of a gauzy material far too thin for the weather, but it looked amazing on her body. Of course, she'd know how good she looked. Bailey would risk catching pneumonia in order to make a fashion statement. The chill in the air made her nipples hard. And looking at the round pebbles of her nipples made Nick hard.

While Nick stared, she pulled her rhinestone-studded compact out of her pale blue snake-skin handbag. He had seen her go through her beauty rituals close-up, but they were just as mesmerising watching from a distance. He knew all the tricks. Now, in the twilight, she was doing those final girly touch-ups that he always liked to watch. Sometimes, he sat on the edge of the bed while she put her make-up on, fascinated by the routine of it. There was something deeply seductive in the way she outlined her full lips with a crimson pencil before blotting away most of the colour. Then she added a swipe of a clear gloss to make those full lips even more kissable.

What he should have done was just exit the car and walk up to her. Before he found out anything he didn't want to know. He could say he was checking in on her, that she'd sounded so tired he wanted to help out. Rub her feet. Massage her shoulders. Kiss her cheeks. He could even give her a way out, say, 'Oh, and it looks as if you're feeling better. Let's catch a quick bite down the block.' His hand was actually on the door handle, ready to open it.

And then, before he really understood what was happening, the front door to her building had opened again and Hunter had come out, his well-worn leather jacket in hand. They'd both been up there together. And Christ, Nick, the moron, hadn't been able to figure it out at first. Why was Hunter with her? Were they talking about him together, had she gone to Hunter with their problems?

Finally, he woke up to the reality of the situation.

Nick, whose cold heart was no longer affected when he tailed cheating spouses. Nick, a man who had become immune to true emotion after watching so many love affairs get flushed down the john, who hadn't believed in the concept of true love any more, not until he'd run into Bailey. It hit him in the same way it hit every client he'd had to come clean with in the past. 'Yes, sir, your wife's been going down on the delivery boy. So sorry to be the bearer of bad news.'

Welcome to Loserville. Here's the key to the goddamn city.

They'd been screwing. No question about it. Because all of those little fix-its Bailey was doing were the same ones she did with him after they made love. He lowered his head, staring down at the steering wheel, wishing he could disappear. He didn't even know which hurt more. Bailey, whose history he knew inside and out. Who he could have expected as much from, if he'd bothered to separate his brain from his dick, right? Because she'd been cheating on her husband when they met. That was her M.O.

But Hunter. Jesus. Hunter. You weren't supposed to do that to your partner. You just weren't.

Chapter Seven

The black sapphire ring was extremely rare, the type of prize photographed repeatedly, so that every jeweller – and every layperson with a jewellery fixation – would be able to know what a true find it really was. The shape of the jewel had been altered over the years, transformed from the largest bauble of its type ever recorded in the raw, to a multi-faceted shape that caught the light from every possible angle. Shaved and polished on the exterior, fire seemed to dance within its centre.

The ring had a history, as well, and this, of course, made the piece even more valuable. If the jewel had simply been worn by some old spinster for seventy years, then passed to her grand-niece, who sold it at auction, the ring would have still been as lovely, yes, but it wouldn't have been as interesting.

And Jodie liked things that were interesting.

She'd studied this particular gem for years, since first coming upon a reference to a similar stone in an ancient Egyptian art class, a vague mention in a foot-note that Cleopatra had worn an unusual fire-black jewel in the setting of one of her elaborate headpieces. Somewhat like an opal, the black sapphire had been of the rarest quality, ever-changing in the light. That mention had started Jodie on her own personal quest for this sort of find. A gem had turned up over the years after Cleopatra's time, finally gaining mention in the bracelet of one of Henry VIII's unfortunate wives. And from her jewellery, the item had been plucked and smuggled to Spain, where word of it was lost for nearly half a century.

What had happened to the stone for those fifty years? Had it been closeted away in some rich woman's jewel box? Or tucked into a safe under the thief's bed? Jodie always wondered about the missing facts in its history. She thought of someone holding the stone tightly in a closed fist, wishing that she could share the beauty of the piece with a friend or neighbour, but being too fearful about the repercussions.

The story went that a fisherwoman cut open an oyster shell one afternoon, to discover not a pearl within, but this same gem. Now, *that* Jodie understood was pure fabrication. Here was a fanciful way for the thief to remain undetected and the woman, whose honour was impeccable, to claim the reward money, which was a large sum at the time. The grand reward was enough to turn a common fisherwoman into a lady of leisure and to set up all of her relatives in positive lifestyles, as well.

A high-level official had purchased the solitary unset stone for his betrothed, planning to have it placed in the centre of a platinum ring, offset by two equally stunning diamonds. But his loved one had died of a rare blood disease only days before their wedding, and he'd had the piece buried with her, set in a simple necklace rather than on a ring for her finger. That should have been the end of the story. The stone and the woman would have rested in the ground for eternity. But Jodie did her research. A stone so worthy, so lovely, couldn't remain in a grave. Not when there were bandits about.

The piece had turned up in the early nineteenth century in America. This time, the jewel had been set in the back of a sterling silver hand mirror that was part of the dowry of a young frontier bride, given to her by a rich robber-baron uncle. The gift had been carefully noted in the bride's journal, with a complete description of the startlingly lovely design of diamonds and precious gems on the back. And the centrepiece – this strikingly unusual sapphire – had been mentioned in great detail. However, the mirror had been lost in the journey across the continent, and little was known about it until the 1920s, when a black sapphire ring was worn by a minor duchess. The sparkle in the jewel was unprecedented. Once again, here was the same stone. Jodie was sure of it.

Now, the ring was on display with the 'Transformed Treasures' collection. Each of the pieces had an interesting history. The write-up in the paper noted the dates and stops on the route. It would start in Europe, make its way to New York, then on to San Francisco. Finally.

Jodie's plan had been in motion for years: a way to get the ring without any risk. Without much risk. Without too much of a risk. Her different schemes had changed with time, and were being altered even now. Jodie's heart pounded as she thought the steps through. Would it work? *Wouldn't* it? The idea seemed plausible. And all of the parts were coming into place. No harm would come from trying. That's what she ultimately decided. Or if there was harm, then at least it wouldn't necessarily fall on her.

Max Sterling, Fine Imports and Exports was run out of an office rather than a store front. Nick learned this fact after several phone conversations with customers of Jodie's, all of whom seemed completely satisfied with their transactions. He pretended to be a prospective client, about to hire Jodie to search for a particular piece for his collection of unusual duck decoys. Not one of the people he talked to had a bad word to say about her.

'She's a dream,' one rich society woman assured Nick. 'She will find anything you ask her for. Anything. And she'll go to any lengths to get what you want.

Max is even more fabulous,' the woman went on. 'His letters detailing research and factual history are unrivalled.'

'You've met him?' Nick asked, surprised. So far he'd had difficulties finding a single person who knew Max in person. The man seemed to be a recluse.

'No,' the woman admitted. 'But I've dealt with him by phone and mail. He is a true gentleman.'

Nick learned the ropes of the import/export business from his careful research. When a coveted item came up for sale, clients either visited the office, or waited for Jodie to bring the object to their house. *Mansion* was probably the more correct term, Nick realised. Max Sterling's clients were in the upper echelon of the San Francisco circle. These were not people who shopped for themselves. They were the clients to whom things were delivered.

So it wasn't going to be as easy as walking into a store and striking up a conversation with the shop girl behind the counter, pretending that he was looking for a gift for his girlfriend as he got more information than he gave. No, Nick was going to have to get to know Jodie in a different, more subtle manner. This was fine with him. He enjoyed diving into a case, using his talents to search out the facts.

He wasn't worried at all that she'd spotted him at Sammy's. One thing he'd learned about the people he watched – and about people in general – was that they rarely paid attention to the world around them. Just look at that study done every so often in college psychology classes. A professor delivers a lecture, as usual, and during the speech a workman enters the room and does some minor repair job, then leaves. The professor cuts short the speech and quizzes the students about the description of the workman. Nick loved this test. More often than not, students were either unaware that a workman ever entered the room, or they gave wildly differing descriptions as to the person's height, looks, age, race, and even sex. This led to all sorts of moral questions when it came to descriptions of people who'd committed crimes. Memories played nasty tricks on people all the time. So Nick didn't mind getting close to his subjects – manoeuvring through their world as a casual observer. But, with Jodie, the question lingered as to how he'd get closer?

After spending several days in research mode, he studied all of the information he'd learned about her so far: Jodie Silver appeared to be the sole American employee of Max Sterling, Imports and Exports. While Mr Sterling was often abroad, running the company's offices in London and Milan, Jodie held the reins in California. A transplant from the East Coast, Jodie had attended the University of Southern California at Los Angeles for graduate school, gaining a PhD in art history four years prior. She had never been married, nor seriously attached to any one lover, although she was known to enjoy male company. Especially handsome male company of the blond variety.

Nick fitted that description without trying. He didn't consider himself vain, but he knew that most women liked the way he looked. Well-built and sharp-featured, he possessed a natural athlete's grace that made women – as well as the men who called the Castro home – do a double-take when he walked by. Being just Jodie's type was luck. Now, he had to think of different ways he could arrange a casual meeting with her. After he paced across the floor of his apartment for over an hour, an idea hit him: he'd join her gym.

Gyms in Northern California were perfect places to make acquaintances. It was easy to strike up a conversation over a marathon run on a treadmill. You asked the person next to you how far they ran a week. Or whether they were in training for some event or other, the Bay to Breakers, perhaps, or Race for the Cure. Everyone liked to talk about themselves when it came to working out. He was sure the plan would work with

Jodie. When he saw her at an event in the future, he'd be able to sidle up to her as her gym buddy, offer a drink, and compare notes on the host or hostess and the items for sale. He could play any part he wanted. That was Nick's main skill.

Jodie's main skill was that she let only a few select people into her inner circle. This became apparent immediately on Nick's second day at her gym. She hadn't shown up to work out the previous morning, which was fine with Nick. He never expected things to go that easily for him. Sometimes he was rewarded immediately for having a good idea – like getting to watch Jodie and Lucas out on the bridge. That had been an amazing bonus for tracking the girl all day long. But other times, he had to be patient. For that first morning at the gym not to go down as a total loss, he'd worked out anyway, limbering his body with free weights before logging five miles on the treadmill.

Today, even though she had arrived moments after he did, he realised that talking with her was going to be next to impossible. From across the room, Nick watched her run, fancy headset in place, music on so loud that he could actually tell what band she was exercising to from where he stood: Nine Inch Nails. There was a surprise. He would have pegged her for the type of San Francisco chick who would listen to all-girl vocals: Natalie Merchant, Annie de Franco, or that new one blasting over the airwaves daily, Poe.

For a moment, Nick admired Jodie from a distance, aware that other men were staring, as well. This morning, she had on tight black running pants that perfectly fitted her lean body, a grey lycra tank top, and a pair of running shoes that had obviously racked up some serious mileage. He liked that. She put her gear through hard-core workouts. Some of the members of this gym showed up for the 'meet market' aspect of exercising. You could spot them easily; the women with full faces of make-up that would streak in lines if they broke even a dew-like sweat. Their male counter-parts could be spotted by hair that looked styled, perhaps even blow-dried. Jodie wasn't one of the fak-ers. That was easy to tell.

Nick moved closer, choosing the treadmill on her right side as soon as it was vacated and starting out at a slow, steady jog. 'I want to take you like an animal –' blared out of her headset. Not a bad idea, actually. Nick had an instant vision of doing her just that way. Bent over, from behind, her naked body glazed with sweat from the early morning workout. The muscles sliding under her skin, pumped and ready. This fantasy was so realistic, he could actually see exactly where he'd move her hair aside, lean forward, lick along the nape of her neck. That was one of his favourite locations on a woman. That erotic curve, the little hidden spot where he always loved to linger before kissing lower. Before biting –

And then what?

Then he'd take her wrists in one hand and secure them over her head. Keep her steady while he took her from behind. He would drive in, working her hard. He had already had a glimpse of the way she liked to do it. Watching her out on the GGB had seriously turned him on. He liked girls who pushed boundaries, and he liked girls who were into the spanking scene. Putting a feline femme over his lap for a bare-bottom spanking was one of Nick's favourite kinky pleasures. He had loved to take Bailey down a notch after she drove him crazy with her teasing actions. Putting the blonde cupcake over his lap had given him the upper hand. When he'd spanked her in public, at a local erotic club, that had been the limit. Now, he pushed thoughts of his ex out of his head and focused on Jodie again.

Aside from the fact that they seemed to be sexually in tune, she had rhythm and ease with motion. He could see that from watching her on the treadmill.

There was no doubt in his mind that she'd be an extremely athletic sexual partner.

Stop it, he told himself. Getting a hard-on in the middle of the gym would be detrimental to his plan, as well as to his ability to keep running. What was he? Some teenager who got hard when the wind blew? Jesus, he had to have more self-control than that. Instead of continuing his fierce fantasy, he searched his brain for a clever opening, a way to get to know her without appearing like one of the other men in the room who was simply content with drooling from a distance.

He considered mentioning that he was a fan of Trent Reznor, but that sounded like something a horny teenager would say, a kid who was desperate to break the icy exterior of this workout goddess. Then he thought of asking her to turn the music down. Perhaps, it was a bit obnoxious that she didn't seem to care whose personal space she was invading with her rollicking music taste. But the nonchalance in her attitude appealed to Nick. If Jodie wanted to listen to her music loudly, then she should go ahead and do so, until someone complained. From the looks of the men around her, it didn't seem as if anyone would dare to do so.

'Hey, Nick,' a grey-haired man said, stopping in front of the machine.

Nick looked up and then nodded to the guy; it was the gym employee who had taken his membership information.

'Looking good,' the man said as he continued on his way.

Loping along, Nick suddenly realised that the lithe brunette was watching him as carefully as he'd been clocking her. Her gaze flickered over to the red-flashing electronic dashboard of numbers in front of him. He understood the look instantly. She was paying attention to how fast he was going. Since he'd been in observation mode, he hadn't thought to seriously work out. But now, aware that she was interested, he upped the speed on the machine, the muscles in his legs starting to warm to the run.

As soon as he'd matched her stride, Jodie pressed the accelerate button on her own treadmill, making the grey rubberised belt move along slightly faster than Nick's. He liked that. She was competitive, and she didn't even know him. Nick smiled to himself as he once again met and passed her stride. This was something he hadn't expected to endure this morning – a race, more of wills than of anything else. Here were two confident people showing off with their athletic expertise. She didn't really think she could keep up with him, did she? Yeah, she looked strong, but she was small.

He'd wear her down in no time.

Jodie's wet hands ran over her naked body in the shower but, in her mind, those hands belonged to the man who had run along next to her on the treadmill. Nick. She'd noticed everything about his hands. The shape, the girth, the length of the fingers. Her running mate had been without a watch, without any rings, and she'd liked that. Nude hands on her nude body. No unnecessary accessories. She didn't go in for fancy guys.

She turned under the shower spray, now lathering herself up with the sweet-smelling rose-coloured liquid soap. This wasn't the place to get turned on, here, in the centre of the shower. Yes, it was a private stall, but that didn't mean much. She could see other gym members through the wall of smoky glass, and that meant that they could see her, too. At least, they could see her silhouette. Most likely, none of the women would guess that she was touching herself inappropriately for the location, but she knew from experience that it wouldn't be long before someone else wanted to take her place.

Yet she still washed herself with long, slow strokes, revelling in every subtle soapy caress. If she were a man, she'd be sporting a massive erection right about now. And she would be unable to deny herself the urgency she'd feel. The need to come. She'd pull on her cock, tug on it, until she shot her milky load against the blue-and-white tiled floor. Oh, the release of a good orgasm would feel so good. So why as a woman was she expected to be any different? Why should she be a good girl and keep her feelings within herself, project a calm, collected exterior when a wave of lust rushed through her?

Screw the people waiting, she thought forcefully, fingers working over herself in rapid random strokes. Screw the gym members who might not like the fact that she was taking over this corner shower stall, steaming it up with the heady spray. Then, just screw me, she thought as she reached her peak beneath that hot shower, her breath coming in a rush, the steam making her feel light-headed and slippery all over.

The pleasure of coming was an instant moment of satisfaction but, as she watched the bubbles circling in the drain, she felt something slipping away. What was missing? That was easy enough to answer – the guy she'd seen. If he'd been in the shower with her, the story would have had an entirely different ending.

When Jodie emerged from the shower, shiny wet hair pulled back in a neat ponytail, face clean and flushed, Nick was gone. Had he given up on her? She hadn't taken that long in the dressing room. Just long enough to come, dry off, and then to slide on her clean clothes. All right, so maybe she'd spent a little more time than usual on her face in the mirror, but so what? She shook her head as she left the gym, embarrassed with herself for being so sure he'd still be there.

As she walked towards the parking lot, she realised that her body ached; she hadn't put herself through a run like that in ages. But the man had been fun to play with, and she didn't have it in her to simply let someone win. Not someone who didn't know who she was or what she was capable of. Maybe that was a flaw in her character, but it wasn't one that she was intent on trying to fix.

He'd proved a fine foe. Matching her step for step. Pounding alongside of her without seeming to be put out. In good shape, he had kept the speed and gone the distance. Ultimately, another gym member had tapped him on the shoulder and, frown in place, pointed to the clock across the way. There was a thirty-minute courtesy limit for treadmill use when others were waiting, and nobody wanted to kick Jodie off her machine, even though she'd been on longer. Pretty girls tended to get away with more than men. Maybe that wasn't fair, but Jodie wouldn't complain.

Her rival, gallant, had tipped his head at her and made his way through the gym. Jodie had followed soon after, certain they'd bump into each other after showers. Both clean, they'd have a chance to flirt a bit more. But it hadn't worked out that way.

Now, as she got into her convertible, she felt an emptiness inside of herself. The race had revved her up, had left her wanting more. On a whim, she reached for the cell phone tucked inside her glove compartment and then dialled a number that she knew as well as her own.

Lucas opened the door to his apartment wearing only a white terry-cloth towel wrapped tight around his flat, muscular waist. Jodie had her hand on the edge of the towel before the door was completely shut behind her. Lucas allowed the petite woman to back him up, but he pressed the door closed behind her.

'Off,' she hissed, pulling the towel down violently to reveal his already rock-hard erection. 'Oh, God, yes,' she said next, breathless. 'You're so fine naked.'

As if in response to her words, his erection strained towards her. Jodie dipped easily on to her knees and welcomed it with her hungry mouth. She wanted something to suck on, and she wanted him to be nice and slick when she rode him. Sometimes, she simply wanted too many things at once. She had to force herself to slow down. Running her hands up and down Lucas's muscular thighs, she felt his rod swell in her throat.

That was exactly what she needed. To be filled, to erase that feeling of longing she'd had as she'd left the gym. Sex completed her. The taste of Lucas's skin, warm against her tongue, made her relax and finally – even for just one moment – slow down. Sometimes slow was good. Sometimes moving at a languorous pace made everything come together inside her. Up and down, the point of her tongue tricked against his straining hard-on. Then she drew her cheeks in tight, sucking hard as if trying to instantly drain him.

'Oh, God,' Lucas sighed, placing his palms flat against the wall to steady himself. 'Oh, yeah –'

Jodie drew as much of her man's cock down her throat as she could. She wanted him to feel the depth of her throat. That was a game she always tried to play. Make him disappear all the way into her mouth until her lips met the base and connected with his skin. She let herself enjoy the pleasure of taking care of him until she could no longer wait. That need screaming within her, she stood and climbed his body as if he were a piece of equipment in her gym. Lucas helped, cradling her ass in his hands as she pushed up and then came back down on him. She hooked her heels against his calves, standing up on him, pressing hard.

She rode him like a wild thing, the vivacity of her need pulsing through her. Even though she liked it when he took charge, when he spanked her, tied her up, did her against a wall, sometimes she had to be on top. Just had to. Now, she couldn't get enough. She needed to slam her body up and down. Lucas gripped her waist, helping, keeping her steady. Even as she worked him, holding on to one of his shoulders to balance herself, she slid one hand between her legs, stroking herself firmly as they fucked. Her clit was still sensitive from her session in the shower. It wouldn't take much more before she came. But that sense of impending release didn't make her slow down. Because now Jodie wanted it fast. She wanted it hard.

When she kissed Lucas, her lips parted. Her teeth bit into his bottom lip, as if needing to impart some of that wild energy from her body to his own. Lucas accepted her, absorbed her, and as always he took everything that she had to give.

Back at his office, Nick glared at the lettering on the front door. He shook his head, entered the small room, then came right back out again with a sharp silver razor in his hand. Slowly, carefully, he edited the gold-lettered words on the door, changing Hudson & Stone, Private Investigators, to simply Hudson on the top line and Private Investigator on the second.

They'd been casual partners for four years, since meeting and liking each other at a police event. Deciding to pool their resources, they had wound up making an excellent team. Now, that was over. He'd already cut Hunter a cheque for half of what was in the business savings account, and he'd sent copies of the legal paperwork that would divorce the man from the business. But after that, he didn't really expect to hear from Hunter again.

Not since he'd sent the pictures of Hunter with Bailey to Hunter's wife.

Sitting down on the edge of his desk, he thought about reaching for the bottle tucked into the second drawer. But then he heard Bogie's voice speaking in his head. 'Take a break, Hud. Get back on the job.' And he knew, as always, that his mentor was right.

Chapter Eight

'So lovely to see you,' the masked hostess said to Jodie. The two women were standing beneath a shimmering chandelier in the centre of a marble-floored living room. Hurrying past on their way to the dance floor or the bar strode men and women dressed in tuxedos and ball gowns. The partiers would have looked like attendees at any other social event, except that to complete the outfits, the guests all wore creative and varied masks to hide their identities. Jodie's own mask was made of brilliant multi-coloured feathers, but the hostess knew who she was, anyway. The woman had paid careful attention when she had entered the mansion, and had focused on the floor-length scarlet silk dress that perfectly fitted Jodie's slim form.

Leaning closer, the woman murmured, 'And where's Mr Sterling?'

Jodie nodded vaguely towards the next room, where other masked guests mingled around two long tables filled with an array of exotic finger foods. 'I saw him head that way,' she added, 'towards the bar. He always likes a drink to start the evening.'

'Don't we all?' the hostess murmured.

Jodie shrugged and looked over the woman's shoulder, trying to spot Lucas in the crowd.

'But what mask is he wearing?' the woman asked next, her voice breathless. 'I promise, I won't tell anyone.'

'That would spoil the surprise, wouldn't it?' Jodie smiled when she spoke, but the woman couldn't see her lips curve up beneath the feathered mask. 'I'll tell you this –' She leaned closer, as if about to impart a fantastic secret, and the hostess tilted her head, anxiously wanting to hear whatever tidbit Jodie would have to offer '– he's in black.' Then Jodie was off in a twirl of fabric, heading towards the second room, hoping to find Lucas quickly and tell him that it was time to slip away. They'd already taken in the layout of the impressive estate, had made their way through each of the open rooms, and a few of the ones that weren't meant for guests to enter. Now was the time to disappear, before anyone grew too interested in their whereabouts.

Later, much later, they'd be back.

They hurried out the door together, then picked up their car from the valet attendant. Jodie drove around one elegantly curving road to another. Parties such as this one always excited her, and she didn't have to tell Lucas where they were headed. She simply sped the car to a deserted cul-de-sac several blocks away, parked between two street lamps, and unzipped the side of her red dress while he watched. Although her foreign convertible was small, it wasn't too small for a quick one. Beneath the designer sheath, she had on nothing and, for a moment, her date simply stared at her nakedness, the way her skin seemed to take on a glow in the bright moonlight that shone down on them.

'Let's get out,' she said, knowing that the suggestion would surprise him. Doing it in public was always a calculated risk, but this was a particularly well-patrolled area. It wasn't the San Francisco police that they had to worry about. Rich people hired their own private services to make sure that no funny business went on in their high-end neighbourhoods. How long would the two of them have in peace before one of the bored rent-a-cops shone his light in their direction? Who could guess? That was the thrilling part.

When Lucas didn't immediately get out of the car, Jodie taunted him. 'Are you scared?' she asked, making

Lucas laugh and follow her on to the sidewalk. She was a little bit of a thing compared to him, yet she let him know that fear of being caught was the farthest thing from her mind.

Of course, that wasn't exactly the truth. It was the potential of being caught that added to the thrill. Pushing boundaries. Flirting with danger. Adrenaline always fuelled Jodie's passion. Now, she unzipped Lucas's tuxedo slacks and withdrew his dick, sweetly fondling the head with the palm of her hand until she brought forth the welcoming signs of arousal. She used this most personal lubrication to firmly grip him while he stared down at her slim, nude body. Jodie had small but beautiful breasts. Her round, rose-coloured nipples were already hard from the chill in the air, and he reached down and lightly pinched one and then the other, making Jodie moan and close her eyes.

The sound of her pleasure, even at a low volume, was startling in the eerie quiet. A soft breeze rustled through the plentiful trees lining the street, and suddenly the two found themselves beneath a shower of pale pink cherry blossoms. Beneath that swirling, natural confetti, Lucas lifted Jodie up and brought her body down on his pulsing dick. He raised and lowered her hips on him, setting the pace.

Everything began to work together: the fragrance of the flower petals; the way Lucas moved her faster, then slower, as if they were still dancing together as they had on the black-and-white marbled floor at the party. Setting her gently against the hood of the car, he slid one hand between their two bodies, using his middle finger now to rub in circles over her clit as he continued to thrust inside her body. It turned her on when they came together, and Lucas knew how to make that happen. He filled her up with his throbbing cock, then tricked his finger and thumb over her button, bringing the two sensations together until she could take it no longer.

As she got closer, she hooked her dainty feet on the backs of his legs and firmly pushed her body upwards. She liked the feeling of taking her pleasure from that of her mate. Physically taking it.

'Pretty baby,' Lucas sighed, looking into her face.

Giving in, Jodie threw back her head and let herself reach the blissful outer limits, grinding her body against her partner's and crying out into the night. If she'd known for a fact that someone aside from Lucas was watching her, she would have come even harder than she did. Because, deep down inside, Jodie Silver had always been a bad girl.

Nick was good at his job. He knew the methods of camouflage, and could blend in with the best of them. That chameleon-like ability was why he'd come to California in the first place, starting his journey down south in the smoggy haze of Los Angeles. He'd originally made the move from the midwest as an idealistic eighteen-year-old kid, thinking that he'd easily break into acting. Maybe he wouldn't be a star right away, but he'd make it. Everyone had always told him he was a sure thing. With his casual good looks and his ability to mimic just about anyone, wasn't he simply destined for the silver screen?

As it turned out, no. To his dismay, he'd discovered that there were a thousand Nick Hudsons already in Hollywood. And, unfortunately, he didn't have as much motivation as the rest of them. Work his butt off at some audition so that some prissy casting director could snub him? Not his speed. Being repeatedly rejected made him want to punch someone in the face. He still had a file tucked away in some drawer with one cruel casting director's comments sprawled across the back of his black-and-white headshot: 'Handsome, in a cowboy sort of way. But nothing special.' Now, there was someone who needed a serious thrashing.

When his initial plans hadn't panned out for him,

he'd bounced from job to job for several years. He'd bartended, dabbled in construction, did a little bit of stunt driving, which was fun except there was too much downtime between gigs. Although he was enjoying himself, he knew that from the outside his life looked like a failure. That is, until a friend had hired him to do a little snooping.

'My wife's having an affair,' Tim had told him over cheap, warm beers at the Firefly Lounge. 'I mean, I think she is. Fuck it, man. I don't know what to think at this point –'

'Why don't you ask her?' Nick suggested. He wasn't married, and had never been able to keep himself interested in anything resembling a long-term relationship. To Nick, straight talking seemed the best way to get the information you wanted in this sort of situation. But maybe Tim didn't really want to know the facts.

'Just can't. I mean, if I'm wrong, then she'll think I don't trust her.'

'Which you don't,' Nick pointed out.

Tim shrugged. 'If I'm right, she's not going to tell me to my face, is she?'

Nick didn't know the answer to that. He'd stared silently down into his beer, picturing Tim's pretty wife, a woman who had a deep true laugh and an uncanny ability to know exactly when you needed another drink. Elaine was fun and friendly, liked to host cookouts and always welcomed Tim's buddies into their home. And she was cheating? Mentally, Nick thanked Christ that he wasn't in a similar predicament. Imagine worrying about something like that and not having the balls to simply ask flat out what was going on. It wasn't until Bailey that Nick could finally empathise.

Tim had continued, taking his silence for interest. 'But what I was thinking,' he started, 'I mean, what I was hoping was that you might be able to find out for me. Follow her for a few days. Tell me where she goes.

What she does when I'm not there. I know it sounds strange, but I'd feel better if I knew a friend was looking out for me, paying attention to my interests.'

Nick had felt dirty at first. Spying on his buddy's wife seemed like a bad idea, any way you considered it. Even a looker like Tim's wife. But he'd gotten past the dirty feeling by plunging himself into the role. Casting himself as a Bogey wannabe, he'd gone so far as to wear an old Fedora on his first hour or so on the job. That was something he'd given up right away. Nothing stood out more than a man in a silly hat. Still, he'd discovered that he liked the detective work. He was good at it. Not only blending in with a crowd, but searching out clues. Later on, he'd even mastered the art of interviewing people, finding puzzle pieces and putting them together. No one was more shocked than he was that the brainy part of the job was often the stuff he liked the best.

He'd learned an awful lot about Elaine in hardly any time at all. The red-headed bombshell had been cheating on her man quite openly with a neighbour from across the street. As soon as Tim had left for work, the neighbour had come over, and Elaine had been more than welcoming, pulling open her front door wearing nothing more than a skimpy little nightie. After a quick embrace, she'd led the lover down the plush peach-hued carpeting to the four-poster bed in the back. Nick had found this out by peering through the bedroom window. The only thing that had been unexpected was the fact that the lover was a woman.

What an amazing fucking sight that had been. The lush Elaine spreading her generous thighs for her petite, brunette neighbour. Together, the two women had slid themselves into positions that captivated Nick. Sweet sixty-nines. Straddling each other's faces. Using strap-ons in ingenious ways. He'd watched for a hell of a lot longer than was actually necessary, unable to move from the spot by the parted lace curtains. To his

surprise, he found that the women were more interesting than porn movies. Their moans sounded genuine,
and their bodies were real. The neighbour's pale skin
was a bright beacon against Elaine's tanned body. The
two women's interlocking curves were straight out of
every man's fantasy.

That first day, Nick had wound up staring until
Elaine had come hard and loudly, thrusting against the
mouth of her seductive plaything. He'd gone back for a
few more days, not only to make sure that this wasn't
a one-time tryst, but because his dick had told him to
get a few more of those sexy images in his memory
banks.

Although he wouldn't have thought it possible, his
first job had actually wound up with a happy ending.
Tim had been so turned on by the thought that his
wife had a female lover that he'd convinced her to let
him watch her with her lady friend. 'It's not her fault,'
he'd told Nick. 'I work all the time. Wasn't paying her
the attention she needed, or deserved. She's a sexy girl,
Elaine is. She needs the release.' Ultimately, the three
had gotten it on together, and Nick had been given a
two-hundred-dollar cheque for his troubles, as well as
the bonus of a new daydream to fall back on during
slow times.

But occasionally, Nick ran into a stickier situation.
Like this new one with Max Sterling. His job was to get
a good feel of what was going on behind the smoked
glass door at 770 Chestnut. He didn't know why the
information was requested – rarely did he receive all
of the facts in his business all at once – but he didn't
mind that. Since the initial phone conversation he'd
only received email communications from his
employer, as well as a wired transfer of an extremely
generous retainer. He'd been given the freedom to find
the facts in his own way, and he appreciated that.

Searching for knowledge was what he liked best. So
far, he knew that the Import/Export business had to be

a front for something. His gut told him that much. But he couldn't figure out exactly what illegal behaviour, if any, was occurring. He also knew that the girl, Jodie Silver, was in on the scheme. She had to be. Working right close with Max for all these years, there was no way that she wasn't involved.

Still, when he'd seen her in action this evening, it was difficult to believe she'd be into anything underhanded. Not someone as put-together as her. Beautiful, yes. But there was more to her aura of self-assuredness than her picture-perfect appearance. The glow in her eyes didn't seem criminal, simply confident. Nick liked confident women. So he'd done the only thing he knew how. He'd watched her. Watched her at the party. Followed, as discreetly as possible, when she wandered into areas not specifically set up for the guests. It wasn't anything that set up warning lights in his head. She was an appraiser. That's the job title he'd discovered. She must have been interested in the varied art around the mansion.

After the party, she had screwed her date close by in the neighbourhood. Then the two of them had gone for a drive to a distant location, losing Nick on the curves of the windy San Francisco streets. Nick had done his best to track their route, but had eventually given up. The girl was good at a lot of different things, he'd learned. Running. Driving. And sparking his libido.

Back at home again, he consoled himself with the fact that at least now he had a brand-new fantasy to come to: a mental movie of Jodie and her man together. Jodie astride the lover and pushing herself to climax, as if needing to take charge of her own pleasure. Nick wasn't impressed by the arm candy. Boys who looked like Jodie's date literally filled the city, especially down by the Marina where her office was located. Strong sailor types, who tended to go along with the Barbie girls. He wouldn't have thought that someone as interesting-looking as Jodie would fall for a Ken doll. But you never could guess what rocked someone's world.

What rocked Nick's was suspense. A sense of not knowing. The moment before he took a woman's dress off to see what her body really looked like. Once he grew accustomed to a situation, it was difficult for him to stay interested. This he saw as his main flaw. He liked the excitement of the new. In fact, when he was really attracted to a woman, he waited as long as possible before bedding her, worried that he would lose interest as soon as he'd discovered her secrets. So far, that's what had happened every time up to Bailey, and then she'd pulled that trick on him instead – losing interest before he had. Served him right, didn't it?

He was tired of learning that people were generally the same, that they fitted into easily identifiable patterns. As soon as you got to know them, they fell into a routine, expecting things from him that he wasn't interested in giving.

Jodie was unique, if he could believe what he had learned so far. She didn't behave like the women he'd dated in the past. She was definitely running the show, which intrigued him. More interesting than that, she looked different every time he saw her. With her hair pulled back in a sophisticated upsweep, or down loose so that she looked like a co-ed, she was constantly shifting. He'd keep an eye on her. Yes, he was being paid to do so, but he thought that at this point he would have followed her anyway. Since the evening he'd watched her indulge in an outdoor spanking fest followed by the morning running side by side at the gym, he couldn't get her out of his head.

Addicted. That's what he was.

And it was a good feeling.

By two in the morning, the party had faded to a few straggling guests, talking loudly and drunkenly in the circular gravel driveway. Jodie and Lucas sat together in her convertible half a block away, waiting patiently, still glazed in their post-coital warmth. They shared sips of whisky from a silver flask, their fingers overlapping as they passed one of Jodie's favourite possessions back and forth. It had been a gift from a silent screen star to her faithful driver, and Jodie loved the fact that Hollywood royalty had once fingered the muted silver. She liked to think that the driver might have been more than simply a wizard behind the wheel. What exactly were the services he'd rendered to be rewarded with such a handsome prize?

Those were the types of thoughts filling Jodie's mind as she waited for the last guest to leave. Once the driveway was empty, and the valet company had departed, she still remained where she was. Timing was everything in Jodie's business. If she misjudged all that she'd worked for might be lost. Lucas trusted her, never rushing, never even questioning her plans.

'Now,' she finally said. 'You wait here.'

'You don't want me to come?' He was only being polite. Jodie never took an extra person in with her. There was no need.

'Just wait,' she said. She had discarded the dress in favour of inky black pants and a midnight blue T-shirt. Now, she slipped a long-sleeved coal-black cashmere sweater over her head and pinned her hair away from her face with a simple lace ponytail holder. With her long hair pulled back, she was particularly striking. Jodie had the features of any fashion photographer's favourite type of model: strong nose, expressive eyes, and a sharply drawn chin that she jutted out defiantly at her partner. 'I'll be back in twenty minutes. Or else come knocking, say that you left your keys by the bar, that you need to find them in order to get into your place.' Always the plan. Create a diversion in case she found herself in unforeseen trouble. That's what Lucas was good for. Although she'd never needed the back-up plan to date, it didn't mean she wouldn't one day.

Quietly, she exited the car and walked close to the well-trimmed hedges and back on to the exquisite grounds that she'd left several hours before. She approached the large, darkened house carefully, aware that there was an alarm system in place, and also aware that Lucas had left a window open for her in the maid's bathroom. If it had still been open when the alarm was set, she would be able to enter with no problem at all. Her heart raced anyway. This was the most exciting part. Getting back in. Once within the confines of the elaborate estate, she had only one stop to make. Nobody would hear her in a palace this large. The master bedrooms – his and hers – were on the third floor. And from the way the two hosts had been drinking, she was sure that they would be out to the world until their post-party hangovers kicked in the next morning.

After climbing through the window, she cautiously stepped on the lid of the toilet and then lowered herself down to the tile floor between the john and the bidet. This early part of the plan went without a hitch. She walked silently through the doorway and found herself in the rear of the house, which Lucas had described perfectly to her. He'd reconnoitred the place while she'd mingled with the guests.

Slowly, she walked back to the main room, where the famous antique pillbox collection was displayed beneath a glass case. Not her style. She didn't even stop to look. This evening, artwork was what captivated Jodie's mind. Specifically, a stunning little sculpture that she'd spied in a corner of the downstairs library. The statue was created of magical pink-veined stone, and it featured smooth polished edges. She closed her eyes for a moment, visualising the exact location of her new desire, then made her way silently down the hall.

What a beautiful piece of work.

How sweet it would feel between her legs.

Once she had the sculpture in her hand, she moved at a faster pace, retracing her steps as she headed down the long hall and back to the maid's bathroom. She had her velvet-gloved hand out to reach for the doorknob when she realised that the door was now closed. It had been open when she left it. Her heart pounded ferociously, but she forced herself to stay calm. Was the maid awake? Was someone in the bathroom?

The sound of a cough alerted her to the fact that yes, someone definitely had woken up during her catwalk through the sleeping house. From the sounds of water splashing into the sink, Jodie could be sure that this person was moments away from opening the door and staring at her eye to eye. With a sense of extreme purpose, Jodie backed against the wall and into the shadows. On tiptoe, she made her way down the hall in the opposite direction.

What should she do?

Different possibilities flooded through her mind. She could wait out the maid, hoping the woman would go back to sleep, would not be hungry, or thirsty, or crave a bit of late-night television. Or she could find another way out. Still with her back to the wall, and the statue in her hand, Jodie moved through the house. She tried to remember the layout of the rooms, but the rush of adrenaline coursing through her body made her forget. There was no fear. Not yet. This was something she'd planned for, a close call. Nothing disastrous had happened, only a change in plans.

After pushing through a swinging door, she found herself in the darkened kitchen. As she stared at her ghostly reflection in the glass cabinet, she realised that the room was almost as big as her entire condominium. She could live here. Sleep in one of the pantries, bathe in the oversized stainless steel sink. Crazy thoughts like these made her feel wild as she stared around the room, until suddenly she spied her one possible exit just as she heard the hall light switch flicked on.

'What happened?' Lucas asked. 'You took fucking forever.'

'Go,' she said, flashing the statue to him as she slid her ankle-length trench coat around her body. 'Just go fast. Get us to my apartment.' Rhinestone-studded buckles on the coat gleamed in the light from the street lamp, sending rainbows dancing drunkenly around the inside of the automobile.

Before starting the engine, Lucas took an extra moment to stare at the prize his partner had brought with her. The thing was positively obscene. In fact, it looked to him like nothing less than an ancient dildo. Shaking his head, he turned on the ignition and steered the car out into a deserted street. He never ceased to be amazed by what people called 'art', and he was continually floored by what they would pay for it.

'I'm going to do you with that,' he murmured, now looking away from the road long enough to see Jodie cradling the ancient Greek artifact in her hands, rocking the stone statue, stroking it. His eyes narrowed as he caught the way she was gazing at her new toy. Strange, but was he jealous of a stone phallus?

'No, baby,' Jodie murmured. 'I'm going to beat you to the chase.'

While Lucas tried his best to keep himself focused on the job of driving, Jodie slid her slacks down her thighs to her ankles, revealing her bare sex already shiny with her arousal.

'Wait for me!' Lucas said, his voice as close to begging as he ever got.

'Can't,' Jodie told him in a rush. She dipped the tip of the marble sculpture between her legs, pressed the head of it against her clit, then slid the rod inside her, all the way to the base. 'Can't wait,' she told him.

Neither could he. Once they were a safe distance

away from one of the most exclusive districts in Northern California, Lucas pulled the car over to the side of the road, unable to drive while Jodie was sliding the statue back and forth between her slender thighs. He watched her, wide-eyed, as she moved the stone statue back and forth, and when she pulled it almost all of the way out of her body, he took it from her hands.

'Let me,' he insisted, and now Jodie kicked off both her black ballet flats and her slacks, then put her feet up on the dashboard. As Lucas pleasured her with the latest acquisition for her private collection, Jodie closed her eyes and sighed.

For the second time in four hours, they made love in public while the rest of the city slept in peace. Now, Lucas slid the impromptu sex toy back and forth between her legs, and then bent down to lick her himself. He couldn't help it. Watching made him so hungry. His tongue flicked out between her pussy lips, meeting her clit and then stroking it with the flat surface of his tongue.

'Keep going,' Jodie urged. 'Do me harder.'

'I'll fuck you, all right,' Lucas said, taking the statue away and pulling out his penis. 'Climb on top of me, Jodie.'

She did as he asked, straddling him in the driver's seat, moving her body up and down his erection. The warmth of living flesh after the stone-cold phallus made her body tremble. Lucas knew just how to do it. Knew just what she liked. Oh, did he ever. As she rode him, he brought the stone phallus up behind her, parting her rear cheeks and touching the very tip of it to her exposed asshole.

'Please,' she said, 'do that.'

'Do what?' He wanted to hear her say it.

'Put it in me.'

'Where?'

'Put it in my ass.'

That's all he needed to hear. With the statue still lubed from her own abundant juices, Lucas pressed the tip further between her cheeks, sliding just the first inch into her rear.

Jodie gritted her teeth and sighed through them. The hiss was of pure pleasure from the extreme sense of being filled as Lucas continued to pleasure her in two holes at once. Giving her just what she needed. In perfect rhythm, he played her, moving in and out of her slippery pussy at the same speed as he probed her ass with the stolen prize. When Jodie started to come, he simply held her, keeping his penis tight inside of her, the statue deep, and letting her reach those gates of pleasure and push through.

Watching Jodie come brought Lucas to climax. The way she seemed to feel the orgasm throughout every part of her body. Her skin glowed, eyes shone, lips parted as if to drink more deeply from the bliss that pulsed through her. She was like a piece of art brought to life. Staring at her made Lucas understand Jodie's thirst for stolen goods. If he could own that look of hers, that expression, he would feel satisfied. He came wordlessly, silently, after her, his body shuddering in the second before she slipped from his embrace and pushed free. It took him a moment to catch his breath, while Jodie seemed instantly contained again. Ready. Waiting.

'So how'd you do it?' he asked as he started the engine, then drove the car through empty streets in a roundabout way towards Jodie's apartment. He was taking his time because he wanted to hear what had happened back at the crime scene. Jodie had let him know that her plans had changed, but she hadn't told him all the facts yet.

'Tell me,' Lucas urged, and now, at his insistence, Jodie came clean, obviously relishing the concept of sharing her dramatic tale. With a self-deprecating humour, she described her horror at hearing the maid's fingertips on the light switch just as she spotted a pet door that led out to the side yard. Sucking in her breath, she'd squeezed through, the grey plastic door fluttering closed behind her as she made her getaway.

'Perfect escape for the Pussycat Burglar of Pacific Heights,' Lucas said with a laugh. Jodie smiled at him, as if she couldn't have agreed more.

Chapter Nine

Case File: 584
Subject: Max Sterling
Job Description: Hazy, at best.

Nick stared at the file on his computer screen. Yeah, 'hazy' pretty well summed his situation up at the moment. He'd been working on the case for several weeks, and he didn't really know what he was doing yet. But although this was a rare occurrence for him, he didn't find the situation unduly frustrating yet. He'd pounded the pavement without immediate success on more difficult cases in the past. It was the vague quality of his assignment that confounded him. Although facts were sometimes sparse, rarely did a client appear confused about the issue Nick was to research.

When people put out the money for his services, they usually had a clear idea of what they expected to find out. Prove them right or prove them wrong, and let them go on with their lives. The suspicions were generally easy to summate. Yes, every once in a while he had to drag the situation out of a client – sometimes people were hesitant to reveal to a total stranger how messed up their lives really were. But if they made their way to his office, then they'd already done the little should-I-or-shouldn't-I dance, had already come to terms with the fact that there was something out there that they didn't really want to know. Maybe there were a few 'ums' and 'ahhs' in their stories. Maybe with women he saw tears and with men dark looks at the ground. He was used to all of that, the messiness of human emotions.

Most often, he'd be hired by an irate husband or nervous wife, some player who had lost in the game of love, but needed facts before finalising an ending. Those weren't his favourite cases, but they did pay the bills. Especially with over fifty per cent of marriages ending in divorce these days, and seventy per cent of the population confessing to having cheated at some point in a relationship. (And how about all those people who hadn't confessed? Were the figures even higher? There was a depressing thought.) With numbers like those, it was clear to see why Nick stayed in business.

Scoping out the truth was his main occupation. It didn't take him long to learn whether a man was cheating, or if his power lunches really did last three-and-a-half hours. Was a wife staying late at the office to give the blow-by-blow to her team, or to give a blow-job to her handsome male secretary?

Over the years, he'd learned that people's instincts were often right on target. A wife who thought her husband was keeping something from her usually got her money's worth from Nick. Photos. Receipts. All signs point to yes, ma'am, sorry to say. You buy your ticket and you take your chances. Although sometimes the secrets were darker or more unusual than the customer had expected. Occasionally, Nick learned that the man *was* cheating – but with a male golf buddy rather than a twenty-year-old bimbo.

Once he'd tailed a woman who'd taken him on a wild ride through several gambling houses in Las Vegas. Yeah, she wasn't coming clean with her husband. But she didn't have a young buck in the bedroom. She had a gambling addiction that set the man back far more than Nick's final bill. Sure, every so often, he came back with happy news. No, sir, your lady's not cheating. She's volunteering for diabetes research at the local hospital. But that was rare. Nick had learned from experience that the age-old cliché held true, although he liked to paraphrase: where there's smoke, there are often two people in bed together who shouldn't be sleeping with each other.

It was Nick's belief that these types of cases were not why people got into the private eye business. Most thought that there was some sort of glamour to the job. And occasionally there was. He'd helped solve a variety of cases that had won him a small bit of press in the local papers. Each time he'd acted in a gallant, stalwart manner, he knew he was giving the PI business a positive name. Showed the population that it wasn't just asses out there who were private dicks. And that pleased him. Because, for the most part, what he did was dig through other people's trash. How sexy and glamorous was that? Not very, because humans were dirty little animals. At the end of the day, their needs and cravings tended to overshadow their moral instincts.

But here was a new situation. He was proud of his achievements, his ability to find the truth among garbage. Yet he hadn't really been given anything clear and clean to work with. What was his job? Again, he stared at the space after 'Job Description'. Then he hit the erase key, removing those three words before typing in what he'd actually been hired to do.

Job Description: Get the goods on Max Sterling, in any way that he could.

That sounded easy enough, didn't it? On paper, it made perfect sense. He'd been hired to keep an eye on Max Sterling, owner of MS Imports and Exports. Apparently, there was a belief that Sterling was involved in some sort of shady business. No hard facts had been found. Nothing could be proven. But his employer wanted to start building a case, to prevent a possible future theft. That's where Nick came in.

Find out the facts, sort them thoroughly, then pass them on to the person who was paying his cheque. That's what he did for his living, yet as he sat at his keyboard, he shook his head. This wasn't right at all. Max Sterling might have been involved in some sort of gameplaying as regards the cold clear facts of the law, but he wasn't even in the country as far as Nick could tell. If Nick was supposed to get a line on Max, then he should be in Europe, trailing after the mysterious man.

No, it was Jodie Silver who was the one to watch. His instincts had told him that from the very beginning, the feeling in the base of his stomach when he had first seen her. And that feeling rarely lied. It was why he excelled at his job. He listened to the little voices in his head. The ones that said 'You're on the right track. Don't blow it.'

She appeared one way on the surface, but he knew already how different she was inside. Yeah, he'd bet money that she had the key to solve the mystery. Even if he wasn't precisely sure what the mystery was. His fingers danced over the keyboard as he opened a new file and typed in a fresh header.

Case File: 584B

Subject: Jodie M Silver

Job Description:

Now his fingers hesitated. Type in what he wanted to know, or what he felt the employer would appreciate?

Job Description: Get into Jodie's head. Get inside her skin.

There was more than that. At least he was being honest with himself.

Bend her over something firm and slide whatever little frilly nothing she had on beneath her skirt. Push the filmy fabric out of the way. Press hard. Drive in. Feel the wetness awaiting him. Make her cry out –

Erase. Erase. Erase.

Job Description: Tail the girl and see if she leads to Max. Take it from there.

All right. That made perfect sense. That sounded justifiable rather than certifiable. But did he really want to follow her because she turned him on? Or was he interested because it was part of his job? As he spread his notes out on the desk, preparing to formulate his weekly report, he realised that maybe the 'whys' didn't really matter at this point. He would give his employer copy A, and keep copy B for himself. If the two cases entwined in the future, then he'd have chosen correctly. If not, nobody would know.

'You ever think of stripping?' Isabelle asked Jodie.

'Right. That's what I think of all the time,' Jodie said immediately. 'I just sit at my desk, gaze out the open window, and think about stripping –'

Isabelle snorted, but she took another sip of her coffee as Jodie continued.

'Sometimes I think about what strippers wear. Those cute little pasties that cover just the tiniest part of skin. Or those itsy-bitsy shorts. You'd know what they're called, right?'

Isabelle nodded. 'Hot pants.'

'Other times, I think about what it would feel like to have a man slide a crisp twenty dollar bill into my –'

'Look, I'm serious,' Isabelle interrupted.

'Oh, I am too,' Jodie said, the sarcastic edge still in her voice. 'Me up on stage, taking off my clothes for a bunch of hungry men. Really shaking my, you know, what's it called? My money maker.'

'You do have a way with descriptions.' Isabelle grinned. 'I mean, I can picture exactly what you just put out there. And I think you'd be damn good, kiddo. You'd probably bring the house down and come home with a few hundred dollars in your pocket, or wherever it is you'd keep the cash. But I'm not talking about doing it for real. I'm talking about doing it for exercise.'

Now, Jodie just stared at Isabelle, waiting for the punch line. This was obviously a joke, right?

'Newest craze, Jo. Everyone's doing it. Even the movie stars.'

'But why would anyone want to?'

'Break from routine. Something sort of sexy. That Tai-bo gets old after a few months, you know? And spinning? I'm so sick of peddalling in one goddamn place without getting anywhere.'

'Where are the classes held?' Jodie asked next. 'The Pussycat Theatre?'

Isabelle handed over the schedule from Jodie's own gym. 'Tonight. Seven. You game?' She watched Jodie carefully.

Jodie didn't have to read the write-up to answer that question. 'For a dare? Always.'

This was how Nick got to see Jodie take off her clothes. He followed the girls from Isabelle's apartment, realising right away where they were headed. He detoured, got to the gym before they did, and suited up in his standard grey sweats. But when Jodie didn't show up in the weight room, he grew suspicious. Where'd they go? Juice bar already? That wasn't like the Jodie Silver he felt he already knew intimately. She put in the work before she relaxed. Maybe Isabelle was a bad influence on her, getting her to do things she wouldn't normally.

He headed to the lobby, checked out the schedule, and immediately found the listing: 'Pole Cats. Work your tail off to some of the best rock music ever recorded. And go home with a new routine to spice up your bedroom life.'

He read on to learn that this was some sort of new exercise craze, like Jazzercise from the 1970s and aerobics from the 1980s. Modern, feminist women were pretending to be strippers. Nothing wrong with that. Not in Nick's book. But could men attend?

'Sure,' the blue-eyed receptionist said, giving him a flirtatious wink. 'Usually, it's all-women. But you know, you're in San Francisco. It's not like we're going to take on some big lawsuit to keep men out of the classes. But the thing is –' and she lowered her voice seductively. 'You have to join in. The teacher won't let you sit back and watch. That would be disruptive to the routine of the class.'

Nick nodded. No problem. He'd stay in the back, right?

Wrong.

As soon as he pushed through the doors, he saw that this was a brand-new style of workout. The teacher was dressed in the most risqué athletic gear he'd ever seen, and she was leading about twenty students through a routine that could only be described as erection-inducing. What was he doing here? Other than getting a hard-on, which wasn't the most effective thing to possess while trying to play it low key. He took a deep breath, thought of baseball, men's hockey, Dame Edna, anything that would keep his libido under control.

Jodie and Isabelle were in the front row, getting into the groove of the music and the actions. They looked like they were having an amazingly good time. Jodie didn't actually peel down to her altogether, but when the class leader pulled her in front, the dark-haired beauty worked her body to the beat. With finesse, she discarded her sweatshirt, followed by her Lycra pants, until she was down to a golden-yellow leotard. She had definitely prepared for the class. Maybe Nick could just stand in the back, move as well as he could to the music, and not catch anyone's eye.

'I need another volunteer,' the frisky blonde instructress called out. 'You. Back there –'

She pointed at Nick. He looked at his feet. For an instant, he felt as if he were at a high school dance. Insecure and not ready to face his fears. This wasn't what he wanted to have happen.

'Come on,' she said. 'Mr Chippendale. You can help me out.'

To the encouraging sounds of twenty women catcalling him, Nick slowly made his way to the front of the room.

'Generally, this is girls only,' the teacher said. 'It's really refreshing to have a guy up here.'

'What do you want me to do?'

She eyed him carefully. 'I won't tell you that. But I'll let you help out here –'

The students didn't actually take their clothes off completely. Not down to bare skin. The class was intended to increase the students' confidence in their ability to move erotically. Perhaps it was a strange concept, but it was not much odder than some of the courses taught at the gym: one based on boot camp, another on playground games. In this case, someone had noticed how much effort good strippers put into their routines; the energy and enthusiasm translated into calories burned. That's what the teacher demonstrated. How to move to the music. How to strut. And how to undress, if a student was willing to peel down at all.

When Nick was finished with his makeshift routine, he looked around, expecting to find Jodie and Isabelle laughing at him. He could already hear it in his head, the tinkling girlish laugh of Isabelle's, the lower chuckle that indicated Jodie's pure pleasure. But when he glanced around the students, the two women had left.

'That was great,' a redhead gushed at him. 'I mean, you were really good.'

He looked at her, surprised, and found that he was blushing. Come on, Nick. Stop being such a freak. Get dressed and get out of here. And never mention this to anyone again. Ever. Christ, was he going to have to find a new gym?

Chapter Ten

Glossy black vinyl jackets kissed each other in Jodie's closet. The material was slick and slippery, and when two items of clothing made of the same fabric butted against each other, the pieces stuck firmly. Jodie had to pry the shiny jackets apart, and she laughed at the sucking sound the material made when she divided the items. It was as if the jackets were happy pressed together like that, and they were letting her know how much she'd annoyed them by stopping their fun.

Her fingertips crossed over the vinyl, dancing towards something more appropriate for the evening's activities. One of Jodie's favourite parts about being a thief was the clothes. Not stealing clothes, but dressing the part. She appreciated the whole cloak-and-dagger aspect of choosing a costume for a night of thievery. The smooth black slacks, the finely cut black turtleneck sweaters. Her dark hair helped her to blend, she knew that. She'd have had to dye it if she'd been born blonde. And she wore the softest gloves to make sure that no fingerprints of hers remained. When she was ready to go into a new place, she always tried to catch a glimpse of her reflection. That was part of the routine, like touching a rabbit's foot for good luck. She'd look in a car rear-view mirror, or in a shop window. She adored the way she felt – like some movie star – clad in a costume that perfectly suited her work.

The other aspect that she adored was the set-up. A difficult plan made her mind work overtime, and she appreciated the mental manoeuvring that had to be done. It was her belief that the thieves who got caught were the ones who didn't put in the necessary research. The sloppy ones who barged into a place, guns in hand, ready to take by force, almost always got nailed right away. Or the ones who tanked themselves up on alcohol beforehand, for courage, and then tripped over themselves to leave clues for the cops. There was no finesse to working like that. No class. She'd read about a bank robber who had handed a note to the teller written on the back of his dry-cleaning bill. A bill that had his name and phone number on the other side. This wasn't a robber from MENSA.

Jodie was unique in her approach: theft as an art form. Rarely would she enter a place without knowing at least three different escape routes. More, if possible. In general, there would be a window escape, a side door, and the old-fashioned front route. People rarely considered that the front door was often the best way in and out. No one expected it. Strangers never thought someone coming or going in this manner was doing something illegal. It seemed too risky.

As a back-up, in case her escape plans went hopelessly awry, she always had an excuse in the rear of her mind, a way to talk her way out of a situation if she got caught.

If. The big if. The if that had never happened to her yet. She didn't count the situation with Isabelle, because that had been planned. A plotted capture. But she hadn't ever had to deal with being caught for real. Thank Christ. Who knew whether she'd be able to convince someone that she had simply found herself in the wrong place? Sometimes, she tried an innocent look in the mirror. 'Oh, my. I must have made an error.' There were a million things to say after that: she'd thought that this was her apartment; she was house-sitting for a friend; she was new to the area; she didn't speak English very well. Or that she was there in a different capacity entirely: as a seducer – a concept that would work only if the person was single and in the mood. Still, she had lots of different plans for each different situation. But the new idea that she had didn't require this type of thorough escape planning. This new concept that she'd been working on was one of the best she'd ever considered. Why she hadn't thought of it before was the only thing to upset her.

Set up Max Sterling?

Now, there was a winning idea.

'It's the old dog and pony show.'

'Excuse me?'

'Bra and Panty show,' Isabelle corrected herself. 'Nothing really that interesting. But do you want to go? I'd love to have some company. It can get lonely wandering the aisles solo.'

'Of course, I'd like to go.'

'Don't get so excited,' Isabelle sighed. 'It's just a whole lot of lingerie spread out in a convention centre.'

'I love lingerie,' Jodie cooed.

'This is different. There will be more lingerie items on display than you've ever seen before in your life. It's pretty overwhelming. You forget which aisles you've already been down. After an hour or two everything starts to look the same. You go into underwear overload.'

'But it sounds awesome.'

'I guess,' Isabelle said, fluffing her hair and making a pouty kiss face at her reflection. 'But I go to these every year, and it's rare to find something truly exceptional. By the end of the day, I leave feeling demoralised, never wanting to see a pair of panties again as long as I live.'

'So where do you get your best stuff?'

'Europe. Definitely. My favourite new designer is this twenty-six-year-old kid from London. She's just amazing. Some people are born with talent, and she's definitely one of them. Usually, designers apprentice with a larger fashion house before going out on their own.

But not her. She just appeared on the scene like magic, and she took over the special corner of the market.'

'Which corner?'

'The one inhabited by women who don't mind spending a fortune on items to be viewed only by a private few. She does these things with bows, and netting, and wraparound style panties.'

'But *you* don't wear panties,' Jodie teased.

'Even I make exceptions, Jo. These are unbelievable. They don't really qualify as panties. They're like outer-wear. Or "only" wear. Put them on, and you don't need anything else. They're art in themselves. I mean, just looking at a picture makes you hot.' Isabelle picked up a four-colour brochure and fanned the pages open for Jodie to see. 'She uses silk imported from Italy, which she hand-dyes herself. Each piece is completely unique. She'll make things fit to order. And she'll create one-of-a-kind styles that blow your mind.'

'Show me your favourite,' Jodie urged, eyes wide as Isabelle flipped the pages. Talking about underwear was making her feel more than a little bit sexed-up. She wondered if Isabelle could tell, but her friend seemed focused on work, pointing out the different styles that she liked the best. There were dotted bikini panties. Opalescent thongs. Sheer tap panties trimmed with rhinestones. Ruffled numbers that looked like something a naughty flamenco dancer would wear. A black set of knickers with zippers running the length of the crotch. Some of the pieces were emblazoned with cheeky slogans across the rear. Others provided almost no protection at all, just slivers of fabric that reminded Jodie suddenly of stripping at the gym. And then Isabelle pointed to a style that Jodie had never seen before.

'See? It ties. The large bow hangs above the waistline of low-cut jeans. So the undies are almost like an accessory.'

'How do you get them off?'

'Your lover unties them and you slide out. But first, of course, you go out dancing or to a club wearing them, and it's like you're in silk bondage gear all night long.'

'Your lover?'

'Come on. You'd have to have a lover if you were wearing those. Nobody would get all tied up in something like that and then stay home alone.'

'Will the designer be at the show?'

'That's the only reason we're going, kiddo.'

'Do you have any of her pieces here?'

Isabelle got a wicked look on her face. 'Why?'

'Just to see. To touch.'

'To try on?'

'If you'd let me.'

And now Isabelle walked to the front of the store and opened the bottom drawer of one of the built-in display cabinets. She pulled out a wrapped package and handed it over to Jodie. 'My gift to you,' she said.

Jodie flushed when she saw the present, flushed darker when she opened the box and saw what was inside. 'You're teasing me. This isn't really –'

'For you. Definitely. But it comes with a price.'

'Doesn't everything?'

'Seriously. You put it on while I watch.'

Jodie nodded, readily agreeing to something so simple, but Isabelle held up one hand. 'That's not the deal. Someone else will be watching, too.'

'Who?' Jodie asked softly, looking around as if some mysterious voyeur would suddenly appear. But in her head, she already knew. All of her work with Isabelle had intentionally led her to this point. Still, she was always pleased when a plan came so easily to fruition.

'Here, let me help,' Isabelle offered, reaching to undo the row of buttons on Jodie's polka-dot blouse. Then she echoed Jodie's words right back to her. 'That would be telling. Wouldn't it?'

'Izzy,' Jodie murmured, her deep grey eyes wide.

With a wink, Isabelle nodded to the camera poised over their heads. 'I have a particularly interesting customer,' she said, 'and he'll appreciate this home movie more than I can say.' This was the truth. Cameron had been asking – begging, really – for a second viewing. Once he'd seen Isabelle and Jodie together that first night, he'd continually requested that Isabelle set up another rendezvous.

'That was by luck,' she'd told him. 'I wouldn't lie to her now. I wouldn't set her up like that.'

'So ask her. I don't think she'll have a problem. Not Jodie Silver –'

'You know her?'

'Of her. I wasn't sure at first. You know when you see someone out of character, it can be hard to place them. But later I saw her at a jewellery show. She's the buyer for Max Sterling.'

'Oh, you rich people,' Isabelle had laughed. 'She's probably bought stuff for your private collections. Is that right?'

'I know her because I know her. Now, introduce us for real.'

This evening, that was exactly what Isabelle did. As Jodie stared into the camera above, Isabelle said, 'Jo, I'd like you to meet Mr Cameron Sweeney.'

Jodie dipped her head and lowered her lashes, suddenly coy. 'But where is he?' she whispered to Isabelle.

'Back there –'

'And what does he want?'

'He wants to watch, Jodie,' Isabelle explained, as if that was the most obvious request in the world.

'I get to keep the tape,' Jodie insisted.

'If that's what it will take.'

Jodie nodded. Then another idea occurred to her. 'This is why you took me to that stripping class, isn't it?'

Isabelle just sat on the edge of her desk and grinned. 'Will you do it?'

'Do I get to meet him for real, afterwards?'

'Sure!'

'Will you put on music?'

Isabelle turned around and slid a CD into the stereo unit behind her desk. As she pressed the button to choose Aerosmith's latest hit, 'Girls of Summer', she heard the sound of Jodie kicking her shoes off. Quickly, she turned back around, obviously excited to watch Jodie slip out of the rest of her clothes. Jodie worked slowly, carefully, her body language letting on that she was playing for the camera, even though she never stared directly into the lens.

When she gazed at Isabelle, she could tell that her friend was impressed. Yes, these were the moves they'd learned together in the class – but there was something else about the way she moved that made the striptease her own. Jodie always knew just the way to play a part. Even a part she'd never played before. Once she'd stripped completely bare, Jodie reached for the open present that Isabelle had set out on the floor next to her. The sky-blue silk panties were just waiting to caress her naked body. '*Now*, help me,' she said.

'Help you what?' Isabelle toyed with her.

'Put these on?' Jodie's voice curved upwards at the end, turning the answer into a question.

'Oh, honey,' Isabelle purred. 'Not yet. Now that you're ripe and ready, we can do all sorts of other things first.'

'Then I want to meet him,' Jodie said again, turning to look over her shoulder at the camera.

'Good timing,' Cameron said, leaving Isabelle's back room and moving quickly to stand next to Jodie. 'Because I've been desperate to meet you, too.'

Watching the watcher. That was Nick's first role of the evening. He had found his place above the skylight in Isabelle's store, giving himself access to a view not available from the street. No, it wasn't the most comfortable location for a stakeout but, from his vantage point, he was clearly able to see Cameron Sweeney – a man he recognised easily from the newspaper society pages – staring into the monitors at the back of Isabelle's lingerie store.

'Naughty, naughty,' Nick murmured to himself. He'd been tailing Jodie this evening and had grown tired of waiting for her and Isabelle to leave the store. What could they possibly be doing in there? Counting panties? When Isabelle had drawn the shades in the front windows, pulling down the blind even over the front door, he'd grown extra curious. For several moments, he'd watched the women's silhouettes moving back there behind the shades. Finally, interest peaked to a fever pitch, he'd discovered a way to scale the wall at the rear of the store. He'd stayed low down, moving along the roof until he'd come to the skylight, and then gazed in from above.

From his spying location, Nick was not only able to see Cameron, he was able to see the monitor that Cameron was watching. Astounded, he viewed Jodie as she put her catlike body through the stripping routine he recognised from the gym. God, she was pretty. She moved her body gently yet generously, her hips rotating, her hands playing peek-a-boo games with her breasts in a faux shy gesture that reminded Nick of photographs of Marilyn Monroe. Jodie knew exactly the effect her body had on her lovers, yet she played innocent. Damn sexy in Nick's book.

After a few minutes, Cameron apparently grew tired of only watching. Nick stared as the man wandered through to the front room. He felt a pang of loss, thinking that the party would most likely continue out of his eyesight. But he didn't leave yet. Maybe they'd play for the camera, so he could continue to catch sexy images. Luck was on his side, because the three players suddenly made their way back to Isabelle's rear store. Now, Nick took a moment to really look around at what Isabelle kept here. He saw immediately that it was filled with the bondage and dominance gear, much more his taste than the items on display at the front of the store. But what Jodie had on this evening was entirely different from the vinyl and leather offered by Isabelle's second business, Undergarments. She was wearing the most intricate pair of light blue panties that Nick had ever seen. They seemed to wrap around her waist and tie in the back, the bow dripping down below her ass. Even though she was partially dressed, she seemed ready for sex. Ready for what came next.

To Nick's utter delight, Cameron and Isabelle spread Jodie out on the sumptuous white rug and each took over a region of Jodie's body. Nick felt his penis grow inside his slacks as he watched Isabelle licking Jodie's pert nipples while Cameron ate the girl through those decadent, otherworldly panties. Jodie arched her body upwards, then reached for Isabelle, pulling her friend into a tight embrace. The blonde allowed herself to be caressed for several moments, as if she knew that Jodie wanted someone to hold on to, and Nick thought he could tell the exact second when Cameron's tongue brought Jodie to climax.

There was no down time between act one and act two of the evening's erotic events. Quickly, Isabelle captured Jodie's wrists over the brunette's head, holding her firmly while Cameron stood and reached for a set of cuffs spilling out of the bottom basket of one of Isabelle's displays. He tossed the cuffs to Isabelle, who slid them into place on Jodie's wrists. Next, the store owner took her position in the centre of the rug, and brought Jodie over her lap, face down. Her fingers nimbly untied the large dangling bow, then spread the blue material open, revealing Jodie's lovely naked ass.

'Oh, Jesus,' Nick muttered to himself. They weren't really going there, were they? He watched, heart racing, for the vision to continue.

Cameron moved aside, watching just as fiercely as Nick, as Isabelle rewarded Jodie for her striptease with a thorough bare-bottomed spanking. The dangerous blonde's hand connected repeatedly with Jodie's sweet ass, until the girl's rear end was coloured a blush-pink all over. Jodie's face was turned to one side, and Nick was pleased to note that although her cheeks were flushed, she wasn't crying. She could take a lot, couldn't she? Isabelle made a motion to Cameron, who handed over a sturdy wooden paddle from a stand on a nearby shelf.

With trembling fingers, Nick lit a cigarette. He needed something to do, something to focus on so that he wouldn't be forced to whip it out right here, on the roof, and come in a white river on Isabelle's skylight.

On the street below Nick, a green-haired street girl paced down the alley behind Isabelle's store. When she reached the shadowy sanctuary of a nearby doorway, she ducked inside. From here, she could see the shape of Nick Hudson bent over and staring through the skylight. She watched for a moment, then dialled a number on her cell phone. After waiting for the beep of the answering machine, she hissed, 'He's looking for you, Max. But maybe you already knew that.'

Chap

Isabelle was right. The conv
lingerie bomb had exploded
gling from every booth were
and merry widows, garters and   was
paradise found. She'd never seen   ny items
all together before, and she turned   ad from side
to side, not wanting to miss out on anything.

'Overwhelming, right?' Isabelle said, nudging her, but Jodie could only nod. Maybe she was overwhelmed, but it was in the best way possible. She wished she had hours to wander the aisles, stopping to touch each piece of frilly finery. To try the most intricate styles on herself.

'Talk to me,' Jodie urged. 'Tell me what someone like you would look for.'

'New items. Or speciality items. Bras with French closures in the backs. Minimisers for women with larger breasts. Maximisers for those with small tits who haven't gone in for the surgery yet. One year, everyone was selling these little silicone packets – like chicken cutlets – for women to use to stuff their bras. Those were huge sellers for some people, but I didn't carry them. They freaked me out a little. The way they felt was sort of creepy. Plus, they really are false advertising. I couldn't help but wonder what would happen when you got home with a new partner and pulled part of yourself off with your bra. How would you like it if a guy similarly stuffed the package in his trousers? I mean, wouldn't that be frightening?'

'We haven't evolved very far, have we?'

...fic than socks or tissues, but
...at fad go away.'

...o much,' Isabelle sighed. 'One of the ven-
...s been in the business for three generations.
...t's their gimmick. They claim that they suited-up
your grandmother, and your mother, and you should
go to them, as well. But the prices are astronomical.
And their colour choices are so bland. Everything is
beige. Or ecru. Or salt. Not what my clientele looks for
at all.'

'But what do *you* like, Izzy?'

'You know what I like,' Isabelle teased, pushing
Jodie's hair off her face to reveal the love bite that
lingered there from the after-work threesome with
Cameron.

'Come on –'

'There are a few new designers on the horizon aside
from the one we're going to see today. One just came
out with these creations made of silk and taffeta. They
look so sweet, and then they have these filthy names:
"rear entry" undies, "undo me" bra, and stuff like that.
Might as well be called "bend-me-over" knickers and
"lick-my-pussy" panties. But women drool over them
because they're sweet on the outside, naughty on the
inside. That's really the number one description of the
ladies who buy from my store.'

A lingerie buzz surrounded the women as they
strolled the grey-carpeted aisle. Jodie picked up words
she'd never heard used in such a way: 'a fusion of
nylon and spandex'. Wasn't fusion usually about
metal? Or jazz? 'Interlocking lace'. 'Air-permeable
micro-fibre cups'. Sounded like something that should
be put to use on the space shuttle. Isabelle appeared
immune to the dialogue, but Jodie found herself both
delighted and intrigued. Here was a world she'd never
known existed. A world in which normal, everyday
colours were given unusual, exotic names. Brown

wasn't brown, it was 'suntan' or 'cinnamon'. Green was 'mint' or 'lake'. Light blue was 'sky' or 'rain'. And Isabelle had been incorrect. There was no beige. There was only nude.

The coolest part of the exhibition, as far as Jodie was concerned, was how focused everybody was on the female form. All of the items were meant to drape, lift, suck in, push up, or display a woman's body. And people discussed breasts and asses with unusual ease.

'Lifts and separates,' Jodie heard.

'Reduces by one full cup size.'

'Enhances by one full cup size.'

Each vendor appeared to have a different gimmick. One supplier featured models decked out to look like Vargas girls. Their hair and make-up mimicked the ripely decadent look of the 1940s and 1950s – wasp-waisted with handfuls of flesh at the hips and bottoms, and full, almost indecent breasts. Their outfits echoed the famed artist's creations. The girls held poses from the pictures: one bent over with a large red-and-white beach ball; another draped on a leopard-print fainting couch. Enlargements of Vargas' art mirrored the girls actions on the walls of the booth.

Around the corner was a supplier of custom-made corsets available in a wide range of fabrics and styles. Jodie noted a sign in the rear of the booth that discreetly assured customers, 'For women *and* men'.

In another booth, an extremely handsome salesman was offering to help dress women as they passed by. 'Let me choose the perfect bra for you,' he said to Jodie. 'I'll find the most flattering style. True fashion starts with the undergarments, you know. The foundation –'

'I'm not a buyer, just a consultant,' Jodie said, motioning to Isabelle. The man immediately focused his attention on the icy blonde.

'You look like a 34C,' he purred.

'Not even close,' Isabelle sneered, dragging Jodie away by the wrist.

'But you are,' Jodie whispered.

'So what? It's like we're at a circus sideshow. Guess my bra size, win a prize. Besides, the fashion show starts soon. We need to get good seats. I want to look at those pieces close up before I decide which ones I'm ordering for the store.'

Jodie stared over her shoulder at the dark-haired salesman, who winked at her and beckoned with a finger. '32B,' he was mouthing, and she nodded, surprised that he had guessed correctly. In a flash, Jodie imagined walking back over to him, stripping out of her simple skirt and top and letting him dress her up in the gorgeous fantasy-inducing attire displayed at the booth. She could almost feel his hands on her before Isabelle caught her attention again.

'No time for that,' Isabelle insisted, shaking her head at Jodie's lustful expression. 'We have to hurry. This is today's hottest ticket.'

Isabelle dragged Jodie past the all-leather booths, the petticoats, the booth dedicated solely to high-heeled slippers, the one that featured only stockings. 'Those are intense,' Isabelle said as they rushed by. 'Fifty dollars for a pair of pantyhose. Supposedly, they never run. But it's a difficult sell.'

'Fifty dollars?' Jodie echoed.

'I went through a whole rack when I ordered them,' Isabelle said, 'but over half walked out on their own. People want them, but they don't want to pay that price. Not even the richest women.'

'But you think they'll pay several hundred for this new lady's lingerie?'

Isabelle found them two seats up front and relaxed as she sat down. 'Yes, I do,' she said. 'Pantyhose are one thing. They seem conventional. Normal everyday things that some people have to wear to work. There's no fun in that. They're not erotic like garters and stockings. Men think they're strange, the way they bind at the top with the band of elastic. But good lingerie, really good stuff, that's something else. Women will pay more for beautiful lingerie that makes them feel sexy than they'll fork out for jewellery. Trust me.'

Sighing, Isabelle pulled a small silver flask from her purse and took a quick swallow. 'I'm already whipped,' she said, 'and we've only just got here.'

'But why do you even bother if you know how much you'll dislike it all.'

'For the chance that something will thrill me,' Isabelle said, handing the flask to Jodie and watching as her friend took a long swallow. 'And I think that's about to happen right now.'

As Isabelle finished speaking, a tall silver-haired woman took the podium at the front of the runway. 'I'm here to introduce today's fashion show,' she began. 'We have six designers on the bill, some of our old favourites, some newer favourites. But I know that most of you are here to see Heidi Linsome's work. We all know that she is the freshest darling to the undergarment fashion industry,' she gushed, fluttering her long, red fingernails towards the heavy drapery that hid the models from view.

'That's Sheila Winston,' Isabelle whispered. 'She's been designing high-end negligées for years. People love her, but she really just rips off stuff from old movies. Edith Head is the true designer of most of her creations.'

Lights flashed and then the room darkened. A loud crash was heard over the speakers, and Jodie jumped.

'That's the music,' Isabelle laughed, nudging her. 'For some reason, they always use techno or dance for lingerie shows. You'd think they'd do something softer. More sensual. Sinatra, or Billie Holiday, or Chet Baker. Instead, they choose Sublime, Nine Inch Nails, Korn, and Nirvana.'

As the music flared out of the speakers, a screen unfurled over the velvety curtains. Images were displayed on this rear screen, photos of the most unexpected items and objects. A blue fire hydrant. An array of lipsticks melting in the sun. A broken windshield, the spider-web cracks filled with rain.

'They try to be all avant-garde,' Isabelle explained, 'as if this were true art.'

A grinding drumbeat heralded the first models on to the stage. Jodie sucked in her breath when she saw them. These women were practically naked, strolling only feet away from her. Their skin had been dusted with body glitter, but beneath the lights, they looked more ethereal than obscene.

Leaning over so that she could speak directly into Jodie's ear, Isabelle criticised the designs. 'Yesterday's news. Just one underwire after another. I'm so tired of push-up bras I could scream. They are all the same. And they all have the same stupid-sounding names. What's so "miraculous" or "wonderful" about the same old bra? Pretty soon, they'll be naming them the "Unbelievable" or the "Catastrophic".' Isabelle definitely had her opinions, and the next designer fared no better to her discerning eye. 'We need lingerie with an attitude,' she said. 'Women can buy regular-looking items at the department store. The plain sets. The conventional numbers. But as the owner of a speciality boutique, what I'm after is the extra spark.'

Jodie kept watching, feeling herself grow increasingly aroused as the different models strutted so close by her. They kept their eyes focused on some unseeable spot on the distant horizon, and their expressions were blank, muted. It was almost as if they were animals at a zoo. Or holograms. Nothing seemed totally real about them.

The music changed with each designer, and the slide shows changed, as well. One lingerie designer had chosen black-and-white pictures of Paris for the backgrounds of her clothing. The music couldn't have differed more greatly – acid rock, so hard and loud that it made Jodie's head ache. It wasn't sexy. And it wasn't pleasant. Isabelle crossed the entire list off in her book. This wasn't going to be the stuff she'd bring into her store.

Finally, it was Heidi's turn. Isabelle held her breath and grabbed Jodie's hand, as if she were about to come face to face with a rock star or a movie screen god, Jodie thought. Isabelle seemed that excited. For the first time during the show, the volume of the music was lowered. Now, instead of the crash-boom-bang noises from the speakers, the lilting voice of Annie Lennox filled the room. This was a song Jodie adored: 'No More I Love Yous'. To Jodie, the lyrics were about stripping down to the bone, being honest with a partner. Was that how Heidi felt about her creations? That they were true, that they were necessary? That beauty and sex were an intrinsic part of life? Jodie thought about the way she'd felt as Cameron Sweeney had tied her into the naughty knickers, and then as Isabelle had untied her. Yes, she had to agree with the concept that sex was definitely necessary.

In darkness, the sound washed over her. Then lights slowly came on. They were golden and glowing, and the curtain parted slowly for the first of Heidi's models. Not amazons like the previous catwalkers, these models seemed different. Why? Jodie wondered. What was it about them? Aside from the fact that they were draped in the most beautiful, refined creations that Jodie had ever seen.

'Oh, my God,' she whispered. 'They are lovely.'

She continued to stare as a sunny blonde in an aquamarine bra and panty set strolled by. A brunette wearing a peachy gauze number with an extra ruffle at the rear hem followed. Finally, an elegant Asian woman took the stage in a sheer cherry-red nightie, with a pair of darker cherry-coloured panties visible beneath. This woman gazed at Jodie, and then tilted her head and gave her a quick, erotic smile.

Oh, that was why they looked different – Jodie realised the answer in a rush. These women weren't coldly focussing on the wall on the far side of the room, thinking about the food they wouldn't eat at the after-show party. They were staring into the eyes of the audience members, making contact, smiling – sometimes slyly, sometimes shyly. Each seemed to have a true personality, differing from the women around them. Unique, that was the right word.

Jodie thought about a strip club she'd been to with a boyfriend years before. It hadn't been a high-end place, where the dancers were lovely but airbrushed looking. No, the Kit-Kat Club had been way out on the highway near the airport, a place that wasn't fancy or exclusive in any way. The women there had made direct eye-contact with the audience. They hadn't all been beautiful, but they'd all been real. The thought of real-life flesh and blood women up there prancing around had made Jodie so wet that she and her man had left after only a couple of dance routines. They'd had sex in the back of his car as Jodie imagined taking the stage herself.

At the lingerie show, Jodie realised that on Heidi's models the hair and makeup styles were different, too, from those of the previous designers. The girls each looked slightly vacant, possessing that sexy bedhead look. Lipstick had been all but kissed off their full lips, leaving only berry-hued stains behind. Remnants of eye make-up darkened their lids, just a shadow beneath the lash line, sprinkles of glitter on the tops. Their skin had an all-over feverish flush to it, as if they'd just had sex. That's what Jodie thought. They've all been somewhere in the back there, rolling around, kissing each other. Touching. Stroking.

She leaned in to tell Isabelle her theory, but Isabelle no longer seemed to be aware of her presence. She was entirely fixated on the models and their outfits. She looked back and forth from the programme to the women walking by, then marked in red on the sheet to indicate which pieces she needed to order. When Jodie looked over, she saw that most of the items had checkmarks next to them. Was Isabelle planning on bringing the entire line into her tiny store? How was that possible?

'I special order,' Isabelle murmured, correctly guessing Jodie's query. 'Many of the items I buy never get a chance to be displayed in the store. They go straight to the end-users. And I have some clients who are going to do backflips for these get-ups.'

As a new wave of models flounced by, Jodie turned her attention to the stage again. The pieces on display now were more seriously turned out in dark materials. Leather with cut-outs. Lace-edged corsets. Studded on the edges or fitted with heavy silver buckles. But, as had the feminine lingerie before them, these items were different from those clogging the aisles in the convention centre. They had character. Even Jodie's untrained eye could tell that. Christ, anyone who knew beauty could see that the woman who'd crafted these pieces understood the female figure.

'Flawless,' Isabelle whispered. 'Look at that. Just look at it.'

How could she not? Jodie was captivated, and she stared almost without blinking until the last model took her turn at the end of the catwalk. Finally, to thunderous applause, a fine-boned blonde siren took the stage.

'That's her,' Isabelle hissed. 'That's Heidi, the designer.'

She wasn't wearing one of her lingerie designs. Instead, she was dressed in a gossamer-light gown, cinched in tight at her slender waist. Jodie could tell that although the dress was outer wear, it had been sewn from the same materials chosen for some of the more feminine pieces on display. One of the models rushed from behind the curtain, arms filled with a bouquet of colourful flowers, which she thrust into the arms of the designer. Then, suddenly, all of the models were on stage, crushing together in a scantily clad group hug.

'That's it,' Isabelle said, standing. 'I have to go and see what I can do about placing this order. Haggle some free freight or extra discount if possible. Want to meet me at Sammy's?' She looked at her watch. 'I'll bet I could be there in about forty-five minutes. And by that time I'll really need a drink.'

Jodie nodded and watched Isabelle join the throng of buyers hoping to win the chance to bring Heidi's items into their store. Then slowly Jodie made her way back through the crowd and to the convention centre.

She had to see a man about a bra.

Nick found it difficult to blend in with the rest of the crowd at the convention centre. For the most part, the buyers were women. That made perfect sense in one respect. Women knew how to choose the dramatic little pieces that would best adorn their bodies. But weren't most of them really dressing for men? Dressing to tease and tantalise? And if so, shouldn't there have been more of the male sex there to offer opinions? To pass on the matronly get-ups, the granny panties and oddly crafted girdles, and point out the colourful tracings of lace and ribbons that made up the most delightful styles.

Just as Jodie had, he found himself overwhelmed by the sheer quantity of bras and panties displayed on the aisles, but he worked to keep focused. He was there because Jodie and Isabelle were there. Maybe this was useless. A waste of time and money. But he wanted to know how Jodie spent her days when she wasn't in the office. This seemed as good an exercise as any.

The salesman was just where she'd left him, beckoning to the ladies as they passed by. Jodie took a moment to observe him undetected from the throng of the aisle. He had dark hair and a perfect, even smile. He looked as good as the male models who'd walked down the runway before Heidi's girls. But there was something interesting about him, a spark to his smile that made Jodie think maybe he wasn't as clean-cut as he seemed on the surface. Generally, she was right about these things. An appraiser of people as well as art, she often noted quirks that were missed by the less observant.

When the man saw Jodie, he stopped his spiel and walked quickly towards her, as if he'd lost her one time and wouldn't let that opportunity slip away from him again. A fierce look ran through his ocean-grey eyes as he automatically sized her up. She could almost read the numbers running through his mind.

'I'm not a buyer,' she said again, confessing. Didn't she always like to confess?

Was there something inherent in her internal makeup that made telling a secret feel so good?

'That's okay.' He had a tape measure in his hand, and he motioned for her to follow him behind an opaque rose-pink curtain. 'I'll give you an accurate reading,' he said, 'if you lift your shirt.' There was nothing dirty about the way he said the words, nothing inappropriate. They were at a bra and panty show, after all. But Jodie got a deep thrill of excitement at the thought of what she was about to do and where she was about to do it. Strip down in public? How delicious was that?

'Actually, if you take it all the way off, that would make things easier.'

Oh, wouldn't it, though? Jodie did so immediately, removing the black silk blouse and then standing directly in front of him, eyes on his. She had pulled an Isabelle today – wasn't wearing a bra or panties. The man didn't seem troubled by this in the slightest. Naked women were his job, after all. His job to clothe, that is. He immediately had the tape measure out and began fixing the cool plasticised material around her breasts. When he had lined the numbers up, he told her the measurement, and that's when Jodie put her hand on his and said, 'Now, let me return the favour.'

This *did* manage to shock him, but he recovered quickly. Smiling at her, he nodded to the curtain, a flutter of fabric which was the only thing shielding the duo from the rest of the convention. People were hustling past them in a continuous stream. With his silent gesture, he was reminding her of the surrounding conventioneers. But wasn't he also issuing a dare?

'Or do you already know?' she asked, eyeing his instant bulge.

'I've got an idea –'

She dropped on her knees, measure in hand, and unzipped his slacks. His eyes were open wide, focused on her as she released his erection and brought the tape from the tip of the shaft to the warm wall of his body. She did an accurate read, extremely pleased by the number she saw. 'Mmm,' Jodie sighed. 'That's exactly the size I was looking for. How did you know?'

Now, the man didn't seem as concerned with the possibilities of getting caught. How often would he have such a sexy chance to play? But he did wait for Jodie to make the next move. He looked down at her and, when she glanced up at his face, she saw the look of anticipation in his eyes. Hungry. Yearning.

Carefully, Jodie brought the first inch of his penis into her mouth. The man sighed and pushed forward, obviously wanting more, but Jodie was ready for him. She liked to take control of situations like this, liked to progress at her own pace. Hands on his thighs, she pushed hard, letting him know that she wanted to do the work. With her actions she told him that if he were willing to let her lead, the pleasures would be innumerable. Sighing, he let her, and Jodie introduced him to the pure wondrous magic of her mouth. She sucked, licked, swirled her tongue up and down the shaft. And then, when she'd gotten him dripping wet, she stood up.

'I always like a matching set,' she said. 'Do you think you have something in my size?' As she spoke, she slipped her short red skirt down her thighs and stepped out of it. Entirely nude, save for her high-heeled mules, she turned around so that he could size up her slim hips, her firm round ass. Her entire package was right there, waiting for his appraisal.

'You're petite all over,' he said, playing right along. It was as if he'd been dreaming of someone like her to come and unleash him from the conventionalities of his daily life. What man wouldn't fantasise in a position such as his? All day long, he was supposed to size up ladies with his eyes and his measuring tape. It was his job to pretend that everything taking place was as innocent as a shoe transaction. But it wasn't. There was the feel of sex all over the convention centre. The scent of it lingered in the air. 'But I'm sure that I have something suitable for you.' As he spoke, he took her firmly around the waist, gripping her soft skin. Jodie reached up to hold on to the metal railing at the top of the curtain, steadying herself as the man thrust inside her for the first time. 'And I'd say you're, oh –' he lost his ability to talk for a moment when he found the wetness that awaited him '– an American size 2. Am I right?'

Jodie murmured, 'Yes,' but she wasn't really answering the question. She was far beyond conversing properly any more. Far beyond doing anything but concentrating on the outrageous session they were sharing. Her 'yes' was an agreement to anything he said, to everything that they were doing. At this point, that was fine. Etiquette wasn't important in situations this heady.

Another sigh, and Jodie slipped her hips back and forth, really lubricating him up with the motion. After she rocked forward, and back, she sealed herself momentarily to his body, gaining the connection that she craved. A harsh thrust against him, and she could tell exactly how turned on he was. Each time she moved, he sighed harder, held her more tightly with his hands on her tender skin. This was almost too good. The way he understood exactly how she wanted him to behave. And she hadn't been forced to spell anything out. The subtleties were readable in the way she took charge, in the way she screwed him, even doggy-style. Pressed her body into his. Pulled her body off again.

She loved the fact that she could see the shadows of all the different conventioneers passing by in a steady stream. What would the others think if they knew that a couple was having sex just feet away from them? What would Isabelle do when she found out what Jodie had been up to while she was conducting her business?

And what would that cute private dick do?

That was the real question.

'Where were you?' Isabelle demanded. 'I've got the most amazing news.' She looked Jodie up and down, and then narrowed her eyes at her. 'And what were you doing, anyway? You look all –' she didn't seem able to find the right word '– dishevelled,' she finally decided on.

When Jodie glanced at her reflection in the mirror behind the bar, she saw that Isabelle was right. She looked like an ad for some sexy bedhead hair product. Use this goo and you'll look as if you've just been fucked. Which was exactly what Jodie had been. 'Extremely dishevelled,' Jodie agreed happily. She slipped on to the round leather stool and motioned for the barkeep that she was ready. 'I'll have what she's having.'

'Dirty Pompadour?'

'That's a drink?'

Isabelle named each of the ingredients from memory, and Jodie nodded gamely. 'Okay,' she said to her friend. 'You tell me yours, I'll tell you mine.'

'We're going to Europe.'

'Is that another drink?'

'To view the whole showroom. Heidi's amazing. We hit it off great. I mean, I already knew we would – we've been emailing each other for months now. But in person it was totally different. An instant connection. I know that you're going to feel the same way. She's invited us to come visit before she does her next show. We'll get first pick. I'm so excited I can't believe it.'

'But what do you mean that *we're* going?'

'You said you had to meet with Max some time this fall. Talk to him in person about the business. Make plans for the coming year. This will give you the perfect opportunity to mix your business with the most amazing sort of pleasure. I mean, I haven't even told you the best part. Are you ready?'

Jodie nodded, grateful to take her time drinking when the Pompadour showed up. Despite its odd-sounding name, the drink was surprisingly delicious. Jodie downed almost half of the concoction before focusing on Isabelle again.

'She wants us to model in her show.'

Again Jodie said, 'What do you mean, "us"?'

'She saw the two of us sitting there together in the front, and she thought we'd be perfect. And here's the deal – she often uses real people as models in her shows, that's why her girls had such a different look than the rest of the mannequins up there.'

'Where's the showroom?'

'One's in London. One's in Paris. We have our pick. Oh, God, Jodie,' she said, gripping her friend's hand. 'Won't it be fun?'

Chapter Twelve

London was the last European stop for the Transformed Treasures display. The jewels had already been to Paris, Hamburg, Rome, and Lisbon. Now the ring moved with the rest of the items on display to London's British Museum, where the show would stay for several weeks on display. But not yet. Another show was in place right now, and the jewellery would remain under lock and key before the pieces were set out once again.

Jodie knew this. Of course she did. It was difficult for her to get her mind off the ring. When she found herself thinking of the fire within it, she'd actually get wet. She imagined touching herself while wearing the famous jewel. Flicking her fingertips over her clit and then gently, slowly, flipping her hand and just lightly dragging that stone against the most tender spot of her body.

What would it mean to take such an item? Could she actually pull off the heist without being detected? Her mind worked on the puzzle at all hours. Subconsciously, she tried to figure out methods in her dreams at night. There were people to pay off. A decoy to be snagged. Each step forwards would mean involving so many extra parties. There was money to be spent. Trust to be gained.

Was it even possible?

Now, that was a silly question. What she'd learned over her years as a jewel thief was one simple fact: anything was possible. The more difficult the situation appeared from the outside, the more likely an easy solution was waiting. If only Jodie could find it.

* * *

Nick was dealing with his employer almost exclusively by email. So when he opened his account and saw a web-site link waiting for him, he wasn't surprised. Sometimes employers became too involved in a case. Rather than turn everything over to Nick, they would parcel out the clues one by one. That was fine. He knew how to process information. Weeding the unimportant from the cold, clear facts.

This website link confused him, however. It was all about jewellery. A jewellery show that would at some point reach San Francisco. This wasn't news to him. He'd been hired as one of the private guards to watch the show. But what did his new employer want him to know about the jewels on display?

He read the descriptions quickly at first, then more carefully. Several million dollars of jewellery would be on display for the masses to see. Nick didn't really care much about the history of the pieces themselves. What did he know about jewels? But he did pay attention to the fact that these were similar to the objects that MS Imports and Exports was known for selling to its most elite customers.

Christ, was Max Sterling planning a heist here?

What wasn't his employer telling him?

Some people drink when upset. Others find they can't sleep, or that they sleep too much, unable to ever feel fully awake. Instead, they walk through life in a haze, starting at loud noises, unable to truly connect with friends or family. Recreational drugs can soothe or smooth over the roughest times for some. But when Jodie was nervous, she didn't revert to conventional behaviours. Instead, she stole even more than normal. Wherever she went, things would disappear off the shelves and out of bins. It was almost as if she had a magnetic force in her core that pulled items to her. No, she didn't *need* a box of paper clips, but while she waited to pay for something at an office supply store, several tiny boxes found their way into her purse. Yes, she already had plenty of lipsticks. In fact, she had a whole drawer full in her bathroom. But that didn't mean she couldn't find use for several more, including the six that wound up in a secret pocket tucked below her belt.

Crazy, she told herself. What's up with you?

It was the thought of what a trip to Europe might mean. Sure, she had told Isabelle that she and Max needed a face-to-face meeting at some time, but that had been a casual comment. A pre-made excuse to explain a disappearance if she found herself with the urgent need to run. Now, she had to make the decision whether she was really going to travel with Isabelle, and open herself up for a whole gamut of new experiences. And the voice in her head kept saying, 'Well, why the fuck not?'

But that was no surprise. Generally, that little monologue was filled with dares. Go for it. Take it. Use it. Fuck it. Nobody will stop you. Nobody will know. So far, that voice had served her well. Look where she was in life – with a beautiful office in one of the most handsome buildings in the Marina. With a lifestyle that could best be described as deeply luxurious. Why not take a week or two and jet to Paris with her new best friend? Really, why not?

When she couldn't come up with any answer to that query – not one that held any true weight – she started packing.

Nick found himself in the most unusual situation ever. He was on a flight to Europe, trying his best to avoid being spotted by Jodie and Isabelle, while trying to watch them, as well. It was really insane. He should have taken a separate flight, he knew, but the way the scheduling had worked out, this was the only one that got in any time close to theirs. He'd have had to arrive several hours later and do his best to find them –

earlier wasn't a possibility, since he hadn't discovered that they were going anywhere until the very day of their journey. It had been Sammy who had clued him in after overhearing the girls discussing their plans.

'Thought you might want to know, Nicky boy,' Sammy had told him over the phone. 'That pantyless wonder you've been watching is on her way to Europe.'

There was one expensive ticket. Well, that didn't matter, either. He'd bill it to the employer, right? Finally, he decided to settle down in the back of the coach section and sleep. The best thing to do was make sure they didn't see him. If she did catch on to the fact that he was in the plane with her, he could fake surprise. Gosh, a gym buddy going to Europe the very same day he was. What were the chances for something like that, do you suppose? There was no reason for her to believe that he was following her.

He was sure that, in Paris, he'd be able to slip after them, losing himself among the rest of the passengers as they reclaimed their bags. He was feeling confident because he'd been to Europe often enough. He knew his way around. Once in the city, he would email his employer, explain the change in circumstances and offer as much information as he had. So far, he'd kept in good contact, but now he wanted the freedom to go deeper. To press further. And this meant he needed to cut the strings. At least, for a moment.

Chapter Thirteen

Heidi was everything Isabelle had promised. Beautiful. Brilliant. And bi. But although she was known for doing it with women, it was immediately apparent to Jodie that she also liked to have a man in the fray, someone to even things out a bit. However, she didn't seem to care if there was an unequal representation of the sexes, if there was more of one sex than the other. All of these facts became apparent within the first few minutes of Jodie's formal introduction to the designer. After gazing around the room, Jodie checked her theory with Isabelle, who nodded.

'That's what I've heard. Her orgies always involve a bit of an assortment to choose from, like some intricate buffet of human bodies.'

'So I *was* right,' Jodie murmured to her friend. 'The models do all have sex before a show.'

'I know.' Isabelle grinned. 'That's the part I was going to tell you about after the lingerie convention. But you weren't really paying attention to me, were you?'

Jodie shook her head, her eyes on a golden-eyed male model across from her. 'Was this why you had us go to that stripping class? Because you knew we might be invited to model?'

Isabelle shrugged. 'I'd had some email conversations with Heidi about the subject, but I thought she was just teasing me. Trying to feel me out to see if I was a serious buyer. Email is such a strange medium. You can never be sure of the inflections in the sentences, whether someone is joking or serious.' Now, Isabelle let her eyes follow Jodie's to see what had so captivated her friend. 'You never did tell me what you'd been up to at the convention centre.'

Now, Jodie just smiled vaguely, her eyes still focused on what might have been the most handsome man she'd ever seen in her life. This model had on a pair of red silk boxers that looked like liquid when he moved. His body was unbelievable, the type of chiselled muscular form seen on billboard advertisements for fitness centres. Yet it was his expression that fuelled Jodie's interest. He looked as if he knew what she wanted. Without saying a word. Without even making a motion. Just his eyes on hers, and that subtle smile. She found herself checking him out further while he watched. This was unreal. Usually, Jodie would play a cat-and-mouse game with objects of her desire, lowering her lashes, trying her best to be cool. But now she simply stared at the model without any sort of shyness. He seemed to enjoy it. Staying in one position, he let her watch him. She looked up and down his entire body, before her gaze came to rest again at the dead centre.

Isabelle was right about fine lingerie. The good quality truly stood out from the normal, everyday variety. Jodie could tell from looking at the man in the silk shorts that if she walked over to him and put her hand on his crotch, rubbing gently up and down, her fingers would tremble at the touch of the fabulous fabric. There was a reason people splurged on fine lingerie, wasn't there? It didn't simply feel luxurious on one's own skin, but looked decadent when worn by a lover.

'Make yourselves comfortable,' Heidi cooed, after coming to stand behind the two women.

'What time's the show?' Jodie asked, her nerves already starting to build. She was excited, and anxious, and aroused, all mixed up together. Then she felt Heidi's hand slide into her own and give her fingertips a quick squeeze. She turned to look at the lingerie goddess, waiting for the woman's response.

'Oh, sweetheart,' Heidi whispered to her, her tender voice soft against Jodie's skin. 'Don't you get it? The show's already started.'

Front row, centre. That was Nick's seat. His only camouflage was a pair of dark glasses, but he didn't think it would matter. The models on stage wouldn't be able to see him with the way the lighting was set up. Bright golden lights pointed at the floor show, illuminating the strip of red walkway. They would most definitely blind anyone who made his or her way down the catwalk.

While he waited for the show to start, he took in the surrounding decorations. The walls featured floor-to-ceiling mirrors, reflecting the audience, the lights, and the as yet empty stage. On the far rim of the catwalk itself, the rounded frame of a mirror dangled in the air, but there was no mirrored glass within the frame. At the foot of the catwalk stood several silk boxes filled with cosmetics. The feeling of the set was extremely girlish and feminine.

From the moment he'd entered the showroom, he'd been fighting off a sensation of total arousal. Stunning girls wearing only the tiniest bits of fabric started the pulses racing as they led the viewers to their seats. Other women, in equal stages of undress, had poured champagne for the viewers. And then, at the mysterious sound of a gong, all of the nymphets had scurried behind the curtain to get ready, leaving the audience in a high state of – well, in Nick's case – erection. Only in Europe, he decided, could a designer get away with something this debauched. This decadent.

Suddenly, a pulse of music entered the room. Nick placed the song immediately: 'Fashion', by David Bowie. And with the music came the first model.

'Oh, my God,' said the woman behind Nick. Mentally, he echoed the statement. This was the most unusual fashion show Nick had ever witnessed. Well, to be honest, he hadn't actually been to a fashion show before. Clothes on display had never seemed that exciting to him. He'd caught snippets on television before cruising along to something more interesting, but if he'd seen a show like this on TV, he definitely would have lingered. Because this was fucking amazing.

Hoarse whispers carried from audience member to audience member. Nick could make out people questioning one another. 'Did you know?' 'Can you believe it?' 'Well, that's Heidi for you –' Because as the lights flashed, a fierce-looking, six-foot-tall red-haired model walked down to the centre of a stage. Behind her, the sheer curtains revealed rather than concealed the rest of the models, waiting their turn. It looked as if the bodies backstage were interlocked, moving together sinuously. There was some additional rustling in the audience. Nick decided that maybe even for France, this was risqué.

The gorgeous Amazonian redhead waited until all eyes were on her, and then slowly she took off her clothes one piece at a time. The music flared up as Bowie crooned, 'They do it over there, but we don't do it here –'

Nick let the music fade from his mind as he focused again on the runway. What kind of fashion show was this? A reverse fashion show, actually. The clothes were coming off instead of staying on. But the trick definitely got everyone's attention. Nick took a deep breath, watching as the model worked slowly, slithering out of the polka-dotted demi-bra. Slipping the panties down her thighs and stepping out. The lingerie created a sexy-looking pool of shimmering fabric on the floor. When she was finished, the model was left wearing only a pair of high-heeled boudoir slippers. She cocked her head for a moment, as if she knew exactly how much the people in the audience were shocked by her actions. Then she walked slowly, hips undulating to the music, until reaching the curtains.

When she was right at the slit between them, a male hand pulled her through to the backstage world. It was easy to see her embrace him, through the semi-transparent wing-like fabric.

Next, a spritely blonde rushed on to the stage. She was entirely naked, and she slowly lifted each discarded piece and dressed herself while the audience watched. She took her time, staring at the empty frame of a mirror that had been placed at an angle on the edge of the runway. She pretended to be watching herself and primping, the way a girl would if she were all alone in her bedroom. But this girl was far from all alone. She was in the centre of a stage, in the centre of attention, and hundreds of hungry eyes were focused on her. What a dark thrill it was to watch.

A box next to the empty mirror held several cosmetics: lipsticks, powder puffs, make-up brushes. The girl took her time, adding a twinkling aura to her skin with a fluffy puff, opening her mouth in a sexy 'o' as she did her mascara. She seemed perfectly at ease out there on the island of the stage, doing the most private little actions.

Nick had watched enough women get ready for dates that he understood she was behaving in a totally natural manner, as if she were all by herself, alone in a bedroom. But she knew everyone was watching. That was part of the fun. And she winked impishly as she walked back to the curtains, and then laughed lightly when she passed through from this world into the next. It seemed as if she possessed a secret – as if she knew that the area behind the curtains was far more exciting than what was going out on stage.

When the model exited, Nick glanced down at the programme in his lap. He was using the folded paper to cover the growing tent in his pants, but now he took a moment to read the words within. The inside cover was filled with sexual factoids, in dark purple ink emblazoned on a lemony background. The words were written in a girlish hand, as if they were notes jotted down in a rush: Number 1 fantasy of the common male – to watch. To play a Peeping Tom and simply indulge in the erotic act of voyeurism. That was what this entire audience was doing. All of the members of the audience were peeking in, as if staring into a woman's private dressing room. He was surprised at how much of a thrill he was getting. But the designer seemed to understand this erotic fetish intimately, because the scene was immediately recreated.

How entirely captivating. Staring at a lovely girl undressing. Staring at an equally beautiful model dressing again. The situation was echoed, as the model hurried from the stage, to be replaced by a giggling couple – a brunette girl and a blond-haired boy, who tripped over themselves to get to the circle of light at the end of the stage. There were lipstick-printed kiss marks along the male model's flat belly, and the waistband of the girl's panties was askew at the hips. What had they been doing 'backstage'? That was an easy guess. In Nick's mind, he saw the two models together; the boy bending the girl over at the waist and getting into her from behind. Now, they worked together to strip each other, strewing the lingerie on the floor around them. Then, still laughing, the models traded clothing – the girl put on the boy's boxers and the boy slipped himself into the girl's knickers.

Nick caught the fact that this lingerie was actually like a work of art. Even his untrained eye could see that the pieces were of a higher quality than those found in your average department store. Was that what this whole exhibition was about? The fact that clothing could be art? That a fashion show could be a piece of theatre? Before he could contemplate these ideas, the show continued.

Here came a towering blonde Asian model sauntering down the catwalk. She had on a pair of clear acetate stripper heels, so high that Nick was amazed at her finesse, her ability to even walk in a straight line. She had no problem at all. She simply strutted down the narrow white space, losing her clothing as she walked – almost violently pulling the items off her body, as if she were so hot that she couldn't wait to be naked. First came the shimmering lavender robe. Then the matching underwire bra. Then, after kicking out of the heels, the lace-edged tap panties. As she took these off, she bent over completely, and Nick was rewarded with the most amazing view of her stunning ass and the private space between her thighs. Oh, he had some ideas of how he'd use that sexy region. First with his tongue, to taste, to tickle. Then, giving over to the demands of his penis, to fill and plunge. And he could tell from the whispering of different people around him that he wasn't the only one fantasising about sex. Before she left the stage, she reached down and pulled the robe's shimmering belt from the loops. This she took with her.

But why?

That question was answered only a moment later. The next model – naked as could be expected based on the repetitive pattern of this performance – was led down the runway by her slim wrists, which had been tied with the rope of the belt. So how was this going to work? Nick wondered. How would the nubile brunette model be able to dress herself? How would Jodie –

There she was. His prize. His prey. Naked in the centre of this European stage, led by the blonde and beautiful Isabelle. He'd been so intrigued by the whole unfolding festival of the show that he'd almost forgotten the true reason he was here. To pay attention. To see. And was he ever seeing. Taking a deep breath, he waited along with the rest of the audience to figure out how the girls would continue with the purpose of the show: to display the lingerie.

No problem. Isabelle beckoned to a man sitting close

to Nick. 'Help me out, Sir?' she murmured, and the man quickly moved on to the stage. The expression on his face was immediately readable. He couldn't believe his fucking luck. 'Hold this,' she said next, handing over the leash. To Jodie, she said, 'Be a good girl for me. I wouldn't want to have to punish you with all these nice people watching.'

That was a lie. Nick, especially, knew that more than anything, Isabelle would enjoy spanking the trembling Jodie while others watched. Disciplining her in front of an audience would add to both of the women's excitement. And if Nick were able to speak for the rest of the crowd, it would add to the audience's as well. But this didn't happen because Jodie remained meek and well-behaved. She seemed to understand that all she had to do was give Isabelle one small reason to spank her and the blonde would make that little bit of fantasy come instantly true. Nick could see it immediately in his mind – Isabelle spreading Jodie over her lap and spanking that slim but haughty ass of hers until it grew as cherry red as the panties left over on the edge of the catwalk. Wouldn't that have been something to see. Unfortunately, it didn't happen.

While the audience gazed on in silent wonderment, Isabelle helped Jodie back into the panties that had been left by the previous model. That stirred Nick deep within himself. He pondered whether the underpants were wet in the centre, whether Jodie's own sexy juices were mingling with those of the pretty Asian model. Then he stopped thinking and just watched the show. Isabelle stood back, as if admiring her work, and then thanked the man for his help. Slowly, she undid the knot at Jodie's wrists, then quickly took the belt and doubled it. Using this folded piece of fabric, she blindfolded Jodie. As a humorous aside to the audience, she said, 'See? These pieces have multiple uses.'

Then she helped Jodie into the bra, helped her into the robe, and taking her hand, led her from the stage.

Nick knew he should excuse himself and try to find the girls, to make sure that they didn't leave while he was playing the part of an aroused audience member, but he found that he was far too captivated to depart now. What was going to happen next? How could that scene be topped? He was sealed to his seat by more than his questions. The hard bone of his erection meant that leaving now would have been more than simply embarrassing – it would have been painfully uncomfortable.

So he stayed, and he watched as the director of the show topped the previous scene with ease. It was as if the designer were on a constant mission to shock and please the audience – and she did. Every step of the way. A male model came on to the stage next. He was wearing street clothes: black slacks and a black T-shirt under a grey button-down shirt. What was his deal? Why did he look so normal? While the women in the audience squirmed in delight, the handsome male model undid the buttons on his shirt and tossed it aside. He pulled his T-shirt over his head, revealing the type of washboard stomach rarely scene outside of a Hollywood gym. Slowly, he undid his trousers and dropped them where he stood. Here was a scene straight out of the Chippendales, and the many girls in the crowd loved it.

Underneath his clothes, he had on only a simple pair of fiery red silk boxers. He stood in the centre of the stage, apparently waiting for something. But what? The seductive sound of bare feet running down the stage made everyone turn. There was Jodie once again, no longer blindfolded, but naked on top, still with the tap pants on the bottom. Didn't she have a beautiful body? Sleek and compact. Stunning in its simplicity.

She reached for the man's shirt and slid it on. So sexy. The large shirt dwarfed her, making her seem surprisingly innocent. But that innocence was all an act, wasn't it? Nick knew for a fact that it was. He'd seen her – oh, had he seen her. With Cameron and Isabelle. With a stranger at the lingerie show. He knew all about Jodie.

The man shook his head at her, and she lowered her chin. Nick understood that this was a theatrical piece, choreographed and planned out to the minutest detail. Still, he didn't have any idea what would happen next, and he was caught off guard when the man bent Jodie over and flipped the shirt up her back, then slowly lowered her panties and began to spank her.

Fuck, he thought. Just that one word, summing up every emotion catapulting through his head. Why couldn't he ever get one step ahead of this brainy brunette? Why did every place they went, every action that she revealed, have to take him by total surprise? Once again, he was thankful to have the programme in his lap, because his erection instantly grew harder and overwhelming in its insistence for release. He would have loved to have taken the man's place. Put Jodie across his own lap and punish her for toying with him in such a dangerously sexy manner. Instead, he made do with watching the spectacle. The model's firm hand flashed against Jodie's ripe behind, and she squirmed with each slap but remained silent. Good girl, Nick thought. No faking a cry before you earn it. He was impressed with her ability to withstand public punishment without putting up a fight. She held herself still as the man spanked her naked ass.

Before too long, the man lifted Jodie across his shoulders and carried her, upended, off the stage.

The lights flashed on and off again, and then Heidi Linsome appeared in the centre of the runway, speaking to the journalists who had gathered there to talk to her. 'It's all about sex,' she said, laughing her soft, delicate laugh. 'People don't always want to admit it, but I can't see why not. There's nothing highbrow here. Nothing kept in the closets. When you peel down to your underthings, sex is in the forefront of your mind.

It has to be. Therefore, my lingerie is all about sex. So why not be real and let the people see what my intentions are all about? Check your inhibitions at the door, if you're going to wear my line of clothing. Otherwise, go buy your items at Veronica's Rumor and leave my clothing to those who deserve to wear it.'

Nick listened for a moment, and then made his way through the throng of believers, off to find Jodie among the models backstage. It took him several minutes to tango his way around the little knots of people who were congregating, drinking champagne and oohing and ahhing at the magnificence of the show. But when he reached the curtains, he found the rear of the show was already empty.

Sighing, Nick turned back to look at the room filled with journalists and fashion editors. A hand on his arm made him glance back, and he saw the blonde Asian model – as tall as he was – with an invitation in her hand.

'Heidi's having a little after-show party,' she cooed. 'Why don't you try to come?'

There was a line for spankings. Jodie saw that right away. Three girls wearing adorable knickers and matching camisoles were standing in line in front of Will, the model who had spanked Jodie on stage. The naughty models were each waiting their turn while a pixie-blonde was getting her bottom smacked. Stinging slaps rained down on her luscious rear cheeks as the girl kicked her feet up in what was obviously mock protest. Jodie felt herself start to blush while she watched, not out of embarrassment for the model, but out of realisation that she wanted to join the line. In fact, she wanted to rudely cut to the very front, certain that this would be the way to ensure a serious paddling on her naked ass. But, before she could do anything, Isabelle slid her hand around Jodie's waist and demanded a conversation.

'You didn't,' Isabelle said.

Jodie understood the statement immediately. 'Of course I did,' she said, her eyes still focused on the spanking scenario going on across the room. Heidi had been right in her little after-show speech. Linsome's lingerie definitely brought out the sexiest side of people.

'But you didn't have to,' Isabelle continued, her voice softening. 'That was absolutely unnecessary. She would have given you anything you asked for in exchange for working the show. Didn't you understand that?'

'I don't like it when people give me things.'

'Some things.' Isabelle smiled automatically. 'You like it when some people give you some things. Right?'

'What do you want to give me?' Jodie asked. She could still hear the sounds of the spanking going on close by, but she now began paying more careful attention to what Isabelle might be offering.

'What are you asking for?' Isabelle shot back, her blue eyes wide and fierce.

Suddenly, there was a sad little cry from the girl in the over-the-knee position. She wasn't crying out in pain, but in displeasure as the handsome male model in charge of the spanking cut short the punishment he was delivering. Quickly, he made his way to the two women and butted into their conversation. 'All right, girls,' he interrupted, standing straight and tall next to Jodie. It was apparent that he'd eavesdropped even while delivering the blonde's smarting discipline. Now, the remaining girls in line moved around uncomfortably. They'd been waiting patiently, but the situation was changing. 'Enough conversational foreplay. I know what she needs. And I know who should give it to her. So let's just straighten ourselves out now, shall we?'

Both Jodie and Isabelle looked up at him, waiting.

'Hand it over,' he said to Jodie, and she saw the look in his eyes, read him instantly. He was going to play this scene out with her to the extreme. Yeah, he'd spanked her out there on the runway but, in a way, that hadn't counted. That spanking was for public consumption. What he was offering with his expression now was something much more personal and to her taste. Slowly, she slid her hand into her pocket, then put out her fist and opened her fingers. A tiny rose-coloured pair of butterfly panties fell on to the floor. The man sighed and reached for them, shaking his head as he did.

'Put them on,' he said.

'You're not serious,' Jodie told him. 'That would mean taking everything off –'

'Put the panties on while I get Heidi.'

They were back at Heidi's studio for the after-show party, with all of the models relaxing in different corners of the room. But Jodie knew that Heidi was nearby; she could hear the sound of the designer's trademark laugh. Low and smoky. Jodie felt the rustle within her, knew just how good this was going to be. 'All right.' She nodded. Standing, she slid her black satin pyjama pants down her legs and stepped out of them. With her eyes locked on Will's, she kicked off the turquoise panties she had on beneath. Then she took the racy, lacy panties from his open hand and put them on. The fluff of fabric did nothing to hide her glorious body. She cocked her hip at him, unable to resist the taunt. 'You're really a tattletale? You're going to go tell on me now?' she asked. Her voice was rich with the sound of a spoiled brat.

'No,' he said, 'you are.'

'Excuse me?'

He reached out one firm hand and locked it around her wrist. Then, with authority, he pulled her after him to where Heidi was seated across the room, seated like a queen with her surrounding court jesters. She watched with obvious amusement as Jodie tried to dig in her heels.

'All right, William,' Heidi crooned. 'What's going on? Are we not having fun yet?'

'Tell her.'

'No.'

'Tell her,' William said, pushing one hand on Jodie's shoulder and pressing her down to her knees. 'Life will be much sweeter for you if you do.'

'How do you know what makes my life sweet?' Jodie responded, tossing her head to make her hair fall away from her light eyes. The move was defiant. She wouldn't give in. Not yet.

'Okay,' William said, nodding to himself as if he wouldn't have expected anything less from her. 'That's fine.' Once again, he picked her up and threw her over his shoulder, so that she was dangling face-down across his back. 'This,' he said, snapping the waistband of the panties, 'this is what we're talking about. She took it. And she doesn't have the nerve to confess.'

As he spoke, he landed one stinging smack on Jodie's near-naked behind, and she kicked out at him violently. But who was she kidding? She was dripping wet already, loving every minute of this crazy scene. Who was this Heidi person, who was so able to collect the types of personalities that Jodie most respected? Outgoing, exhibitionist-style people who were ready to play. Ready for anything.

William set Jodie down on the floor, but he kept her wrists captured tightly in one of his large hands. 'So?' he continued, looking at Heidi. 'What do you say?' The blonde-streaked beauty regarded Jodie with a careful expression. Her eyes were cold for a moment, and then she smiled and warmth flooded into them as she said, 'I'd have given it to you. You know that, don't you?'

Jodie shrugged. William nudged her. 'Answer her.'

'What is she, a queen?'

'No, she's the hostess. Show some respect.'

Jodie looked down. She wouldn't.

'You have choices. You understand that,' Heidi said.

'You can leave at any time. This is a party, for heaven's sake. Nobody is forcing you to be here.'

Yes, of course, Jodie understood that. She wasn't a captive. She was just part of the festivities. She sensed that others in the room were paying attention now, carefully watching what was going on in the centre of this large play-space.

'Fine, then. If you stay here, you play by our rules. That means that my friend William, here, is going to spank that naughty ass of yours until I determine it's red enough.'

Jodie trembled all over at the words. Christ, this was going better than she could have hoped.

'Do you understand?'

Jodie nodded and William nudged her again. 'Yes,' she said, 'I understand.'

'Fine then, we don't really have anything else to discuss, do we?'

'No,' Jodie said automatically. 'No, we don't.'

William picked her up again while she was still speaking, and he brought her to the same spanking chair he'd used before. How she'd wanted to feel the sting, herself, as she'd watched the blonde. Wanted to be punished for both the pleasure of others and the pleasure of herself. But now that it was actually happening, she found herself in the same scary place that she'd been before. Anticipation was an incredible turn-on. But there was a moment or two before the action began that always made her heart pound at triple speed. Could she take it? Would she fail him?

William spread her out cleanly across his lap and then lifted her gauzy shirt at the back, once again revealing her bottom, her cheeks separated by the lacy floss of the butterfly-style underpants. He lowered the stolen panties down her thighs, then let his hand connect with her ripe flesh in a rapid series of stinging blows. Jodie held on to his legs as he spanked her, trying to steel herself for the whole ride. Trying to behave in a way that would make him proud of her. Wasn't that crazy? She didn't know him, didn't have any connection to him, yet it was deep within her to behave – as one who misbehaved – in a way that would give him the most satisfaction.

She could feel that he was hard, and that each time his hand met her skin his penis seemed to throb against her. That made the spanking even more exciting, because she knew how aroused he was, and she knew how aroused *she* was becoming as well. She wondered, fleetingly, where Isabelle was and what her friend was thinking of the whole situation. Then thoughts of the shopkeeper fell away as William let his fingertips dance between her cheeks to land against her most sensitive flesh. Slapping her there once, twice, three times, until Jodie let out her first moan of the evening.

As she gave herself over to being punished, Jodie thought about the way it had felt to be spanked out on the runway, and then she thought about the rest of the models in the show watching her right this minute. Urgently, she slid her hips against William's lap, and he gave her a final series of stinging smacks before helping her to stand. But that wasn't the end, was it? They'd created a connection together, one of dom and sub, and Jodie wasn't finished yet. She needed to continue in her role of pleaser, needed to show him how much she appreciated the spanking she'd won from his stern hand.

William rumpled her hair with one hand and called her his good girl. And then Jodie got down on her knees in front of him, waiting somehow desperately for the first taste of him. Why did she want it so bad? She couldn't answer that. She just wanted to suck him and then slide her mouth up and down that rod. And when he was wet from her mouth, she wanted to stand and turn around, bend over so that he could take her from behind. Reward her for being – for being herself. Her lips worked over the head of his cock and down the shaft, and when she was the one to make him moan, she felt a sense of pride within herself.

Before she'd even had enough of him, Will's hands were on her shoulders, lifting her. As if he could see the image within her mind, he turned her around, bending her over and running his fingertips along her still-warm ass. The sensation rippled through Jodie and she caught herself in a half-sob, half-sigh.

'That's right,' the man said, 'you let yourself go.'

She swallowed down on the next groan, one that would have been loud, would have reverberated around her, and then he parted her sex lips with his fingers and slid inside her. She'd never felt such an immediate reaction. She tightened on his cock and held him within her, and when he plunged even deeper, she couldn't help herself any longer. She started talking, almost without thinking, urging him, begging him.

'Yes. Oh, please. Yes.'

As he took her, she wondered whether that private detective had made it to the party. She'd had an invitation passed to him, but she wasn't sure whether or not he was among the throng who watched. If so, was he pleased with what he saw?

Nick, standing in the doorway at the other side of the room, gazed with great interest at Jodie as she came. He didn't worry that she would see him, because she was far too busy focused on the pounding she was receiving. Besides, with all of the different types of people around him, he knew he blended in.

As he stared at her, he suddenly saw her in a different place – with long red hair, and green eyes. What was his memory telling him? He tried hard to put Jodie in another scenario, mentally cast her in a memory, but he failed.

Chapter Fourteen

Nick was sure that Jodie would lead him to Max. That was what he had planned for, why he'd followed her all the way to Europe. At least, that's what he told himself. And he believed himself. For the time being. Why would he think he was lying? Mental mumbo jumbo conversations like that made him want to slam his head against the wall. He recalled passages in classic Raymond Chandler novels in which Philip Marlowe, Chandler's ultimately cool PI, had hazy, surreal conversations with himself, but they generally happened after he'd been drugged or sapped with a nightstick.

So what was Nick's excuse? He couldn't even begin to give himself the alibi that he was falling for her. Not even. Not yet. So he consigned himself to having these ridiculous mental chats, knowing that there was still a shimmer of truth in the basis of all that nonsense. His instincts told him that she had an ulterior motive for being in Europe, one aside from lingerie-infested orgies. He thought she'd go to Max, and then he'd know where the man was, would at least have something to tell the client – something to justify all this time and money spent.

But although Jodie and Isabelle did split off from one another after the show, the slinky brunette didn't seem as if she were doing anything but shopping. Shopping and walking. Nick followed after her as best he could, ducking into doorways when she turned around, slipping into the same Metro cars as she took, finding himself way out at the edge of Paris, at a famous flea market made up of several rows of tiny stalls. This was a little like a movie set, he thought, the perfect place for a secret rendezvous with the mysterious Mr Sterling. But although Nick kept Jodie firmly in his sights, he didn't see her talk to anyone as she walked through the open-air market.

What she did do, he saw immediately, was steal a wide variety of different items. Although risky behaviour, her actions didn't take him by surprise. Jodie seemed incapable of making her way through any situation without stealing. On this day, she appeared to be in high gear. She didn't walk by a stand without sliding some small trinket up her sleeve or down her pants, never into her red leather purse or the pocket of her slim-fitting slacks because that would be the first place an irritated shopkeeper would look. 'Empty your pockets,' someone would insist. Jodie could do that without a problem, revealing the lilac silk lining that proved her pockets were empty.

She was good. He'd give her that. She had a way about her, occasionally pulling out money and paying for one item, then snaking a more expensive bauble while the shopkeeper sorted the change. She was pleasant in conversation and so lovely to look at, and he could tell that the majority of those who interacted with her were charmed both by her lilting French and her sweet manner. Besides, most shopkeepers had their eyes on the teenagers who flocked to this flea market for bargains. They didn't think to look carefully at someone as high class as Jodie.

But she wasn't so sweet, was she? Stealing from these people. One after another. These were hard workers who carted their belongings way the fuck out to the edge of Paris to try to make a profit. And yet he wasn't upset by her behaviour at all, was he? In truth, he simply felt a pang of anxiousness hoping that she wouldn't get caught. Where was that boy scout now?

Where was the man with the strong moral sense who always knew right from wrong?

Long gone, he realised. Long gone as soon as he'd spotted the prize that was Jodie Silver.

There was that old saying, 'Never judge a person until you walk a mile in his shoes.' Well, Lucas had come up with his own personal version of it. 'Never judge a person until you slip into her panties.' Or something like that. Because 'judge' wasn't the right term, either, was it? No, he thought, as he admired the way his ass looked in a pair of Jodie's sapphire blue hipsters.

God, he wasn't even sure what he meant at this point. All he wanted to do was come. Again and again. Surrounded by Jodie's sinfully delicate belongings. He knew that he was on shaky ground, because these panties wouldn't be usable again once he got through with them. They were stretched and misshapen over his ass and his bulging erection. Never again would they cling to the hips of Jodie Silver. Ah, but he couldn't help it. He'd been living in Jodie's bedroom while she was away. Truly lost in the world of her possessions the way a sugar-fiend would have felt if locked over-night in a candy store.

The funny part was that he was in her apartment with a purpose, to care for her plants while she went abroad. But now that he had free rein of the place, and the knowledge that she wouldn't be able to surprise him at his dirty games, he was almost in sensual overload.

He didn't restrict himself solely to the lingerie in her hamper now. He wanted to touch everything, to lie down on a bed strewn with every single item from her drawers. He wanted to roll in the soft finery, crush it with his body, roll over and shoot deep into the turbu-lent mess of silks and satins.

As he pushed through the finery in Jodie's drawers,

he found several items that confused him. A single gold cufflink with the initials MJS. A brochure dedicated to the Transformed Treasures exhibit – with the 'Unforgiving Heart' highlighted in yellow ink. And a list of names – Isabelle, Lucas, George, Cameron, Nick – with checkmarks by each one. There were notes in Jodie's handwriting: Exhibit. Talk to Liz. And an address in Pacific Heights that Lucas didn't recognise. He had no idea what that all meant, but he couldn't waste his time wondering, either. An urgency built within him that was too strong to deny.

From Paris, Jodie and Isabelle took the hovercraft to England. Isabelle had several more designers to visit in London, and Jodie wanted a look at the Transformed Treasures exhibit first hand. Nick followed after the women, buying his ticket and then choosing a seat several rows behind the girls. He settled himself in for the journey, tipping his hat low over his face and preparing for a nap, but after only a few minutes, he peeked under the brim and saw Jodie making her way back towards him.

Quickly, Nick hunched down in his seat, trying to play invisible, yet Jodie obviously wasn't buying his camouflage act. She perched on the armrest at his side and gazed down at him. 'Work out lately?' she purred at him, and he found that he did have to work out, mentally work out, trying to figure out what the correct response would be.

'You go to my gym, right?' she asked next, and he just nodded and made some hurried explanation about business. Travelling for business. That sounded fine. She didn't know anything about him. Why shouldn't he be in Europe at the same time that she was? Nick noticed that Jodie seemed much more self-assured than he was feeling. She appeared to be completely in control and, as soon as he thought that, some sense of self-preservation kicked in. For a moment, he forgot that he was working on a job and focused on the fact that he was talking to a woman who captivated him.

'And you do know about challenges.' She grinned.

He smiled back at her, and once again in her face he saw someone he'd seen before. Couldn't place her, though. It was just a suspicion, a glimmer of a concept. 'I liked the race at the gym,' he said. 'You're a tough foe. I would have liked to pushed on to the end.'

'But I'm not an enemy,' she corrected him, 'I'm a competitor.'

'There's a difference.' He nodded, agreeing with her.

'Are we both going after the same thing?'

'That's the question,' Nick said, catching on to Jodie's hand and pulling her down in the seat. 'Isn't it?'

He thought of all the different Bogie movies he loved, and detective movies in general, in which the tough-talking dick was mesmerised by a beautiful woman. He didn't want to go down the same messy route. Fall for the girl and spoil the case. But what did he have to lose right now? He wasn't officially after Jodie, just her boss. Getting to know her was probably the smart way to go. At least, that's what he told himself as Jodie leaned into his arms and pressed her lips against his.

Chapter Fifteen

To Nick, the story sounded quite a lot like the plot of *The Maltese Falcon*. Wouldn't those writers from Hollywood in the 1930s have approved? A rare art object passed from one hand to another, stolen from the proper owners, who had most likely stolen it from someone else. To the point at which there really were no proper owners any more, only people who laid claim to the piece. But no one seemed to have more of a legitimate stake than anyone else. Yes, they had their paperwork. Their insistence that each was the one who deserved it. Yet an Austrian museum had ultimately won out in a court battle, and now the black sapphire was on display – for all to see equally.

Knowing this history, Nick bought his ticket and waited in line outside the British Museum. He remembered reading of the queues for the Tutankhamun Exhibition. People had wrapped around museums in tight bands waiting for the sight of the treasures stolen from a dead king. He'd never had much interest in this sort of thing, but he knew that Jodie did, so why not try to forge an appetite for what made her excited?

Besides, he had a feeling. He didn't know if it was possible, but he had such a strong feeling that Jodie was checking out the exhibit with a purpose. Maybe Max had his eye on the piece. That wasn't too far-fetched. Although museums seemed unlikely places to rob – there was such intense security – that didn't mean it couldn't happen. Just look at the thief recently nabbed in Brussels. One man had stolen over fifty masterpieces during the past twenty years. Countless pottery, jewellery and paintings had all been taken from museums. When he'd been caught, his eighty-year-old mother – who kept the prizes in her old farmhouse (you really couldn't make this stuff up, Nick had thought when reading the article) – had cut the artwork into tiny pieces and thrown the scraps in the pig bin. The harder-to-dispose items had been tossed in the nearby river, where authorities had fished them out. But the canvases were gone forever.

How had the man done it? He'd been a common waiter; nobody would ever have supposed that he was the most successful art thief in modern history. And all the items stolen had been taken from museums, some of the largest museums in the world. So Nick wouldn't put it past this Max Sterling to try something similar. Not at all.

As he waited to enter the museum, he stared at the girls he was following. Now that Jodie had spoken to him on the ride to England, he felt less of a need to hide from her. They were definitely engaged in a game, neither one willing to reveal too much. But her kiss – that had surprised Nick, and he knew deep down that the feeling of her lips against his own was the main reason he was watching her this morning.

Jodie and Isabelle entered the exhibit together, gig-gling like teens as they stood in line. Giggling because they'd just snuck behind the building and got stoned together on a joint that Heidi had given them as a going-away present. Jodie felt like a high school kid, giddy and happy as she and Isabelle made their way through the exhibit hall. They held hands, falling into one another when the security guard waved them through.

'What is all this shit?' Isabelle asked in a stage whisper loud enough to be heard by several other nearby adults. Her obscenity won her several mean glances. A woman turned around and said, 'There are children here.'

'I pity them,' Isabelle responded to the lady, then turned to Jodie. 'Why'd you take me here? You know that I'm not into art the way you are.'

'I wanted you to see beautiful things.'

'I haven't been in a museum since grade school. I just don't get the point.'

'And it shows,' Jodie laughed. 'Your manners are atrocious.'

'At least I'm stoned. These places bore me to death.'

'But this won't,' Jodie said, 'I promise you.'

Isabelle put her arms around her friend and pulled her tight to her body. 'Do you?' she hissed. 'What else can you promise?'

Jodie turned her face upwards, gazing at her lovely friend. 'You're getting bold.' Jodie smiled. 'Usually, you don't like to mess around in public.'

'Usually, you don't drag me out to museums,' Isabelle sighed.

'This will be worth it. You've never seen anything like this. Not ever.'

'Besides,' Isabelle continued, 'nobody knows us here. We're free to behave as well or as badly as we want to.'

Jodie liked that sound of that. 'What are you trying to tell me, Izzy? Have *you* been a bad girl for once?'

Nick stayed one room behind the women, watching them more intently than he looked at the items on display. Their conversation had been innocent on the surface, but both knew there was something deeper going on, didn't they? He found himself enjoying the tease of the situation, now that they were being more open about who was doing what to who. Well, maybe not entirely open. He didn't tell her that he'd been watching her for weeks now. But perhaps she knew that already.

He shared Isabelle's distaste for museums. Once you'd seen one suit of iron, you'd seen them all, right?

The one area that he always found interesting were the rooms dedicated to artifacts of ancient Egypt. Maybe he'd stroll up the stairs to view those exhibits when he'd finished tailing Isabelle and Jodie.

That was his plan, anyway. But when Jodie and Isabelle stopped in front of the black sapphire ring in the centre case, he found himself as captivated by the stone as he had been by the embracing women. Which sight was more beautiful? That wasn't an easy question to answer.

Chapter Sixteen

Jodie knew full well when someone was stealing from her. How could she not? Stealing was her life, after all. Her passion. Taking things from the rich and giving to the ... well, giving them to herself. She wasn't poor. Couldn't claim that was why she took things. She stole because she needed to. Now that she had returned from her trip abroad, she could focus on the fact that Lucas was definitely pilfering from her own stash. Not big things. No jewellery or expensive items, objects that he could sell to someone else to make a profit. Christ, he wasn't even taking things that made any sense. If he wanted to score an extra buck on the side, it would have been easy enough. Grab a ruby-and-diamond bracelet, or one of her prized paintings. Something that had value.

If he ever did decide to seriously steal from her, he'd get away with it. Who could she possibly go to? Not the police. 'I'd like to report a theft. My partner in crime is stealing items that I've stolen.' Yeah, that would go down well at the station.

But he wasn't taking any of the items they'd stolen together. Instead, he'd focused on the types of inconsequential belongings that she might not even notice were missing if she were a different type of girl. Items that she would think she'd misplaced, and forget about, sure that they'd turn up after a while. What he didn't understand was how organised Jodie kept herself. She always had a concept of where things were, so when she couldn't find a pair of panties that she liked, it made her pause and then consider who else had access to her world.

First, her frilly white panties went missing – a pair that she'd bought on a shopping trip to Italy. She liked them well enough to know that they were really gone, not caught in the bottom of the hamper, or lost in the jumbled chaos of a lingerie drawer, because there was no chaos in her drawers. Everything was neat, carefully placed, exactly where she could find it when she wanted it.

After several different personal belongings disappeared, she decided to talk to Isabelle about the situation. What would her friend do if a beau was stealing from her? Whip the crap out of him, most likely. Jodie could imagine that scene easily. Isabelle clad in some high-end dominatrix gear, wielding a crop like a pro. But that wasn't really Jodie's style. She hoped Isabelle would have other advice to share.

Catching a shining red cable car at the corner, she rode up one of the steeper hills in the city, clinging to the thick golden bar as she stood. The tourists gathered around her pointed out the different sights to one another, but she ignored their conversation. She enjoyed being a San Franciscan. Although not a native, she'd assumed the identity as her own. But she could understand what the people were chattering about. San Francisco was a city like no other. The cable cars were just one of the many little pleasures found in this unusual setting, which included rollicking hills, acres of greenery and an actual herd of buffalo roaming in Golden Gate Park.

As the cable car crested one hill and began the steep ascent of the next, she recalled reading a fact about San Francisco in the 1960s: it had been illegal at the time for women to stand during cable car rides. Only men could experience the flying quality of traversing the hills while hanging on to a thick metal beam for support.

Thank God they'd advanced past that, Jodie thought, feeling the breeze sliding up under her short suede skirt. She loved the freedom of the ride, the heart-stopping free-falling sensation of cruising down one of the hills. It reminded her of the breathless quality she got when stealing. And that made her wonder about Lucas. Did he steal for the same reasons she did? Was he taking because there really was no other fucking choice? If that was the case, then she had to treat him with care and respect, because deep down inside herself she understood.

But first, she would explain the situation to Isabelle. The women met at a coffee shop. A favourite hangout for the young hipster crowd, the place boasted a living room style decor: worn leather sofas; rounded end tables; shelves filled with an assortment of interesting paperbacks and hardback art books. The clientèle was equally eclectic – from rock stars to real estate agents to the exceptional jewel thief with a problematic boyfriend.

'What else did he take?' Isabelle asked after hearing the facts, and she was surprised to see Jodie flush. This was unlike the dusky beauty. Outside of the bedroom, Jodie's facial expressions rarely gave any information away, rarely let on to what she was thinking or feeling.

'A photo.'

'Of you?'

'Polaroid.'

Isabelle's honey-blonde eyebrows went up in a curious arch.

'Yeah, *that* kind of Polaroid,' Jodie admitted, her voice dipping down low. 'Why? What's wrong?'

'I'm just surprised. You don't strike me as the type.'

Jodie leaned back against the comfortable green leather sofa. 'Why do you say that?' She was genuinely interested in this answer. Her friend had seen her in a variety of compromising positions. What did one photo matter?

'You're too careful. Don't seem to let yourself out of the box. Maybe you'd let someone take your photo, but

I'd have thought you'd be sure to get every copy, every negative, for yourself. Just like with the video tape we made with Cameron.'

Jodie contemplated that concept for a minute, and then she smiled. 'You think you know me pretty well, don't you?'

'I'm a good read. You really have to be in my line of work.' Isabelle took another sip of her mocha, and then gazed back at Jodie before continuing her explanation. 'I have to know if someone's worth my time and trouble. It doesn't take a brain surgeon to tell the browsers from the big sales.'

'But you don't really know me,' Jodie said, and there was a tease in her voice.

'So surprise me,' Isabelle challenged. 'What don't I know?'

Jodie popped the silver clasp on her green leather wallet and pulled out three creased black-and-white photos. She fanned them out to give Isabelle the quickest of views before spreading the pictures face-down on the distressed wooden table, like a pornographic version of the sidewalk shyster game Three-card Monty. Isabelle grinned, watching Jodie. 'A card game?' she asked. 'Looks like fun.'

Jodie shuffled and waited for Isabelle to pick. The pretty blonde's ruby-red fingernails traced over the backs of the photos carefully, as if she were trying to make this moment last. The pleasure of anticipation flickered in her eyes. Finally, she chose the card on the end.

'Turn it over.'

The first one made Isabelle catch her breath. After staring at the second one, she just looked up at Jodie in shock. 'Really?' she asked finally.

'Yes.'

'This is you? For real?'

Jodie nodded, quite obviously pleased that she'd managed to surprise her friend so greatly. Then Isabelle did something to put herself back in the game. Rather than pick up the third photo, Isabelle reached into her own purse, riffled through the contents for a moment, and took out a folded yellow paper ticket. She placed it on top of picture number three. On the back of the ticket were three Xs.

'I was there,' she said. 'I saw you.'

Club Triple X catered to the high-end players in the S/M world. People to whom aesthetics were as important as orgasms and anonymity was the top aphrodisiac. The steely eyed bouncer at the door turned away contenders not only for their inappropriate dress styles but for their overall attitudes. Wearing red rubber from head to toe? I don't think so, the bouncer said with a shake of his head. Clad in brand-new gothic gear, so fresh and clean it sparkles? Then you're not a real player, are you? One needed to fit all the rules to make it through the doors – even though once inside the rules were ultimately made to be broken.

The first time Isabelle attended, she'd taken her time choosing her attire. She'd heard the stories; models refused entry because they were too coked out to behave like humans; millionaires turned away because they pulled an attitude with the manager. Cool wasn't something you could buy, and it wasn't even something you could fake. For once, Isabelle felt insecure. She'd tried on high heels and a black zippered PVC dress from France, but shook her head at her own reflection. Trying too hard. That's what the outfit screamed. Disappointed in her selection of choices, she'd stalked back and forth in her store, searching out something that would make her stand out from the crowd without making her seem as if she were playing a role.

Finally, after hours of preparation, she was ready. To offset her lovely blue eyes and glistening light hair, she picked a fiery pink lace bra and garter set. It was one that she'd had in the window of her store that out-

priced even the top names: Molta Bella. Tristease.
Nuance. So now it was hers. Maybe that's why she'd
marked it up so much in the first place; she had not
wanted to see the set go to a home other than her
own. Was it crazy that so many of the items in her
store ultimately found their way into her own lingerie
stash? Sure it was – especially because, as she'd told
Jodie, she rarely bothered to wear panties. That didn't
mean she didn't like to own them.

The colour of this set was perfect. Not only would
black have been clichéd, but dark hues tended to be
too harsh against her milky skin. She liked pink, also,
because it seemed safe. Girlish. Naive, even. All of the
qualities that described Isabelle on the outside,
although what was contained beneath her innocent
appearance was completely different.

She'd gone with Cameron and a girlfriend, knowing
that it would be easier to get past the bouncer if she
and Charlene spent their time in line making out. And
she was right. The chisel-cheeked bouncer had kept
them in line just long enough to enjoy the show of
Isabelle necking with her gorgeous red-haired play-
mate, and then he'd grinned and said, 'All right, Blon-
die. I like your style.' Lifting the black leather cord, he
had allowed the trio access into the dreamy world of
XXX.

Once inside, Isabelle took in the dangerous glow of
blue neon over the bar. The moving picture show on
the far wall showed black-and-white images flickering
over the huge white space. Images that projected on to
naked dancers, as well.

Charlie and Cameron had gone to the bar to score a
new drink – Voluptuous Vixens – while Isabelle made
her way through the throng of dancers, looking
around. Taking everything in. She'd seen the main
stage right away, seen Jodie in black, bound, mask in
place. A different Jodie.

Where had the pictures come from? Isabelle shut her

eyes now in the coffee shop, trying to re-create the full memory in her mind. She'd seen Jodie, her hair long and shimmering in a red-gold wave down her back. The stage was white marble, and Jodie had been right in the very centre of it. A spotlight, ever-changing from blue to lilac to gold, found her body over and over. It swung out to caress the crowd, and then moved right back again to Jodie's face, distorted by a black silk mask over her eyes and a gag between her glossy vamp-red lips.

Jodie was bound in place while a man issued commands to her. Isabelle moved towards her, needing to see her more clearly, to hear the words the man was saying. 'Take it,' he demanded. 'You take it for me, girl.'

Staring up, Isabelle had memorised his face. Handsome. So handsome. Different from many of the doms she'd seen around clubs in the past, he looked almost like a movie star. But the problem was, he seemed as if he were acting. When Isabelle had stared at Jodie she'd seen that this was no act for her.

'Take it,' he said again, bringing a crop up high in the air. 'For me –'

But Jodie had taken it in a different way. She'd made a move for him to undo the gag, and he had. Then in a whisper loud enough for Isabelle to hear, she had made her request. 'Untie me.'

'It's going to hurt, baby.'

'Then untie me,' Jodie had begged. 'Let me feel it.'

'That was you,' Isabelle murmured again. 'God, it *was*. It was you. Why didn't I realise that before?' She tried to answer her own question. 'Because you didn't seem real. I never thought to look at you like that. The girl up there – and it was you, right?'

Jodie nodded.

'The girl up there was too perfect to be real. And the long red hair and dark green eyes – yeah, I knew they were probably fake, but they looked so perfect.'

Jodie had impressed them all, hadn't she? Taking the pain without the bindings. Holding herself totally still, not moving. Not flinching. Isabelle had nearly creamed herself watching, and when Charlie and Cameron finally joined her, she hadn't even acknowledged their presence. She had been immune to Charlie's hands running up and down her body, holding on, and had hardly felt Cameron gripping tightly on to her fingers. The three of them sharing their heat while they absorbed Jodie's world.

'Who were you with? That wasn't Max, was it?'

'Lucas,' Jodie said, as if that were the most obvious answer in the world.

Now, Isabelle flipped over the picture, knowing inside herself exactly what she'd see on the frozen frame of paper. Jodie. Eyes shut. Lips open. The moment. *That* moment.

'Does that change anything?' Jodie asked.

'What do you mean?'

'The fact that I didn't tell you before.'

Isabelle shook her head. And then, as a thought occurred to her, she said, 'But you knew I was there, is that what you're saying?'

Jodie just smiled and slid the photos back into her purse.

Chapter Seventeen

Once again, waiting for Nick on his computer was a new site to check out: www.yoursforthetaking.com. He was getting used to the fact that his odd employer enjoyed offering clues rather than issuing commands. Usually, clients had one question that needed answering. That's why they searched out his services. This was something brand new, and he found that he enjoyed the game. Still, he felt a little bit as if he were in an Agatha Christie mystery. When would all of the facts come together to make any sense? At some point in the future, would he gather the players together in his office and point to one of them. 'It was you, Professor Pink, in the garage, with the bayonet.'

He read the opening note that stated the website wasn't intended to urge anyone to commit thievery. It was simply a site dedicated to the art of the take. The codicil continued to say that the site contained a work of fiction, and, as such, couldn't be taken seriously.

What an odd concept, he thought. He wondered how many sites there were dedicated to the art of the catch – catching the criminals, that is. He did a quick search on the Internet and came up with several hundred thousand sites regarding catching shoplifters and other criminals. Yet there were only five sites that he could find about the pleasures of thievery.

He poured himself a glass of whisky and then got down to reading through the articles on the website. He'd actually visited this site before, when first hired by the Artone Museum to work an upcoming show. But now he really paid attention. There were movie reviews, write-ups about recent thieveries throughout the world, and first-person articles about the thrilling rush of breaking the law. And, as he read, he wondered why his curious employer had sent him the URL.

Part of San Francisco's endless appeal to Jodie was the fact that the great outdoors was only minutes away. Where else could you be so deeply entrenched in an urban environment and still be able to witness the pure beauty of pristine nature, mountains, the water, the endless sky – to own that view from a simple apartment? Her diaphanous curtains, more form than function, were open right now, and from the centre of her mattress, she could see the endless blue sky and the rolling hills in the distance.

But Jodie wasn't a country girl in the sense that she wanted to go out hiking in the wilderness. She only liked to appreciate the view from afar. When she wanted relaxation, she didn't strap on heavy boots and slide into a polar fleece. She found peace in the form of some of the city's best-known spas, or shops, or – as she was experiencing right now – sex sessions with willing partners.

Yes, she thought. Plural. Partners.

Lucas and Isabelle were getting along better than she'd ever hoped. With herself as the creamy filling in a dreamy sex sandwich, the threesome had made a culinary creation fit only for the passionately hungry. Isabelle had her long arms wrapped around Jodie's body, holding her firmly in a spoon embrace, so tightly that Jodie could feel Isabelle's sexy wetness against her ass.

Jodie knew that one of the reasons Isabelle was so turned on was the fact that she'd revealed herself as the girl at Triple X. But she also knew that Isabelle was excited about meeting Lucas, and learning more about his true character before offering her advice.

In this position, Lucas entered the lovely brunette

from the side. He could stare into Jodie's eyes or, if she ducked her head slightly, he could look at Isabelle. Jodie liked that thought; the way she could orchestrate the situation, becoming more or less personally involved in a very personal situation. What she most enjoyed was the fact that she'd made this whole thing happen. She'd discussed the idea ahead of time with both of her friends – both of her lovers, truly. And, as she'd thought, they had each been interested in the concept. But you never knew how people would react once something like this was actually happening. Talking dirty was one thing. Acting on an erotic impulse was something else entirely.

And just look . . .

The threesome moved and glided in a dreamlike manner. Although strong wills prevailed when Jodie was with Lucas on her own, or with Isabelle one-on-one, there was no one person dominant in this event. Each member had equal play and equal say in what they did and when they did it. Like now, as Jodie arched and pulled back from Lucas, letting his penis slide out of her. He shot her a questioning glance, but she just smiled, slipping out from Isabelle's embrace and moving lower on the mattress. This left Lucas with the perfect opportunity to inch closer to Isabelle, who opened herself up to him, letting him know with her actions that she was ready. Jodie watched as Lucas entered her friend, and she sat up on her knees, so that she could see every frame of the erotic play as it unfolded.

So sweet. So pretty. The way her two blonde playmates looked as they slid against one another. The raw fabric of Jodie's white comforter was the perfect background to the tanned duo. They looked as stunning as if they'd been positioned by an erotic photographer. Or directed by an X-rated film maker.

'You like this?' Lucas murmured, slipping deeper into Isabelle.

'Oh, yeah,' the blonde whispered back. 'Just like that.'

Jodie held her breath and watched the situation grow steamier and steamier. What was it about watching that was such a turn-on? Why did it make her so wet? She couldn't answer that. She simply widened her eyes and got as close as she could without intruding. This was simply too powerful not to stare at. Sighing, she slid her own fingertips against her pussy, pressing into her hot spot as she watched.

Isabelle moved on to her back and Lucas got on top, in a missionary style position, and from this angle, Jodie simply couldn't help herself. She had to get back in there, had to do something. Quickly, she slid between Isabelle's legs and as Lucas lifted up, she gave his balls a flick with her tongue then darted her head down to caress Isabelle's inner thighs. She moved away, letting Lucas take over for a moment. Then Jodie moved further up the bed, to kiss Isabelle's breasts, then to kiss her friend's open mouth. She was small and slight and could fit wherever she wanted, making herself an important part of both of her friends' pleasure.

But as Lucas grew more excited, Jodie found that once again she had to simply sit back and watch. The show was too good not to. She found it even more exciting to be an audience for once, rather than to be the main-featured event. She saw how carefully Lucas rolled Isabelle over on the bed, pushed her into a doggy-style position, and drove into her from behind. His large hands held her waist firmly, and his muscular arms bulged as they gripped Isabelle's golden skin. The look on his face was exquisite – that vision of almost coming. The approach to Nirvana. Jodie had seen that look often enough when it was from something she was doing with him, or to him. But this time was different.

Isabelle lowered her head and her long blonde hair fell forward, hiding her face from Jodie. That was no good. Jodie needed to see. She held Isabelle's long hair back with one hand and gazed at her friend's lovely jewel-toned eyes. She saw the hunger there, and the desire.

'Kiss me, baby,' Isabelle crooned, and happily Jodie made her friend's simple request come true.

From the corner of 14th and Valencia, it's only a short step to reach Venus, or Saturn, or Mercury. Depending on the quality of the night and the clarity of the heavens above, and depending on whether or not the Sidewalk Astronomers are out. Because this evening the sky was dark and clear, without clouds or fog, Nick hoped the astronomers would be there. It soothed his mind to glance through one of the amateur astronomer's powerful telescopes and view a world so indescribably far away from his own that his mind couldn't fully process the fact. Where problems didn't seem to matter any longer.

More than simply being able to see into the distant heavens, he liked the concept that there were people who were so involved with faraway places that they wanted to share their knowledge. The sidewalk astronomers didn't expect money, only a bit of awe. They brought out their equipment as a way to share the pleasures of feeling at one with the universe. Sometimes, it made Nick feel tiny and insignificant. And that could be a good thing. Other nights, he was simply struck – star-struck, really – by the beauty of the skies above. So often was his life about dirt and muck and secrets that he forgot to even look up. The sidewalk astronomers, with their tools and their gentle way of describing serious science, managed, somehow, to bring him a sense of true calm.

As he approached the corner, he saw the motley grouping of tourists and locals, crowding around the large, white telescope. There were teenagers, each wearing the ubiquitous hooded sweatshirt, trying to look tough. You could tell by their attitude that they felt invincible. Give them a couple of years, Nick thought, a couple of heartbreaks. That was cynical, he knew, but true nonetheless, wasn't it? Besides, they were no different from their leather-jacketed prede-cessors, were they? The rebels – still without a cause.

Tourists stopped to see what the commotion was about. It was easy to guess which region the different people were from, simply from observing their outfits. There were hipsters from the east coast, drenched in ennui, as well as heavy-set couples from the midwest, clad in T-shirts with slogans on the front and clinging to each other for safety in a big city. Nick took them all in, and then turned his attention to the astronomer.

'Venus?' he asked hopefully. The blue-green planet was his favourite. Inky gases swirling in vapour clouds. He liked it more than Saturn, with its dancing rings, and more than the red hot Mars.

'Look hard enough and you can see Uranus,' said one of the jokesters nearby, before heading off on his way to the bar across the street, but Nick didn't even bother to glance up at who was speaking. He wanted escape, and that meant gazing when it was his turn, not engaging in some testosterone-loaded exchange. Staring upwards, he tried, somehow, to find the peace that left him wanting. But this evening, even after spotting the ethereal rings of a distant heavenly body, Nick couldn't banish Jodie from his thoughts.

It's why he ended up at the Outer Mission, at a little joint known as Airhead.

Although Jodie had invited both lovers to join her in the bed, Isabelle came prepared for a little inspired action on her own. After Lucas climaxed a second time, sprawled between the two beauties, breathing harshly and blinking a little in stunned appreciation at what had just taken place, Isabelle said, 'I've got this craving –'

'For a little after-sex snack?' Jodie teased.

'For a little man-on-the-bottom action.'

'Meaning?' Lucas asked, rolling over to face Isabelle.

'Meaning I'm wondering if you're game –'

It was obvious that she wasn't going to offer any more details unless Lucas agreed. This was a flat-out dare, and with his lips curved immediately into a half-smile, Lucas nodded. 'Whatever you're offering, Isabelle, I'm more than up for it,' he replied, nodding his head to indicate that he was speaking for all parts of his anatomy.

At his response, Isabelle slid out from his embrace and walked naked to where her large black purse lay on one of Jodie's leopard-print chairs. She riffled through the massive bag for several moments, then withdrew a long, vibrant pink vibrating dildo. This she attached easily to a slim harness and buckled the harness around her waist. When she faced the bed again, she cocked her hip and stared at Lucas.

'Still game?'

The expression in his gold-brown eyes had hardened. Jodie gazed at him and saw someone she didn't immediately recognise. Lucas wanted what Isabelle had to offer. That was easy to see. But could he admit it to himself? All three partners seemed unsure of the answer to that question.

'I won't ask again,' Isabelle murmured, her hand casually stroking the pink shaft of the toy. Her fingers caressed the synthetic penis as knowingly as if the prosthetic device truly were a part of herself.

Lucas watched for a moment. Then, without a word, he rolled over on the bed and stretched his arms over his head, offering himself over to her. Jodie felt something twist inside the centre of her chest. He was being subordinate, in the style that she often was, and she couldn't believe how sexy he looked in that role. But that wasn't what caused the topsy-turvy sensation within her. It was the fact that Isabelle was going to give him something that she wouldn't have been able to offer herself.

'Get him all ready for me, Jodie, will you?'

Now that she had a mission, Jodie was able to stop the noisy conversation within her thoughts. Quickly, she straddled Lucas high up on his back, facing his ass. She parted those fine muscular cheeks and trailed her fingertips along the crack between. Lucas sighed and bucked up, taking Jodie on a mini-ride, but she stayed where she was, spreading him open for Isabelle. Licking one finger, she traced the tip around his opening.

'Use this,' Isabelle said.

Jodie looked up. Her blonde friend tossed over a bottle of lube. Jodie caught the deep blue bottle and flicked the cap open with her thumb. Carefully, she poured a slim river of the glistening liquid down the valley between Lucas's cheeks. Her man bucked again, shuddering at the chill.

'You think he's set?' Isabelle asked, coming forwards.

'Not quite,' Jodie said, slipping off Lucas and positioning herself in front of his mouth with her thighs spread wide apart. 'Now,' she said, 'I think now.'

'Wanna hit?' a street kid murmured in a low, cagey tone as Nick approached the cafe. He shook his head slightly at her, catching just the startling shade of her blue hair and the paleness of her skin, before his hand found the door. She wasn't so easily dissuaded. When she pressed forwards with her body, urgent in voice and action, he answered more tersely. 'Not interested.'

'Best stuff in the city.'

'No thanks.'

'But I've got something that will really rock your world. And there's a money-back guarantee, of course.' She said this in a rush, but with a smile, as if she knew she were making fun of herself. Nick had no time for nuisances. He didn't look back, but he heard her mutter to herself as he pushed open the door to the oxygenated cafe. 'You paying for air, dude? Come on, don't be an idiot. Air is free.'

'Not this air,' he said as he left her behind. Pure, clean oxygen. Hits of the stuff were the new yuppy sensation. Breathe freely. Breathe deeply. Or some such shit. Maybe the whole thing was the modern-day version of The Emperor's New Clothes. Everyone knew the concept was a joke, but nobody dared to be the first person to point a finger. That street kid outside, she was the only one. Because what did she have to lose? What hadn't she lost already?

He looked around the room. Turquoise-painted walls were echoed by tinted mirrored ceilings and a deep blue floor. Gauzy-dressed waitresses with the flowing hair of mermaids moved among the lounge chairs, offering various elixirs in tiny glasses that looked like test tubes. Nick knew the drill. These were potions created entirely of oddly named herbs. No hardcore stuff was sold here. Alcohol and drugs were strictly forbidden in a place where the body was considered a temple. But after breathing the real air, not the clouded garbage hanging over San Francisco, even a hit of wheatgrass juice could make you feel light-headed. At least, that's what the true believers would have you think.

When it came right down to it, Nick didn't have a great deal of faith in the stuff at all. Drink someone's ground-up lawn for pleasure and not a dare? He was much more in tune with the violet blue-haired girl working the streets and alleys. Want to get higher than high? Shoot some speed. Want to get crazy? Try a hit of X or the good old-fashioned down-to-earth buzz of Colombian Gold. For Nick, the best relaxation technique in the world didn't involve praying to a Buddha or imbibing a herbal apothecary's creation. He preferred Jim Beam to any other buzz on the market – including, he might add, air.

Inside the air cafe, customers reclined in comfortable-looking chairs. If it weren't for the nozzles fitted into their noses, the clientele would have appeared the type you'd find in any other bar in the city. But the face-mask attachments made the people look, to Nick, like outpatients from a hospital. They didn't seem healthy, even though the air cafe prided itself on its positive mind-body outlook. But in the alien-green glow of the lights, the men and women all looked ill.

What Nick would give to be in a dimly lit jazz bar on Fillmore. Bantering with the bartender and doing magic tricks with a glass of whisky. Now you see it, now you don't. At his favourite pub, the bartender sometimes made a napkin 'dance' along the bartop, a lemon hidden beneath the folds giving it the swing-sway motion. There wasn't anything fancy about Sammy's; which was why Nick liked it.

With a wry smile, he tried to imagine what his number-one hero would think about a place like this. If Bogie were looking down (or up) from wherever he was, would he laugh his ass off? Would he think he'd landed on another planet? That was more likely. Would he think that he'd been slipped a Mickey and wound up without his senses? 'Get out of there, Hud,' he heard his mentor whisper to him. 'This isn't your scene.'

It's exactly how Nick felt. But he'd heard that Isabelle and Jodie were fans of Airhead. And what he most wanted was a hit on her. A straight-up swallow of Jodie Silver. Christ, he'd mainline her if he could.

Lucas pressed his mouth against Jodie's pussy, licking and sucking as Isabelle drove the latex toy deep inside him. Each time she thrust, he worked Jodie harder with his tongue. It was as if he needed something to keep himself busy, something to focus on to keep his mind off the fact that a beautiful blonde goddess was taking him like this.

Jodie would take a licking for any reason at all, and

she could look directly into Isabelle's eyes as her friend had her boyfriend. But was he her boyfriend? That term didn't really make much sense. He was her partner. That was for sure. Partner in crime, at least. But he wasn't linked to her in any passionate way – other than the fact that they'd always seemed in tune with each other's desires.

Yet maybe he'd been acting a role that hadn't been suited to him. Maybe he'd better serve Isabelle's needs – as she was serving his. Was that the subconscious reason that had made Jodie orchestrate this situation in the first place? Did her heart know something that her mind didn't?

Jodie found these thoughts rumbling through her head too quickly for her to ignore, yet too quickly to pay much attention to, either. Because Lucas was coming, rubbing himself against the mattress beneath him and shuddering all over. At his first true moan, Isabelle turned on the motor inside the vibrator and hummed the thing into life. And as Lucas came, he breathed hard on Jodie's fur, spiralling her off into a world where thoughts and worries had no place and pleasure was queen.

'What next?' Isabelle asked, crushed in between Jodie and Lucas and staring up at the ceiling. The three were washed, haphazardly dressed, and ready for something else.

'I know,' Jodie murmured, 'we'll go somewhere for a drink. We'll act normal and sane, and nobody will know what we just did.'

'And what was that?' Lucas asked, rolling over to stare directly into Jodie's eyes.

'Screwed each other senseless,' she said, grinning, and the threesome started to laugh as they stood and made their way to the door. It was all going to be all right, Jodie realised. You could strip yourself down, expose your inner core, and then hide it again in a heartbeat. No harm. No foul.

There was no reason to think that Jodie would be here tonight. Just because he was in the mood to see her didn't mean he'd linked into her thoughts. But, for some reason, he felt certain that she was here, or that she would be soon. Generally, he was right when he had a nagging feeling like this. Generally.

And then he turned the corner and saw her coming through the door with Isabelle and some guy. Saw her and looked away, then looked back just to make sure that it was really her. Yes, there she was, gazing at him with an impish smile, head cocked. Her eyes told him that she knew more than she was letting on. Why couldn't he just walk over and put everything flat out before her. If they each laid their cards on the table, wouldn't life be so much simpler?

No. He needed to know more about Jodie before he could proceed with the case. The non-case. That was the funniest part. As far as he could tell, she hadn't done anything wrong. Maybe she was planning on it. Maybe she was strategically setting out the scene for the heist of her life. But right now, all she appeared to be doing was choosing an azure leather recliner and getting ready to breathe. He couldn't fuck with her for that, could he?

He walked closer, without appearing to be looking down at her, eyes fixed on the mirror on the far wall. Still, he saw her, saw everything. She wasn't wearing the stupid nozzle. No, she was breathing regular air, just like he was. Isabelle, on the other hand, was letting herself be hooked up to an oxygen tank, sucking that air down as if each breath were her last. Lucas seemed unsure as to which way to go. Follow Isabelle's lead, or stick with Jodie? After a minute or two of trying to act as if he belonged in the joint, Nick took his leave.

'Going so soon?' one of the ethereal air hostesses

asked him. Nick turned to face her, and he saw the look in her eyes that he always associated with religious fanatics. This wasn't a woman he could have an actual conversation with. She would never listen to his point of view, yet he let her speak her piece. 'You haven't really experienced the scene yet, have you? In order to find your true centre, sometimes you need to be pushed off balance.'

All right. What did that mean? 'What I really need is a breather,' Nick said, pushing open the door and walking out into the dark, possibly polluted, night. He sucked in a breath of San Francisco's salt-tinged air and smiled as he made his way to his car. This was the real stuff. This was what he liked. And when he thought about it, he realised that's what Jodie liked, too. If she were in the place right now, it was only to humour Isabelle. Jodie's world was the same as his. Maybe the other side of the tracks than his, but the same, nonetheless, and that's what put the smile on Nick's face.

'He was here, Max,' the blue-haired girl said quickly into her cell phone. 'Looking for you, I'm sure.'

'Why are you so sure? Are you the detective now?'

'Come on, he had that expression in his eyes. You know it. He's on to you. Or after you. Or something.'

'And what are you on?'

Low chuckle from the street saleswoman. 'What are you looking for?'

'Stop by later and you'll find out.'

Chapter Eighteen

Nick walked alongside the water, trying to put all the information together. He knew that Jodie was playing around with him. The way she teased him with her glances whenever they met. He'd understood the whole time that she was a step ahead of him. As long as he ultimately figured everything out, he didn't care if it took him a little while. His brain roamed over the facts until he got down to one shiny idea.

Max Sterling was in town. This was the only concept that made any sense to Nick. The man was carrying out high-end thefts under the cover of his import/export business. With Jodie at the helm of the company, Sterling had time to plot and work through his heists. Since everyone believed him to be in Europe and nobody seemed to be exactly sure what he looked like, the man easily flitted in and out of society homes. Or he used information gleaned from Jodie when she went to auctions and parties. If Max was any good at disguises, then Nick might well have already run into him somewhere.

Lucas could actually be Max, right? That wasn't so far-fetched.

Nick wrote this theory down as clearly as possible in his notes: Max is here. Follow up. Check hotels. Airport records. Re-read guest lists at gala auction events. Note Jodie's location at said events.

He realised, as he looked over his notes, that he was doing everything he could to make Jodie appear innocent. Wasn't that what Bogie had done in *The Maltese Falcon*, all the way to the very end? That wasn't the way to go at being a detective. Not a good one, anyway. It was a lawyer's job to prove the innocence of a client. Nick's job was to gather the facts, regardless of what they might prove or disprove.

Hell, but knowing that didn't make life any easier.

Cameron Sweeney was a man who knew his mind. Isabelle appreciated this particular character trait. He never hesitated over items that didn't suit his personal desires. With a shake of his head, he simply moved on to the next object that Isabelle spread out for him. Although Isabelle and Cameron were occasional sexual partners, she knew that he had a troupe of other women in his stable. Names were linked to him in the society pages, girls coming and going as the seasons passed. He never spoke to Isabelle about the women he dated, but he did buy a variety of lingerie for the mysterious women. There was no jealousy in Isabelle's curiosity about Cameron's life. She liked the fact that she had a part in it, although occasionally she wondered how the other women felt about sharing such a prize.

Isabelle could always tell when a new girl was in play. That was her detective instinct kicking in. Cameron bought different sizes, concentrating for a year or so on a 34B with a small panty set. Then suddenly requesting teddies in a 32A or bras in a 36C. One girl out, another one in, Isabelle always thought.

The other quality that Isabelle liked about Cameron was how well he understood the clothing. He touched the seams, stroked the laces, searched for the best-made items that she kept in stock. If Cameron really liked a piece, he'd often buy several. That was what happened this afternoon. As he made his way through the supplies in the back room, he kept everything completely professional, even when he was talking about the most erotic concepts. 'Does this lace all the way up the back?' he'd ask, fingering a whale-bone corset. 'How comfortable is it to wear? Especially when bent over...'

'So comfortable. I've heard only the best comments.'

'But have you tried it?'

'Not me. No.'

'What have you tried lately?'

She showed him, knowing that if he liked the items, he'd buy them. But today was different. Nothing suited his tastes. 'We're low,' she said finally, shrugging sadly at the items on the rack. 'New shipments are coming soon, but I've sold out most of my favourites.'

He smiled at her, and then he slid a white envelope towards her across the back counter. She reached for it, then looked back at him, eyebrows raised.

'I'm having a party,' he said.

'I'd love to come,' she responded automatically, not even opening the envelope. Then she felt herself blush; Cameron hadn't invited her to his house before. They either had sex in her apartment or, more often, in her store.

'I'd like more than your presence,' he said, taking a step closer. 'I'd like your clothes.'

Now, Isabelle just stared at him. She didn't understand.

'It's a dress-up party. I'm inviting my favourite girls, and I'd like you to provide the outfits. Certainly, I'll buy all the pieces ahead of time. But I thought you could sort of play the hostess. Help each of my ladies get dressed.'

The way he said the words 'my ladies' made Isabelle instantly picture some sort of harem. Was that how it was with him?

'I'll pay you for your time, of course,' he said. 'And if you have a friend, someone who could help you, I'd pay her, as well. Maybe Jodie –'

Now, as he quoted a price for the evening, she

nodded. And, as soon as he left, she reached for the phone. 'Jo,' she sighed. 'Have I got an offer for you.'

Jodie couldn't believe it. She'd wanted to get into Cameron Sweeney's house for years. But with the security system that he had installed – not just electronic, but also human – she'd never taken the risk. Now, she was actually an invited guest, a paid guest. She'd be able to scope the layout, see whether she would want to try for a return trip. Of course, she told none of that to Isabelle, saying instead that she'd be more than happy to help, and that she would do it free of charge.

'Just for the excitement,' she told her friend. 'I can't wait.'

Isabelle special-ordered the items that Cameron requested. She chose them in the sizes he stated on his fax, and in the colours that she knew he appreciated. As she prepared for the party, she realised, from the files that she kept on all of her customers, that all of the sizes and colours matched the ones he'd bought over the years. Had he actually been dating a multitude of women this whole time? Was that possible?

No, she didn't feel jealous in the least. They weren't tied to each other in any way except for sharing the occasional tryst. But she'd assumed that he'd move on from one girlfriend to another. Now, she rethought her theory. What if he were with all these girls at once? It was very Hugh Hefner of him, wasn't it? Except, unlike Hefner, who seemed at ease with the public knowing his private life, Cameron kept all of this undercover.

It was about to come out in the open, though.

Isabelle and Jodie chose their outfits together. As true dressers would, they settled on simple selections: slim-fitting black slacks and matching sweaters in the softest cashmere. They carried garment bags with them and, when they arrived at the mansion in Pacific Heights, they found that their host had set up the living room perfectly. A black iron rack waited for them to hang their clothes on. There was chilled champagne in the corner. Glasses stood on one table. Jodie counted the glasses: ten. It would be a small, tasteful party, Jodie decided.

Once they'd set up, they stood next to each other, waiting. Isabelle was nervous, and she paced in front of Jodie, who was taking in all of her surroundings. She saw the Tiffany-glass lamps, the ancient statues, the gilded vases. Walking around the room, she saw the collection of snuff boxes, the tiny Japanese erotic figurines, the tiles imported from Greece. Suddenly, the doors swung open and six women entered the room, each one blindfolded, all holding hands. Cameron stood in the centre of the group.

'Today is my birthday,' he told Isabelle and Jodie. 'And I've prepared my own present. I want my beautiful girls to be wrapped like delicious gifts. And then I want to slowly unwrap them at my leisure. You two are the designated wrappers.' Then, to the women he was with, he said, 'Ladies, you may peek.'

Jodie watched the girls' faces when they saw the frilly collection of luscious lingerie Isabelle had assembled. All had the same expression: instant joy. They started peeling off their clothes immediately, not embarrassed at all to be naked in front of each other or the strangers. With Isabelle's help, the girls found their sizes and began lacing and tying, fastening hooks, slipping into each of the different items.

As the women dressed, a bell sounded. Within moments, another woman had arrived, this one carrying suitcases spilling over with shoes. Had Cameron gone around the city to his favourite stores and created the dream date for his girlfriends? That's how it appeared. Jodie tried to keep her eyes on the women – watching one, then another – but she grew dizzy at the quick changes that were taking place. Corset on. Then off. Merry widow replaced by bra, panty, and garters. Who could choose? The clothes all looked beautiful – equally beautiful – to Jodie. How did one decide that something worked better than something else?

That's where Isabelle took over. She eyed each one of the lovely women, then went to work: assisting with colour choices; helping to fasten a wayward lace. She treated the women as if they were dolls or mannequins, taking in their hairstyles, eye colours, body types, and then nodding as she handed over outfit after outfit.

Jodie looked around the room, overwhelmed, and then realised that the host was gone. Mentally, she counted the women. None were missing: there was the blonde with spiky hair; the brunette with silky waves that cascaded almost all the way down to her perky ass; a redhead whose fierce expression was softened each time she laughed; a tiny honey-haired nymphet, who had chosen a polka dot number immediately and was now prancing around in a pair of pony-skin boots, tripping over herself to get to the champagne.

Without looking to see if anyone was watching her, Jodie made her way to the double doors. Maybe she'd be able to have a quick peek before someone caught on. What she wanted most was a glimpse of Cameron's most famous collection of faux jewels. If anyone found her, she'd simply say she was looking for the ladies' room. That was the plan, anyway.

But Cameron Sweeney had other plans entirely.

'I didn't choose anything for you,' he said softly, coming up behind Jodie in the echoing hall.

'Didn't know my size?' she asked, teasing as she turned to face him. Christ, but he was handsome, those dark green eyes and thick black hair, going silver in the most genteel way. He seemed unaware of how good-looking he was, which wasn't really possible, she knew, for someone who was so often in the public eye.

He must spend hours putting himself together, yet he looked rugged and uncomplicated. 'Or weren't you sure that I'd come.'

'That wasn't it at all,' he said. 'I simply didn't want to hide your beautiful body beneath too much lace.'

'You're not really into lace, are you? From the things you've picked out there,' she gestured towards the main room, 'I'd have to say that leather is much more your speed.'

'And yours? What's your speed, Jodie Silver?'

She tilted her head as she looked up at him. There it was, the answer in his eyes. She'd known men like this before. Men who had a way with women, a special understanding, a bond, even. 'You know, don't you?'

'I'd put you in something red. And let me see. You're about –' He took a step closer, as if to put his hands around her breasts to measure her.

'You can eyeball my size, can't you?'

'But I could guess it correctly if you let me touch –'

'That's the question, isn't it? Will I or won't I?'

Cameron laughed. 'Not much of a question at all,' he said, 'because we both know from pleasurable past experience that you will.'

Now, Jodie laughed. She felt more on his level than she had in the situation in Isabelle's store. This time it felt as if they were on equal footing. As Cameron led her back into the large living room, Jodie glanced longingly over her shoulder at the rooms she'd been unable to see. But when she gazed at Isabelle, surrounded by the bevy of beauties, a brand new idea occurred to her. One of Jodie's best abilities was to roll with new concepts, to shift her plans with ease when a new situation arose.

When the rest of the women had left, it was down to Cameron, Isabelle and Jodie, all crashed out in the multitude of pretty finery. Champagne bottles lay upended near the sofa. The girls had become rowdy by the time all of the clothes had been tried on. Few items remained on the hangers. The rest reminded Jodie of wrappings at Christmas time. Colourful bits of different items were draped and remained dangling all over the furniture in the room: a bra over one end table; a Merry widow wrapped around one leg of the sofa.

'That was fun.' Isabelle grinned, unconcerned about the way the room looked. This wasn't her home, after all. And if this was the way Cameron wanted to spend his time and money, then let him. She was just along for the risqué ride.

'Was it, Izzy? Was it fun for you?'

'Of course. I like to see pretty women wearing the clothing that I pick out.'

'So do I,' Cameron said, nodding in agreement. 'It's one of my favourite sports. But I didn't really get a lot of chances tonight.'

'What do you mean?' Jodie asked. 'You were surrounded all night by all these beautiful girls in gorgeous styles of dress.' She grinned at him. 'And undress.'

'I was the host. I never wasn't moving.'

'And now?'

'That's what he wants you to think,' Isabelle laughed. 'He wants you to think, "Poor Cameron. All these dolls to play with and he's still a lonely boy." My heart bleeds for you, baby,' she said, tousling his hair.

'No,' Jodie said. 'That's not it at all. He wants us to put on a show for him. And that's what he wanted the whole time, isn't it, Cameron? Buying the lot of your back room supplies was simply his way of begging for a private show.'

The man nodded again, eyes focused intently on Jodie.

'What type of show?' Isabelle purred, getting in on the scenario.

'A dress-up show,' Jodie said, and she locked eyes with Isabelle and sent her friend a silent message.

They would ignore the host, in order to give him the most pleasure. He liked to watch, right? All three of them knew that. Well, let him watch this.

'I didn't see anything I particularly liked,' Jodie continued. 'But maybe I missed something.'

'Oh, you did,' Isabelle said, catching on right away and hurrying over to the rack. 'You can't have seen everything I brought. Let me pick something perfect for you. I'm sure I can find just the right item.' While Isabelle perused what remained on the lingerie rack, Jodie began to strip off her clothes, taking off her sweater and the thin black T-shirt beneath. She heard Cameron sigh behind her, but she refused to look in his direction. Moving directly next to Isabelle, she watched as her friend searched through the different lacy and racy items. Jodie got right next to Isabelle and whispered something in her ear. Isabelle nodded once, then said, 'Take off all of your clothes, and I'll give you something to change into.'

Instead of obeying, Jodie stepped on the hem of a lacy get-up, tearing the lace off the bottom. Isabelle heard the sound of fabric ripping and was on Jodie in an instant.

'Clumsy girl,' she said, immediately leading Jodie to one of the large, over-stuffed cream-coloured sofas.

'It was an accident.'

'Whatever,' Isabelle said, 'I'll give you something to remember so that you'll think hard before you make that sort of mistake again.'

Didn't Isabelle always know exactly what to say? And how to say it?

Jodie allowed herself to be bent over her friend's sturdy lap, and she sucked in her breath as Isabelle lowered her black slacks down her thighs. Beneath, Jodie had on a pair of leopard-print silk panties. Bikini style underwear, they completely covered her ass in a way a thong wouldn't. Isabelle left them on for a moment, giving Jodie a sharp spank on top of her panty-clad bottom. Jodie groaned and rubbed her body against Isabelle's lap. Yes, the two women were putting on a performance for Cameron's pleasure, but that didn't mean Jodie wouldn't enjoy herself during the scene.

'Such a bad girl,' Isabelle murmured. 'And you know I'm not just talking about tearing a little slip.'

As her friend continued the spanking, Jodie felt herself growing more and more aroused. Being on display made the punishment even more erotic to her. How much could she take? How far would Isabelle go? Oh, a bit farther now, Jodie realised, as Isabelle took the time to peel Jodie's panties down, revealing her naked thighs and ass. Striking against her bare skin now with her open palm, Isabelle began to really heat Jodie up. Then, after only a few blows, the blonde dom spread Jodie's ass cheeks and slapped with four fingers between, catching against the lips of Jodie's sex.

'That's right,' Isabelle murmured as Jodie raised her body up to meet Isabelle's firm four fingers. 'You reach up and get it.'

Was this what Cameron wanted? A private peep-view style show? It seemed that way, because even though Jodie wasn't looking at him, she heard him sigh darkly, heard the sound of a zipper travelling down the familiar route to the crotch of his slacks. He was going to play with himself while Isabelle punished Jodie, and that was the image that brought Jodie to climax. To be used for another's pleasure while she wrung her own pleasure from Isabelle's lap made her cream. Because, for Jodie, a spanking wasn't the same without someone watching.

Chapter Nineteen

From an article in the *San Francisco ART Weekly*:

Transformed Treasures has finally made its way to San Francisco! These pieces, all of which have been stolen at some point in their 'lives', are travelling together in a single display. The transformation in the title refers to the way the jewels had been hidden – reworked, re-faceted, reset from their original placements. When possible, pictures show the original settings. If not, drawings and written hypotheses accompany the items.

Several famous thieves have been arrested during different eras for attempting to steal the items on display. Police records accompany some of the pieces in the exhibit. Mug shots from the 1920s show a group of thieves who succeeded in stealing the Unforgiving Heart, but who failed to get far away from the site of the theft. The ring, which was hidden for two months in the bottom of an apple cellar before being recovered, is now the centrepiece of the display.

Additional pieces on display include:

- The ruby stone from the sceptre of King Wallace the third
- The diamond believed to be the engagement setting of Dame Judy Lawson, stolen from her finger on her wedding night
- The Deathstone, an opal named for the fact that so many women met their untimely deaths while wearing it

Yet most of the crowds will be there to see the Unforgiving Heart –

Jodie stopped reading the article. She scanned the notes she had about the exhibit. There were several private security companies in charge of added protection for the jewels. But she knew something that they didn't. She knew the curator. And she had an idea of how to make this exhibit the best in the world. A memorable situation, that would drive up the press and bring the crowds in force.

Elizabeth Carson had been Jodie's friend since college. She was one of the people like Jodie who also shunned the 'Greek system', in search of a more eclectic university experience. Now, Jodie called Liz on her private line and asked her to meet her for lunch. There was a cafe around the corner from the museum. When Liz agreed, Jodie ensured she arrived promptly. She wanted to have a few moments to gather her thoughts; this was an important presentation.

'You want to what?'

'Have the jewels stolen.'

'Come on, Jodie,' Elizabeth murmured. 'You're talking crazy.'

'I'm talking instant publicity. You won't believe the write-ups in the paper.'

'And then what?'

'You have one of the private security companies "find" them.'

'With no jewel thief. No arrest?'

'Remember when the Oscars went missing? Everyone was up in arms. Then that man found the statues in the dumpster, and they flew him to the show to watch the award show in person. It was revealed later that his own brother might have been in on the heist. Nobody was arrested, but the publicity for the Oscars that year was amazing.'

'But the Oscars don't ever need added press. I think that everyone connected to that scandal was more embarrassed by the end of the day.'

'Right. That's true. But the audience loved it. They liked every single part. The heist. The loss. The recovery. The aftermath. Something like that wouldn't hurt you, would it? Even people who aren't interested in museum exhibitions would pay attention.'

'How would I make out? Supposedly, we have the tightest security in the museum system. I'd be the curator at the only museum to have lost a piece during this show!'

'Lost and found.'

Liz hesitated, obviously liking the way that sounded. 'I'll think about it.'

That was all Jodie wanted to hear. She had plans within plans and, for the first time in months – maybe years – the need to thoughtlessly lift items from every shop she went by subsided. She made it all the way back to the office without stealing one thing. Then she collapsed in her leather chair, feet up on her desk, and waited for the phone call she was sure to receive. Elizabeth would be too intrigued not to follow up. Jodie was sure she could win her over. When the phone rang, she gave herself several seconds, then answered with a smile.

'Tell me more,' Liz insisted.

'I can give you someone. But the thing is, you won't have a person, just a name.'

'Go on.'

'Max Sterling.'

'Max? Are you serious?'

'Don't worry. He'll outsmart your team. You'll find the jewels and Max will return to Europe, undetected.'

'That actually sounds OK. We can pass the buck to the European police. But you have to tell me this. Why are you doing it?'

'The thrill,' Jodie said.

'You still might get caught. I can only protect you so much.'

'I know. All I want is a shot.'

Chapter Twenty

At the next high-society event, Nick found himself not only slightly confused but more than a little aroused. He was captivated by the tantalising tango performed by the character he was watching, but each time he felt as if he had a handle on the situation, something happened to shake his confidence. There was Jodie, looking stunning as always, refined and elegant with her gleaming dark hair up. Her make-up was so subtle that she simply looked as if she possessed a warm, healthy glow, the type won from a day basking beachside, or an afternoon romping bedside. And he knew what she looked like in the midst of a powerful, passionate clinch. Even now, simply watching her glide through the crowd was enough to give him an instant erection.

This evening she had on a violet cut-away dress that fitted her body in a way that only a very beautiful woman could carry off. The back featured a large oval opening that dipped low enough to show what he had heard was called rear cleavage. No way was she wearing panties this evening – not only weren't there any panty lines to give her away, but another cut-out shape high up on each thigh left no question about the fact that she was bare down there.

It was obvious from the way she moved that she knew all eyes were on her. When she strode across the room, both men and women turned to check her out. Risky, he thought, especially with this type of stuffy crowd. It was why he admired her even more. She didn't let social protocol impede her from dressing how she liked. Not all the women in the room were as appreciative as Nick. He saw the scowls, the head-shakes. But he would have bet money that the men all wished Jodie was their date. Even momentarily.

But who was she with? The blond Adonis at her side resembled her date from the previous event, to the point that, for a moment, Nick had assumed he was the same man. But, on closer inspection, this date looked different. Same body type. Same sharply cut blond hair. Same expensive tux, even, if Nick could believe his eyes. So on the surface, Jodie had found the exact same date. Yet, to Nick's trained eye, the man wasn't the same person at all. What was different? Nick didn't really know. A sense. A look in the man's eyes. A subtle change.

As before, Jodie and her date split off into two directions, both observing the various articles out for auction. For a moment, Nick wasn't sure which person to follow. After a second, he chose the man, since he still couldn't be sure that his eyes weren't playing tricks on him. Was he the same date or wasn't he?

He followed the tall man into the great room. There, the evening's wares were on glorious glittering display. Diamonds caught the light and sent rainbows dancing around the room. Ropes of rubies dangled from the necks of antique mannequins. Other guests were busy checking the items out, as well, and it was easy for Nick to stay safely within a little crowd of people. Easy, at least, until Jodie's date turned to face him.

'Come here often?'

Nick smiled at the pick-up style question. 'To this mansion?'

'To this event?'

Now, Nick shrugged. 'I'm just learning about the scene. Getting a feel for how it works. This is my first time here.'

'It's easy,' the man said. 'You covet an item. Someone else wants it, too. You both make greedy fools of yourself and one walks off the winner. In fact,' the man said, speaking a little softer, 'it's kind of like a dating triangle.'

'Dating?'

'Never easy. Usually, there are several people involved, right? And one makes a play, the other counterplays, complicating the situation greatly.' Here, the man put his hand on Nick's shoulder and squeezed hard. Nick's eyes opened wide. What, precisely, was going on?

'Like I'm doing right now.'

'Excuse me?' Nick said, taking a step back. The man didn't seem to mind. He simply came forward, now even closer in Nick's private space. Nick's eyes narrowed. He couldn't figure out what was going on, and he felt lost. This wasn't the way a private investigator was supposed to behave, he knew. But he couldn't help himself. There'd been no clues that something like this would take place in Jodie's world.

'Making a play for something I covet –'

'I'm sorry,' Nick said automatically. Sure, men had come on to him in the past. He lived in San Francisco, after all, and he had the strong, magazine-quality good looks that many gay men appreciate. Yet he'd never fully got used to the concept that he was attractive to other males. This fact played out in a light flush over his cheekbones that Jodie's 'date' instantly took as a sign of encouragement.

'You don't have to be sorry for anything,' the blond said. 'Unless you've done something naughty that you haven't told me about. Then, I'd be all ears. I love a good confession.'

'I don't even know you,' Nick said.

'Easy to remedy. I'm George.' A strong hand gripped Nick's and shook it. 'I'm in the computer business. And I'm here because I like to look at beautiful things.'

Jesus, it was like an AA meeting. Say your name. Confess something personal. And wait for the supportive response from your audience. Nick returned the handshake just as firmly and then tried to drop George's hand, but the man held on. 'Nick,' he said, shaking again and pulling free. 'I'm a researcher. And I don't –'

His sentence was interrupted by a loud bell, as the hostess called the guests to be seated.

'You don't – ?' George whispered in his ear, taking a seat at Nick's side. Before Nick could finish, he saw Jodie hurrying over, and he bit off the rest of his statement. Why give out too much information? Jodie winked at him as she took the seat at his other side. Now, he could sit right next to the little minx and see exactly what she was up to. It wasn't long at all before he had an idea.

Plain and simple, Jodie was up to no good.

Jodie's main team – and that's how she thought of them, as a team – consisted of herself, Lucas, and George. She had other helpers spread throughout the city, people she could contact whenever she was in need. Some of her assistants provided special jobs. Others were randomly connected to her by favours owed. But the trio was her core team. They worked together in several different styles. Sometimes, Jodie would take a single man with her, as a 'date'. Other times, the men would go together, or the trio would travel as a threesome. Rarely, did she allow either one of the men to actually enter a house or a building with her during a heist. She used the two handsome males as decoys, while she did the most dangerous – the most exciting – work herself.

There were many different ways to engage in the delight of thievery, successfully. Jodie's favourite was to remove an item that wasn't on constant display, something that wouldn't immediately be missed. She most liked to do so several days before a large event, so that afterwards the host or hostess might believe that a sticky fingered guest had absconded with the item in question. Another way was to have a replica on hand to replace the true object with. Do a quick and successful switch and it might be years before the fake was detected. In fact, the decoy might never actually be discovered if the replacement was well-crafted.

Jodie had heard of a story in which a married woman was seeing a lover on the side. The lover stole the woman's diamond earrings, replacing them with fakes. The swap might never have been noticed except that, when the woman died suddenly, her husband planned on selling the earrings, and had them appraised. Upon learning that the expensive baubles were worth hundreds not thousands, he was shocked, and he drove himself crazy trying to find out why. Ultimately, he'd chosen to believe that his daughter's fiancé was responsible for the switch, causing all sorts of commotion in the style of a French farce. Jodie had heard that story first hand from Lucas. He had the original earrings still in his possession to prove that the story was real. Lucas shared her passion for dabbling on the wrong side of the law. He'd been an amateur before meeting Jodie, but together they created a strong match.

Where George came in was difficult sometimes to put into words. He was the extra, the added bonus. The one who added spice to the trio, who was as 'out there' as Jodie was on the inside, while appearing icily calm on the outside. He was dashing, in the old-style definition of the word, debonair, like a movie star from the 1940s. He had a way of lighting and smoking a cigarette that captivated those around him. What Jodie appreciated most about him was that he so closely resembled Lucas that people were often fooled into believing that one was the other or, more truly, that there was only one handsome blond who accompanied Jodie to events. And, because she never really revealed too much information, most of the people believed

Lucas was Max. Jodie never did anything to undermine this belief.

Just as she'd never let on what was in her hand when playing poker, why should she give out more clues than were necessary? Especially to a private detective.

'Where's your normal date for the evening?' Nick asked Jodie as they stood in line at the bar.

'Define normal,' she said, teasing him. She was having fun playing with this handsome man, and she wondered whether or not he could tell how much he was entertaining her.

'The other blond bombshell you like to show off.'

'Do you mean Isabelle?'

'Is that what he calls himself?'

'Oh.' She grinned. 'Lucas. He's all tied up tonight.' She laughed softly, as if it at a private joke, then looked at the delicate diamond-crusted watch on her equally dainty wrist. 'At least, if he's not yet, he will be soon.'

'You say that as if you have prior knowledge.'

'I do,' Jodie said, taking a sip of her Martini. 'Yes, I do.'

There was a special note for Lucas waiting in the bottom of the laundry bag. His hand found it by accident, and he pulled it out to see what the slip of paper could possibly be. A receipt, he thought at first, or some grocery list that had fallen out of Jodie's pocket when she'd tossed her laundry into the bag. But that didn't make any sense, because this wasn't a net bag of street clothes; all the items inside were her frilly undergarments. So what was this paper doing here?

Lucas held the letter in his hand, looking at it. Here was a folded-over white piece of paper, lipstick imprint on the seal. His hands trembled as he held it, because he realised exactly what this meant.

Fuck me, he thought, she knows. She's known this whole time.

That didn't stop him from sprawling out on her bed, holding the note in one hand, and a pair of pastel-pink panties in the other. His mind spilled over with possibilities. If she did know, and she hadn't said anything to him, then that meant she didn't mind. Right? She was teasing him, playing his own game, and that was fine.

But what should he do first? Treat himself to the most pleasurable sort of hand job with her sweet satiny panties, or read what might be an embarrassing letter about his personal fetish? He had his pants open, hand on his dick, rosé-coloured satin panties wrapped around it, when he stopped. No, he couldn't wait. Anticipation about what might be in the letter was too tantalising, and too much to deny.

With a slight sense of remorse at making his organ wait for release, he set the panties on top of his cock. Then he quickly cracked the seal, unfolded the mono-grammed stationery, and read the letter. His eyes grew wide as he read the note a second time. Not at the words written there in her fine handwriting, but that someone was reading those words aloud with him.

Isabelle.

'Bad boy,' the letter said. 'Stealing all those pretty panties for your own naughty pleasure. Playing at being in charge, when we both know it's not you at the helm. It's your cock. So prepare yourself –' and Isabelle added her own low chuckle as she walked into the room. 'Because, Lucas, honey, it's going to be a long night.'

Lucas set the letter down and looked over at the stunning blonde dominatrix. He felt extremely exposed; panties draped over the hard-on straining upwards, making a little lace-edged tent over his penis. But, from the look on Isabelle's face, he could tell that she wasn't shocked in the slightest.

'Jodie asked me how I'd deal with a thieving boy-friend. And I said, "I can't tell you. But I can show you." Would you like me to show you, Lucas?'

Christ, this was why Jodie had taken George to the auction as her date instead of him. She'd set him up. Knowing that he'd feel left out, feel a need to act on his own. She'd read him so clearly – well, then, why should he fight it?

His voice was deep and hollow sounding as he answered the question. All it took was one word. 'Yes.' With that simple word agreeing to whatever Isabelle had to offer.

'Then take those pants the rest of the way down.'

Was she going to screw him again? What sort of punishment would that be? He leaned up on one arm to stare at the goddess in the doorway, and then he saw the belt dangling from her hand. An instant tremor ran through his entire body, and he ran one hand over his eyes, then down his face, finally resting over his mouth. He'd played the role well enough, hadn't he? Taking charge of Jodie had been one of the high points of his life. But if he were to admit his darkest fantasies to himself, then this was the way he truly wanted to play, and to be played with.

'What's your answer, Lucas?'

Without further hesitation, he rolled over, sliding his slacks down his thighs to his calves, and offering himself over to the wrath of Isabelle. He couldn't think straight. All he could do was behave for her, praying silently that she truly knew what she was doing.

'How long have you been taking things?' she asked. He didn't turn his head to look at her directly. Instead, he stared at his reflection in the round mirror over Jodie's 1920s vanity unit. Was it crazy that he was going to embark upon this dirty scene in his lover's own bedroom? He supposed so, but wasn't everything about being with Jodie a little bit crazy?

'Since the beginning.'

'The beginning.'

'Our first weekend together. I stole a pair of white cotton panties that she'd worn under this little school-girl skirt. It was a naughty outfit, a tiny little plaid mini-skirt, but those were pure, pristine panties. I needed them.' He paused, trying to make sense of his explanation. 'I mean, I just needed them. You under-stand that, right? Haven't you ever seen something that you had to have?'

Isabelle ignored the question by answering with another of her own. 'How many things have you taken?'

He shrugged. 'I don't keep 'em.'

The belt landed hard on his ass.

Again, he felt that delicious tremor wash through him. 'Not most of them,' he said, amending the lie. 'Maybe a few. The black ones with the red lace. God, those were amazing. The blue silk tap panties with the polka dots. They're still in my dresser drawer. But mostly, I use them and then bring them back. Clean. Slide them into the bottom of her bag. Never thought she knew.'

'But you hoped she did.'

Now he did turn to look at Isabelle, making direct eye contact. 'I don't know what I hoped. I knew she couldn't give me precisely what I wanted.'

'Which is?'

He closed his eyes. The muscles in his back tensed, and he could feel his penis digging deeper into Jodie's cloud-like down duvet. This. This was what he wanted. Exposure. Punishment. Pain. All of that would equal pleasure for him. He'd been able to convince himself that fantasies were enough. Now, he realised that he'd been denying the truth, keeping himself away from what he wanted more than anything else.

'Say it, Luke.'

But he wouldn't. She couldn't make him, could she? If she and Jodie were so goddamn pleased with themselves for setting him up, then Isabelle could just go figure it out herself. Faced away again, eyes shut, he waited. But not for long. He felt Isabelle move closer to the bed and reach for his wrists. Then he felt the cold bite of metal close over his skin as she snapped the cuffs into place. Immediately, he strained against the bindings, like an animal testing the boundaries of a leash, and he discovered that she'd locked him up as tightly as she could.

The belt found its mark again, and Lucas's body contracted into one tight rod of muscles. He wouldn't make a sound. Not yet. Not for a long time. With each blow, his body grew warmer, his cock harder. Impossibly hard. Until he wasn't really feeling the pain any more. He was above or below it – beyond it. He knew the sensation. Sometimes when he worked out with heavy weights, he achieved this strange mental level where he knew his muscles were too weak to lift any more, but he did it anyway. Mind over muscle. Something like that. Forced himself to continue beyond the point of no return. When he stood up after a routine like that, he felt as if he were floating, or flying. Felt as if the world wasn't really there.

Isabelle knew how to take him to that same level with the belt. Swing hard and land firmly, then let a light blow fall directly on a growing bruise. Push him past his preconceived limits, break through any boundaries. He shuddered when she caught the rounded part of his ass, and arched when she landed the belt right at the sweet spot. His body spoke for him, because he refused to give in to her with his voice. That was as much resistance as he had left in him.

She was good, this girl. Standing right next to the bed, swinging and landing in all the right places. She acted as if this were the most natural thing she'd ever done. And maybe it was. Maybe, with the really good doms, this type of situation came naturally. He'd seen things like this at clubs, had watched, awestruck, as some dom dressed in black pushed a sub to the brink and then some.

Isabelle was different, though, because unlike those scenarios he'd viewed and even acted in at Club Triple X, she appeared real. She understood. She knew just what he needed, and figured out how to take him there. Speaking to him in an undertone, she encouraged him to confess.

'Be a good boy for once, Luke,' she murmured to him. 'Tell me your secrets.'

Yet she didn't seem to mind that he remained quiet. Maybe she had figured out that the language of his body was more powerful than words could ever be. He gave himself up to her, letting her know that he would take what she had to give. And, oh, could she give. Never heating him up too much in one particular spot, just warming him all over. He pressed his face against the pillow, the muscles in his back tight as he waited for the release he understood awaited him.

Nick and Jodie shared their second kiss against the wall in the sprawling kitchen of the estate. Black-and-white tiled floors. Amethyst glass-fronted cabinets. The scent of tuberose in the air. But, most importantly, there were no guests, only the possibility of the help coming in to catch them, and that wouldn't have been the worst thing in the world.

Nick gripped Jodie in his arms and lifted her on to the cool tile counter. He wanted to hold her as tightly as he could, dig his fingers into her arms, bite into her bottom lip, and force her to make a noise – to let him know exactly how she was feeling.

But this wasn't the place.

They could hear the sounds of the partying guests making their rounds through the different rooms: hitting the bar, the buffet, the displays with high prices marked out to show the winning numbers. But those sounds were just background noise. All Nick wanted to hear was Jodie. Hear her talk. Hear her breathe.

She was the one who'd led him back here, the one who had stood on her tiptoes to give him the kiss, starting them both on this road where his heart was pounding so loudly in his head that he couldn't hear anything else.

'I know you,' she said, pulling away and looking directly into his eyes.

'From the gym.'

'From other places. I've seen you.'

Was he that bad a private detective? Had she known all along that he was following her? And if so, what would that mean to her – to him – to the job he was on. His brain had rationalised this already. He was looking for Max, right? Well, what better way to look for Max than to get to know his sole employee. 'Get to know' was in quotes, of course. There were so many ways to get to know someone, and what Nick wanted was the most base way possible. He wanted to get to know her from the inside out. But what did Jodie mean that she'd seen him?

'At a club,' she continued, offering more clues in her sly little way.

Now, he stared down at her, trying to place her. Was she telling him secrets? Letting him in on a bit more of herself, a bit more information for him to process.

'Which club?'

'You know,' she said. 'I only go to one.'

So it had been her. At Club Triple X. With the long red hair and those fake green cat-eyes. He wondered whether she had seen him there with Bailey. And if so, what she'd thought of their exchange up on the stage. He couldn't remember everything about the night – because it had been the last night. He'd blocked as much of it from his mind as he could. That's why his brain hadn't wanted to place her in the past. More unwilling than unable.

'You're not with her any more then? The wisp of a blonde.'

Yeah, she had seen him with his ex. What did that mean?

Nick shook his head, waiting for Jodie to continue with her questioning. When had the power shifted? Why was she the one doing the interrogating, and why did he not mind in the slightest? Maybe because, with each question, she rubbed her body up and down along his, sliding the seam between her legs along the centre of his own body. She sent a charge of electricity through him each time his hard-on pressed against her crotch, even with both of them still completely clothed. He could only imagine what it might be like to slide against her when the two were totally naked. And that was easy to picture: heaven. It would be pure heaven.

'How long did it last?'

'Not long enough,' he said, surprised at how truthful his answer was.

'And then you broke it off.'

He shook his head again.

'She left you?'

Now, he gave her the smile of a loser. Half-turned-up lips, nod of the head, a shrug as if it didn't really matter. Not any more. Yes, she'd left him. For his partner. What did that make him sound like?

'Can't believe it,' she said.

'Wasn't meant to be –'

George entered the room as he spoke. And he glanced from Jodie to Nick to Jodie again.

'You're captivating my date,' he said to Nick. 'You really shouldn't do that. Not unless you're asking for a duel.'

Nick looked down at Jodie, expecting her to answer the man. He thought for sure she'd tell him that she was the one who'd started their little kissing session. But Jodie remained silent, her eyes wide and innocent, waiting to see what Nick would do.

Confused again when Jodie didn't explain, Nick took a step away from the counter. 'Sorry, man,' he said, staring at Jodie instead of George. Why did she just sit there, looking at him? Daring him. He didn't need that. 'Sorry,' he said again, palms raised outward, 'won't let it happen again.'

When she was done with the belt, Isabelle kissed each fiery stroke that she'd marked on Lucas's skin. She made everything better with the wet heat of her mouth, with the way her fingers danced over those deep berry-red lines. Her tongue flicked up and down, creating the most stirring sensations within him. Pain and pleasure crumbled into one another. Each flick of her tongue brought the hurt of the blow right back up to the present. And each time she pressed harder, he throbbed against the mattress. He thought he'd come right on the bed; that he wouldn't even need her to slide one hand beneath his body, to work him with a few knowing jerks. He'd climax without her ever touching him directly.

But he didn't.

Isabelle knew how to make the most of the situation; how to make it last. Lucas didn't have to say anything, didn't need to tell her what he wanted or ask for any wish to be granted. She simply knew. And she made him fly with the unfolding waves of pleasure she imparted.

'Roll over,' she told him finally. He sighed at the sound of those magic words, and achingly slowly, he obeyed. He could feel the welts cushioned by Jodie's soft blanket, and he could feel his erection, bone-straight, pointing towards the ceiling.

'Oh, lovely,' Isabelle murmured. 'That's just what I needed.'

Without another word, she climbed astride him, placing her hands on his chest and arching her back to slip up and down the velvety sleek pole. Lucas wished that his arms were free so that he could help her, cradle her waist and do the work for her. But that wasn't what would bring Isabelle over the top. She left him cuffed to Jodie's headboard, continuing to over-power him even without a weapon in her hand. From staring into her eyes, he saw the force there, and he understood that she would take her own pleasure from him. Wring it from him.

Let her, he thought. Just let her.

Chapter Twenty-One

Nick couldn't get Jodie out of his mind. That was a fact. No matter what he did. No matter how many old movies he played. He sat in his apartment, staring at the computer, re-reading the notes he'd made thus far about the case. But there really wasn't a case, was there? He'd been asked to keep an eye on Max Sterling and, when Max refused to reveal himself, he'd turned his eye on Jodie instead. And now he couldn't turn away.

So what did that mean? In the past, when a case kept him up at night, he'd thrown himself deeper into it. The only way out, he'd learned, was to go through. Just keep on ploughing forward, often not even knowing what he was looking for, until the clues finally sorted themselves into the proper order.

That's what usually happened. He'd only failed on a few cases, and those times, he'd run into dead-ends that couldn't be resurrected. But this was a different problem. This time he had too many live leads: Jodie; Isabelle; Lucas; George.

What the fuck?

He thought about what George had said to him the previous evening. He was in computers, web design. Curious suddenly, Nick went to the computer and typed in the URL for www.yoursforthetaking.com. He scrolled through the different pieces of information at the bottom of the page until he found the web provider. And finally – though he was scared to admit it – things started to make sense to Nick Hudson.

Humboldt was cow country. Nick had never seen so many heifers before. They stood by the roadside, heads poking through barbed-wire fence, munching on the greenery on the street side. Did cows behave like so many of the people that Nick ran into? Did they *also* think the grass was greener on the other side of the fence? Now, there was a crazy thought. But it seemed as if most of the bovines preferred munching in the most awkward positions imaginable. As he passed the different herds, he met the gaze of several black-and-white bossies. No, they didn't look as if they had a thought in the world.

'Must be nice,' Nick muttered to himself. Here he was, with so many thoughts in his head he couldn't keep them straight. Wouldn't he rather be somewhere else, lost in a big field, gazing up at the striking blue sky, thinking of absolutely nothing?

No, not really. Relaxation didn't suit Nick in that way. If he were honest with himself then he had to admit he liked confusing situations. He liked chewing on facts rather than cud. This drive gave him plenty of time to think, but by the time he reached his destination, he was ready for a break from the car. It seemed a totally different world from the high-end bustle of San Francisco, and yet he was still in California, even after six hours of driving. What a difference from the east coast, where six hours would win you a pass through four or five states, all crammed together in a tightly packed seaside corner.

As he parked his car in front of Wolverine Web Service, he realised that the country was changing. Even though the pungent smell of animals perfumed the air, this particular street was dominated by the electronic age: a computer store on the corner; a cell phone hook-up centre; DVDs and CDs filling the racks of a once-hip vinyl record store. Nick was a throwback to an earlier time. Although he'd finally upgraded to a high-end media centre, due to his love of old movies, he still relished the feel of real records, even the skips in slightly warped LPs. It was with great sadness that he watched the demise of his favourite vinyl stores.

Shaking his head, he pushed his way through the glass front door of Wolverine. He found himself in a tiny lobby, fitted with two space-age modular chairs that looked distinctly uncomfortable, and a white plastic desk in the shape of a lima bean. Behind the desk sat George, the man who'd been Jodie's date at the most recent gala.

'Long time no see,' the handsome creature purred, turning away from the monitor and setting his chin in his hand. Today, George was dressed in a slippery-looking long-sleeved green shirt with a whisper thin yellow tie. He was fairly high fashion for Humboldt, Nick thought, and he wondered what the locals made of this city-slicker style. 'You change your mind, baby? Rewire your synapses?'

Nick shook his head automatically. Here he was, confronted with the link that he thought he'd discover, but still he felt overwhelmed. Why did every encounter with Jodie or her associates leave him in a state of near-total confusion?

'Then you must need web service? I could design something for you, Nicky. The perfect website. You said you were into research, wasn't it?'

'Something like that. Right now, I'm looking for someone –'

'Aren't we all?'

'The person behind www.yoursforthetaking.com.'

Now, the honey-blond stunner was the one to shake his head. But he didn't appear the least bit surprised by Nick's request. 'Can't give out that sort of information. Confidential, you understand.'

'To the police, maybe?'

Again, the little headshake. 'We could only tell them that we receive an anonymous electronic payment each month deposited directly into our bank account. There's nothing illegal about the site – nothing even slightly pornographic, which is legal anyway, you know, as long as the viewers are of age, and of course, we all know what kids are like. Who's to stop someone from claiming to be twenty-one or over? You should see the stuff you can get away with.'

'I'm not interested in sex.'

'That's not what I heard.'

And again, Nick just stopped and stared.

'Why don't we go get a coffee somewhere,' George suggested. 'Just the two of us. And I can tell you all I know.' He made a little click with his tongue against the roof of his mouth. 'Every dirty little secret –'

'You wouldn't though,' Nick guessed. 'You'd tell me some of what you know, enough to cloud my mind a bit, and then you'd put your hand high up on my thigh and whisper sweet nothings to me. And I'd tell you again that I don't swing that way.'

'But you *do* swing.' George grinned. 'Don't you?'

When he returned to his car, Nick felt a wave of confusion run through him. What had he learned? Nothing really. Nothing absolute. Only that the providers of the site about shoplifting employed George, a friend/acquaintance/casual date of Jodie Silver's. He stopped his Jeep in front of the most cow-filled field and stared out at the grazing heifers.

He had a strong feeling that Jodie was behind the site, but so what? George was right. There was absolutely nothing illegal about posting pretty pictures on the web, about writing reviews and columns.

Was he a step closer to Max? No.

Was he a step closer to having sex with George? Not in this lifetime.

He gazed out at the grazers and sighed. A wasted weekend. That's exactly what this had been. But then, why didn't he feel more disappointed? That was the big question. It seemed that as long as he was concentrating on Jodie, he felt electrified.

Chapter Twenty-Two

'I have a confession to make,' Isabelle said as she poured Jodie a glass of chilled white wine. 'A secret, maybe, more than a confession.'

'A secret?' Jodie cooed. 'I love secrets.' When Isabelle stared at her, waiting, Jodie grinned. 'I understand. Don't worry. That means you don't want me to tell anyone, right?'

'It's a risk, I know. But I trust you.'

'You're not really a woman.'

Isabelle's deep blue eyes widened. 'That would be a magic trick, Jo. Not a confession. You've been down there yourself enough times to know the real thing when you taste it.'

'I was just fucking with you.' She took a sip of her wine and sized up her friend. 'All right, let me try again.' Jodie contemplated the ceiling fan as she thought. 'Actually, you do wear underpants. You were only saying that to shock me.'

'Like I'd try to shock you.'

Jodie giggled. 'But you do. You always try. Even though we both know I'm completely unshockable.'

'That's a lie. I'm not even going to go there.'

'All right. You've reconsidered your position and you are going to prosecute after all.'

'Right. I'm going to the police about those panties you stole. They'll lock you away for, oh, seven minutes or so –'

'I give up.'

'I think I'm falling for Lucas. No, that's not it. I know I am. Definitely.'

Now, Jodie actually did look shocked. 'And you're not kidding me, are you? You wouldn't tease me about something that serious.'

'How does that make you feel?'

'Why, is that a secret?'

'Not from you,' Isabelle explained. 'From him. If Lucas knew for sure how I already feel, then he'd have more power over me than I want him to. But again, Jodie, I need to know how this makes you feel.'

Jodie thought about it before answering. How did she feel? Christ, ecstatic. Isabelle was perfect for Lucas, wasn't she? Lucas and Jodie had never really been more than casual sex partners who really, really liked each other. 'Liked' in the way you liked your best friend, not the way you hoped someone would some-day feel about you: knocked down by a combination of love and lust for you. What she was craving was a different emotion entirely.

Isabelle took Jodie's silence to mean the opposite of what it did. 'I'm sorry,' she said. 'You hate me.'

'I could never.'

'Then you're sorry that you introduced me to Lucas, and that you asked me to take care of him for you.'

'No,' Jodie said, shaking her head. 'I couldn't be more pleased than if I'd planned this outcome myself.' There. That was almost the truth. Because she had planned it herself, hadn't she?

Even though Nick was making progress, he was still having a difficult time figuring it all out. In fact, he was sick with it. Sick of even trying. The employer was now appearing more sinister than the prey. He could get no information from the client, except to keep going forwards. But there was no forwards as far as he could tell. There was only this stagnant place that resembled his version of hell. No action. No satisfaction.

He'd headbutted on cases before; coming to a brick

wall and then crashing into it. He never stopped in time. He always wound up with cuts and bruises; battered scars to his well-wounded ego. But this was different, because this time he felt that he was being constantly steered in the wrong direction and pointed to places that made no sense.

What he should do is just confront Jodie and have it out with her. Do you like me, Jodie Silver? Are you just messing with me for fun? Are you fucking Max?

He tried that sentence again, slower, with a different inflection.

Are *you* fucking Max?

Was she Max?

Could that even be possible?

And, if so, what did it really matter? All he knew was that she liked to play around with blond men, bringing different ones with her to different auctions. He knew that she liked to kiss him in public places – first the hovercraft and then at the party. And he also knew that she liked to steal, but he'd never caught her in the act of taking something big, yet. Nobody had, as far as he could tell.

His head hurt. He sat down in his living room staring at the black-and-white movie that flickered there. Finally he gave up for the night, grabbed his leather trench coat, and headed to the Triple X.

At least *there* he'd find some release.

To Nick, San Francisco was like a woman: coolly beautiful, yet curiously ambivalent. A woman who, more likely than not, wouldn't deign to date him but who would flirt like hell just to let him know what he was missing. Each city he'd lived in had a different human feel. New York was all male: towers; spires; pointy and phallic. Los Angeles was bi, definitely: bi-sected by highways; bi-sexual, with its feminine valleys and vistas and masculine asphalt and architecture. He liked to think of his homes in human form, because it made his surroundings seem more personal for him. But San Francisco was difficult to peg. Yes, the city felt like a she, but it was a she who was busy with her own inner turmoil. And, in this city, it was a she who might once have actually been a he.

Moody and unpredictable, the city was divided into poetic sounding regions: North Beach; Seacliff; Russian Hill; The Sunset; Potrero Hill. This jewel by the bay was a compact, walkable city. Salt-tinged air and a constant shroud of silver fog created a mysterious ambiance.

Unlike the sprawling mass of Los Angeles, with its intense buffer zones surrounding the ritzy neighbourhoods, San Francisco was a true melting pot, a free-for-all fondue. Turn the wrong corner in what the locals called 'Ess-Eff', and you could wind up in a frightening environment. An unexpected place where street people walked in front of your car, not caring that you could mow them down – not even seeming to be aware that if they ever actually decided to start a battle between human and automobile, the car would win every time. Here, the fanciest stores in Union Square were only three blocks from sidewalk crap games. Here you could walk out of an elite department store and throw a rock into the centre of a homeless haven.

Well-manicured parks provided business sites for drug dealers. Some of the city's most famous architecture butted up against its seediest situations. In SF, you could dine at one of the four-star restaurants, then walk to one of the city's many famed sex show theatres for a little after-dinner lap dance.

What all this meant was that to find a dark spot in the city, you merely needed to turn the corner. What you craved – whatever you craved – was always only a few steps away. Take Triple X, for instance, the sex club that catered to the most upscale fetishists in the city; it was centrally located down the block from the hotel favoured by foreign dignitaries, up the street from the best heroin in the city and around the corner from the Modern Art Museum. Whatever you wanted; it was all there.

That was, of course, for a price.

Isabelle was the one to suggest a night at Triple X.

'I'm not in the mood,' Jodie sighed, wrapping the lavender terry-cloth towel tight around her still-wet body. Steam from the shower curled the hair around her face, turning her dark tresses into an ornate frame.

'You're uptight. It'll help you unwind.'

Jodie shrugged. 'You really want to go. That's what this is all about, isn't it?'

'I really want to go,' Isabelle agreed, parting the wing-like flaps on her black trench coat to reveal the skimpy outfit beneath. Jodie smiled when she saw how much thought Isabelle had put into the evening.

'All right,' she said finally. 'Help me get ready and we'll go.'

'You look perfect.' Isabelle grinned. 'Just the way you are.'

'Totally naked?'

'You'll raise a few eyebrows, maybe, but isn't that the point?'

'How am I going to get there? Taxis pick up naked people on street corners?'

'They'd stop for you.'

'Be serious.'

'Slide on your coat, wear some killer mules, and we're out of here.'

In the car on the short ride over, Jodie leaned against Isabelle's tight body. 'I know why you really want to go.'

'Then tell me.'

'You want to see the transformation.'

'Can't I see that at home?'

Jodie laughed. 'There's a power in an audience. You understand that just as well as I do.' She turned to look out the window at the passing San Francisco architecture. Rows of multi-coloured Victorians, slammed together in an array of pastels that, during the daytime, appeared like something from a fairy tale. At night, the houses simply seemed too close together, pressing one on top of another, like Jodie crushed into Isabelle's body. A tremor ran through her.

Would he be there tonight?

Lucas was playing the part of amateur detective on his own. Or, more honestly, he was playing the role of horny dick. He trailed Jodie and Isabelle in his own car, following the women to the club and then sitting hunched over to watch them pass by the bouncer with no trouble at all. Jodie had simply flashed open her coat and the man let them in. What was she wearing underneath? Lucas could only guess.

He, on the other hand, knew exactly what he had beneath his clothes: a pair of Jodie's panties, ones he'd never be able to return now, because they were seriously stretched out over his muscular thighs. He loved the way they felt beneath his slacks. He loved slitting the zippered crotch of his expensive suit pants and running his fingertips over his cock, clad in those lilac silk panties. Having sex with Isabelle hadn't made his need to purloin panties any less real.

Maybe he should go into the club, too. Act as if he'd shown up on a whim. He thought about that for a moment before opening the door.

Intense blue light filtered down on the crowd, making the dancers look as if they were moving underwater. The lights changed with the beat of the songs, but the colour never varied, only the intensity: pale sky blue; watery ocean blue; the deepest cobalt; the brightest sapphire. The colour tied everything together – made the motley assortment of people momentarily share in their appearance. Skin colours had no meaning. Clothing all melted into blue.

Then a new DJ took the floor, bringing with him a new light designer for his shift. And the world became more normal again, or as normal as could be expected in a situation such as this one. Lights swirled over the crowd in shocking pinks and electrifying greens. The beat of the music intensified – it was almost 2 a.m., now, and this DJ's job was to keep the energy on the rise.

Several stages were already busy with sexual activity. Three handsome women worked together on one stage, engaged in light-hearted sexual spanking. On another circular platform, two men made a human sandwich out of a nubile young blonde. The lights flickered over this stage, illuminating the girl's face, her eyes open wide, her lips parted dramatically. She was moaning – that was obvious – even though the sound of her voice was drowned out by the raucous rhythm of the dance music.

At three o'clock, the main stage would be lit, and the music would become secondary to the art: the art of sex. That stage was dark now, but in the centre was a wooden horse, with straps to capture trembling limbs and, leaning against the horse, a bone-tipped crop.

Isabelle and Jodie moved closer to that stage. This was where the real action was going to take place.

'Don't you want to dance?' Isabelle asked.

Jodie shook her head. 'I want to wait.'

The lights in the entire club dimmed, and then a golden spotlight came on over that stage. Still, it remained empty. This was the challenge. Who from the audience would take the dare? After a moment, Jodie pulled herself free from Isabelle's embrace and made her way up the stairs to the stage. Isabelle sucked in her breath as she watched, remembering Jodie from the time before – the succulent redhead with the arresting green eyes.

In the centre of the stage Jodie stood and waited. The music faded and the DJ took the microphone and launched into a quick ad-libbed spiel. 'Here she is, ladies and gentlemen. A feline-looking brunette with silvery eyes and a lean physique. Who is going to top her tonight?'

While many of the patrons looked as if they'd spent hours preparing for the club, Jodie appeared perfectly at ease in her unusual situation. It seemed from her sense of self that she had simply emerged from the outer world into this strange, dark place, with no need for transitioning. The lights flickered over her again, and she stood up even straighter. Here was the question. Who would join her?

Not Isabelle. Not Lucas, who had made his way into the club and stood next to the killer blonde. Finally, Nick worked his way through the crowd, climbed up the steps, and stared into Jodie's eyes.

You game for this? his expression seemed to say.

Jodie nodded.

They audience was quiet. They were all here to see a show, weren't they? That's why they'd paid the extravagant cover price. It's why they were still here, in the wee morning hours, rather than home in bed like good little girls and boys.

Jodie, such a gorgeous submissive, was obediently cuffed into place: legs bound; wrists captured. Yet she seemed so at peace. Isabelle was captivated by her expression. Eyes open. Back straight.

'You ready?' Nick whispered to her. Still, Isabelle heard. She was that close.

'Yes, sir.'

'Good girl,' he said, and Isabelle felt her pussy tightening at the words. Because this was the start; this was the very beginning. Something good was about to happen. Something that would make her come. As Isabelle watched, the man lifted the crop and brought it down on Jodie's naked ass. She arched forward, but kept her mouth closed. She didn't cry out. Didn't cry at all. Her eyes took on a hot glow. She seemed to be processing the sensation deep within herself.

The man immediately lined a second blow beneath the first. And then a third. Jodie remained contained the entire time. She didn't make a noise. She didn't beg for mercy. That wouldn't have been expected anyhow, not so early in the night, but still ... There was no reaction at all. Isabelle had seen many shows like this one – she'd been in them herself. Never had she witnessed a sub so completely in control.

'You want something else?' the man said.

'Yes.'

'You want to be free?'

She nodded, not responding.

'You think you can take it?'

Her face held a defiant look that Isabelle admired. She liked strength.

'Ask nicely then,' he said, and now the dark-haired submissive shut her eyes. She was looking inside herself for the right response, Isabelle thought. She was searching it out. If she asked nicely, would that get her what she wanted? If she disobeyed, was that the way to play?

Jodie bit her lip. She squirmed for the first time, testing her bonds and finding herself firmly caught in place. Then she tilted her chin down, opened her eyes, and did what she always did best. She did what came naturally to her. In a heartbeat, in a breath, Jodie Silver stole the show.

Nick understood. Finally, he understood. She had been testing him this whole time, because she was waiting to see if he would take charge. As soon as he realised this, that power flickered inside him. Because yes, he could take charge. When he wasn't so deeply lost in a case, confused and confounded, he was a very admirable top.

With Jodie, he let her free and then watched her take what he had to give and, as she pleased him, he knew – knew for sure – exactly who she was.

Back at her apartment after the show, Isabelle slid her body over Lucas's. She let him feel her – all over without using his hands. She let him see her, even though the blindfold kept out any bit of light. Sight wasn't only for eyes. True vision could take place in the sole caress of skin on skin. But, most importantly, she made him wait, even though she knew that he'd been waiting for this moment for a long time. She let him wait even longer, because anticipation was the most important weapon she had to use. If she could make him tremble before her initial touch then he would be hers forever.

'You'd beg me if you could, wouldn't you?' she murmured, firm fingertips stroking along the gag that separated his lips. He was silent. She saw his body shudder, though, unable to hide the flinch that flickered through it. Words didn't compare with the language of the human body. Words could lie but, as far as Isabelle was concerned, the body could not.

'You'd beg me to start, because waiting is the hardest part.'

Now, he nodded, almost in spite of himself, and she took her time gazing at him. God, he was stunning, lovely, even, if one could safely use that word to describe a man as masculine as he was. And she knew all about him, which made the evening even more enjoyable. Sometimes, learning while doing was fun. Digging deep into a new lover's psyche was always exciting, searching to see if she and a new mate would be a match, if their desires echoed one another. As time passed, she would delve deeper, uncovering more and more of the fantasies of her new bedmate. But having the upper hand, as she did now, gave her an extra charge of pleasure.

'I'm going to set you free,' she whispered. And now he did respond. Clearly, she heard the word 'no', even against the thick fabric of the gag. She laughed. 'No, baby. Don't worry. I don't mean that I'm going to release you from those bonds. I mean that I'm going to set you free. Entirely different. Just wait,' she said, 'and see.'

Lucas had loved every minute of taming Jodie. Playing the dom to her sub had rocked his world. But it hadn't been honest. It had only been a game. With Jodie, he'd been incapable of denying her any desire. And what she'd wanted was a strong man with a firm hand. She was in charge of so much in her world, she needed the relaxation that came with relinquishing her power.

Giving himself over to the domination of Isabelle made him harder than anything ever had before. She knew exactly what he wanted, and that made him feel safe. Safe enough to relax into the pain of the belt against his skin. Safe enough to actually cry when he came. Her mouth working on him, her fingers digging into him. She created a pain-pleasure mix that had him riding higher and higher until he couldn't hold back. At the moment of climax, she made a satisfied humming noise with her mouth, and those vibrations further enhanced his orgasm. He saw flashes of light behind the blindfold, heard his heart pounding as loud as the drumbeat of an acid-toned garage band.

As soon as he'd come, she was on him, pulling away the blindfold, undoing the cuffs, as if she knew what he'd want next was to move. He picked her up in his powerful embrace, rolled her over on the bed, and plunged inside her, growing hard again while surrounded by the warm, wet heat of her willing pussy.

Isabelle's ocean blue eyes held his gaze as he took her, Missionary-style. He slammed his body into hers, trying to change that expression on her face from one of passive acceptance to one of untamed bliss. Could he do that?

Her cheeks took on a warmer glow as he slid his body against hers. The warm wetness of her mouth beckoned him. He leaned forward to kiss her, then bit her bottom lip and made her moan.

Yes, that was it. That was right.

He drove in deeper, using his fingers to part her he slid one finger up and down her hot spot, rubbing lightly, giving her the friction that she needed to reach that final reward. She let him take charge of her pleasure, which was precisely what he desired right now. He couldn't always be the one to give himself up. He needed the sense of accomplishment that could only come from being on top – regardless of whether that was only an illusion.

How did she know? He wouldn't linger on that thought right now. He'd simply take what she had to give and sort out the rest in the light of day.

Yet beneath it all, another question nagged at him. Why had Jodie given him away? Because it was obvious that's what she'd done. She had used him until he no longer suited her, then passed him along to the next owner. Was it how she behaved with all of her belongings? Taking, using, admiring, discarding?

Chapter Twenty-Three

Right. Steal something. Then he'd understand. That made perfect sense, didn't it? If he lived in a galaxy far, far away, maybe. Come on, now, he thought, mystery writers didn't actually have to kill someone in order to think like a murderer. Why should Nick have to steal something to get closer to Jodie Silver?

Because she loved it. That was why. She wanted him to immerse himself in her world yet, at the same time, she obviously didn't think he was capable of doing it. So that was the dare: the thrill of it all. And what was the big problem? He could always mail a cheque to the store for the damage done. Taking was more important than keeping. Slipping something up his sleeve and down his pants – whatever. Making it out the door undetected.

Christ, who was he? Where were these thoughts coming from? He'd never been so oddly influenced by someone before. Never been the kind of guy to do something based solely on peer pressure. He hadn't tried hard-core drugs when they were in. Never dropped acid. Never pretended to like a rock group just because everyone else was into them. Hair bands? Yeah, right. Heroin? No thank you. So peer pressure didn't have much of an effect on someone like him, who seemed to have based his entire life on emulating a hero in a movie. What would Bogie do? Who thought like that?

But she wanted him to try it. He understood that from reading the words on her website. In order to get closer to her, he had to do it just once. Was that the definition of peer pressure? Was that what this was? Everyone else was doing it – everyone he had his eye on, anyway: Lucas, with his exotic and erotic panty raids; Isabelle, trying her hand at being a thief in order to please Jodie; and Jodie herself, the Queen of the Thieves, unable to pass by anything that wasn't pinned down without sliding some prize into her pocket.

When he thought about it like that, then there was no question. He didn't have to take something because he didn't have to prove anything to her. This was who he was – good at heart. Maybe he liked some kinky things in bed, but he didn't force anyone to do something unwanted. He was kind, compassionate, caring. Jesus. Get over it, Nick, he told himself. Take the fucking thing and be done with it. Nobody will know. Nobody but you.

And maybe her.

That was right. She re-read her words, nodding to herself. Then she saved the text as an html file and uploaded it to her website. Give the poor boy a fighting chance, right? It wasn't fair to play him in this manner; to toy with him as if he were someone useful only for her amusement. No, he could be so much more. If he set his sights high enough, he could reach the very top. That's where he wanted to go, wasn't it? That's where she could take him.

Do it. Take it. You know you want to.

Nick stopped reading. Oh, fuck. Was she writing to him directly. Urging him on?

Cut the bullshit and face your fear. That's all it is. Fear. And you can get through fear. That's the trick. Get through it. Not around it. Not over it. But through it.

Yeah, it seemed as if she might be. Because, from the sound of it, she knew all about him, didn't she? Knew that, more than almost anything else, he hated the thought of being afraid. But he hated the fear of failing even more. Still, he took his time reading once again through the different articles on her site. There was one that claimed a shoplifter was caught an average of once for every 49 times spent stealing. Was that possible? And why was it even up there on Jodie's site? She wasn't a shoplifter at all, was she? She was more like a magician – making things disappear.

She'd done a good job with his sanity, hadn't she?

Pulling his leather jacket on, he headed out of the apartment, not even bothering to sign off.

There were several schools of thought when it came to messing around with criminals in the movies. You had your Bogart style – denying his own passion when confronted with what was morally right. Christ, did Bogie ever get the girl? Not in *The Maltese Falcon* or *Casablanca*. In the first, he got to keep his sense of respect. In the second, he was left only with his buddy. Was that what being a good sport meant? If so, then Bogie could have it. Nick didn't want to go through life like some fucking choir boy. Always doing the right thing and winding up on his own. It's what had happened with Bailey: it wasn't going to happen with Jodie.

There were other styles of Hollywood thieves, as well. Clint Eastwood's ageing jewel thief in *Absolute Power* – taking for the pleasure of it, but well-off enough that he no longer needed the money, only the thrill. There was class in that, wasn't there? Like a master puzzler, Eastwood just needed to prove he could do it. And then he could return the loot. Give it all back, like some sort of game.

And then you had the ever-gallant Cary Grant who'd given up the crime scene years before the story of *To Catch a Thief* even took place. He'd taken the high road, joining society at a level that allowed him to flirt with

Grace Kelly. Or the cunning thief of *The Thomas Crown Affair*, not needing to steal, at all, but doing it for the rush and then returning the goods.

But what happened when the criminal wooed another over to her side? What would have happened if Bogie had taken both the bird *and* the girl? Would that have been so unbelievable?

Chapter Twenty-Four

From a 'what's hot' column in the *SF Wild Side*:

Fashion is like love; transient and inexplicable. Something popular one day loses its power to captivate the next. But fashion is also fickle. Trends come and go quickly – but they do come and go. Leopard spots make their appearance every so often. Artillery belts come into play, and then fall by the side to make room for something new. That's art. In one day, out the next.

Fashion shows are art, as well, which lingerie creator Heidi Linsome knows extremely well. This twenty-six-year-old *fashionista* exploded on to the scene by first staging lingerie shows in strip clubs. She paid the 'models' to wear her one-of-a-kind pieces, while the audience paid for the girls to take them off. As soon as Linsome grew more well known (read more 'accepted') she had to find a way to upstage that concept. And she did so without a problem. At her recent shows in Europe, Linsome showed models dressing and undressing on the stage, while the titillated audience watched, mesmerised by the sight. Women wanted the pieces for themselves. Men wanted ... well, they wanted what it is that all men tend to want.

But now, Ms Linsome comes to San Francisco, and her artistry as a theatrical director of fashion continues. Her new show will be displayed as part of the Transformed Treasures exhibit. 'What?' you say. 'Lingerie and art combined? How is that possible?' According to Elizabeth Carson, curator at ARTone, Ms Linsome's lingerie *is* art.

The show, a benefit for community art programmes,

is by invitation only, but the ticket is a hot one. We've already learned that thousands of dollars have been offered for entrance into this sensual explosion of art and eroticism.

Stay tuned.

From Heidi's show in Europe, Jodie had learned how to capture the attention of a crowd and, with Heidi's help and Isabelle's experience, the three women staged what could only be called the fashion show of the season. Held at the ARTone museum, amongst the Transformed Treasures exhibit, the lingerie became the framework for the jewels themselves.

The models for the show were supplied generously by Cameron. Or, rather, Jodie had access to the women because of Cameron. The girls had all readily agreed. The finishing touches were the fact that all of the women were wearing replicas of the jewellery displayed in the cases. In order to have the pieces made, Elizabeth had allowed Jodie private access to each and every piece.

That was the first trick.

Nick was in the museum as a hired employee. His job was to guard the jewellery on display while looking like one of the guests. In order to blend in with the upscale crowd, he'd had to go shopping. This evening, he had on a pair of maroon pants, a black shirt, black belt, and black engineer boots. He looked hip, like any one of the millionaires milling around the room but, unlike the rest of them, his eyes were focused on the gems.

Yet his mind was focused on a different jewel entirely.

What was Jodie up to? He knew she was involved in the event, yet he couldn't figure out her angle. With everything so carefully protected, how was she going to pull a heist here? All he could do was watch. That was OK, since watching was something Nick never grew tired of.

Jodie entered the room first, dressed in a filmy silver negligée. Her dark hair was down and straight. Her eyes were painted in an elaborate Cleopatra style. Directly behind her came Cameron's six girlfriends, followed by Heidi and Isabelle.

The women moved through the crowd as if they didn't see the people around them. Each model was wearing at least one replica of an item on display. As the girls moved to stand by the cases where the real gems were displayed, Nick followed Jodie, knowing somehow which corner she would reside in. No surprise there at all. He knew she would choose the place that was the centre of attention: the Unforgiving Heart. How perfect was that.

For over an hour, the models moved through the crowd. Exotic drinks were served to the guests in tall glasses, and the rustling whispers of the attendees let on to how pleased people were with the show. For this event, Heidi didn't have the models robe and disrobe in public. That would have been too much for this particular crowd. However, she did bring out items that raised more than eyebrows among the viewers. Nipple-revealing bras; and panties that showed the cleft of a perfect ass. Although this was the first showing of the jewellery in the Bay Area, very few eyes were on the display cases.

An order sheet listing the names and prices of the lingerie items was passed out to those who wished to buy. Customers made small check marks by the items that intrigued them. Then, at ten o'clock, the lights suddenly went out. There was a rumble of shocked whispers through the crowd, as people reached for one another. When the lights came back on, the models were gone – their lingerie left in puddles of rippling silk where they had stood – and the display cases were empty.

Headlines screamed about the jewel theft in the morning editions – in San Francisco's main newspaper, the story even appeared above the fold. By the afternoon edition, however, tempers had cooled as the museum announced the full recovery of the items missing. Detective Nick Hudson was interviewed by several stations about his part in recovering the stolen gems. He was thoroughly questioned about what he knew about the situation, and how he had managed to crack the case so quickly. That was what everyone wanted to know. How many people were behind such a clever heist? Why had the gems been taken at all?

Standing in front of the police station, Nick stared into the TV cameras. He hadn't slept yet, and he looked scruffy in a gangster way. A small smile played over his lips as he announced that Max Sterling, famed importer, had been named as the lead suspect in the case. Sterling, who now seemed to have disappeared to Europe, was also believed to be responsible for several other recent break-ins. The jewels themselves had been recovered quickly – not one item was missing. People were welcome to come see the jewellery display first hand at the museum. With a wave, he brushed off further questions. That was all he had time to say.

'Mr Hudson –' a reporter called out as he made his way down the stairs.

'Excuse me,' he said, pushing past, 'I can't talk any more. At the moment, I have a pressing engagement.'

Nick stood at the threshold of the Marina condo, waiting. Beyond the crash of the Bay only blocks away, he thought he could actually hear the sound of his heart pounding. The level of insecurity pulsing through his body made him feel nervous as hell, but not willing to flee. To calm himself, he mentally replayed all he'd learned over the past months. What if he was wrong?

But then again, what if he were right?

When the door finally opened, he took a step forwards and said, 'Max Sterling?' His voice was both hoarse and husky, and he found it difficult to keep up a steady eye contact, but he forced himself not to back down. But bending down, now that was something else. Bending on one knee and looking up. Yeah, that was something else entirely.

So he'd found her out. Uncovered her secret. And it hadn't made him run away, hadn't done anything except bring him closer to her. Bring him exactly where she wanted him. How was that for the work of a master planner?

'Will you?' Nick whispered. 'Will you, Maxine Jodie Silver?'

Jodie nodded, unable to keep the smile off her face as she watched Nick kneel before her and offer over a little black velvet box. When she opened the tiny container, her smile broadened. It was the black sapphire ring. *The* ring. Jodie slid the band on to her finger and admired the beautiful jewel shining through her tears.

Nick had discovered her secret, hadn't he? But then, she'd stolen his heart. And in the end, that was a fair enough trade for the pussycat burglar, wasn't it?

Epilogue

The real treasure wasn't something to be stolen; it was a secret to be discovered. And Nick's world was filled with secrets. Yet this one was different. Because this one was inside him. The secret need to be with Jodie. To do to her the things that she needed to be done.

She looked beautiful naked, wearing only the ring on her finger and nothing else. Nick started slowly. He was amazed that he had the presence of mind, the power of mind over body, to make it last. Somewhere inside himself, a voice told him to just get the initial fuck out of the way. Slam his body into hers, meld it with hers, and then afterwards go slow and steady. But that would be a waste. He wouldn't let his dick take control of his mind.

Nick thought about the way Jodie had behaved at the club. Bound until she'd broken free of her bonds. Tamed until she'd proved that she was untameable. The fierceness in her eyes had captivated him then, and it struck him now how steadily she always looked into the face of the person she was with. Unflinching. Unbending. That was rare for a sub, wasn't it? There was a power in that, he realised. A strength in obeying. She obeyed him now: every word, every command, and that made him even harder than he was at the start. Watching her bend over the bed, offering up her back, her thighs, her ass. Where to start? Where to start?

He was still dressed, and that gave him an edge. When he pulled the black leather belt free of the loops of his slacks, Jodie sighed. It was the first real sign that she was as turned on as he was. He hadn't stroked her yet at all, hadn't touched between her legs to feel the wetness, but her sigh let him know, and that was all he needed. He moved closer, then pressed his body to hers. She sighed again and arched her hips, offering herself up even more obviously, making it clear what she wanted from him.

'I won't tie you yet,' he said. 'I'd like to see what you can do.'

'What I can do?'

'What you can take.'

That was different, wasn't it? Two different concepts. He wouldn't push her too far right now. Not at the very start. But he was intrigued to see how deep she would let him go, how much of herself she'd let him see. This was an entirely different situation than at the club, with the audience all around watching. This was one-on-one. More private. More personal.

Was it easier for a sub to behave when others were observing the show? He'd always wondered that. It was easier, by far, for him to keep himself in check when he knew that other doms were evaluating his performance – not that he generally gave a flying fuck what people thought of him. But some part of his ego wouldn't let him put on a bad show, as it wouldn't let him fail on a case. It was a feeling of moral responsibility, if that made any sense.

Oh, she was trembling. Here he was, taking his time, simply enjoying the view of her nude body as he moved against her. Rubbing up and down, he let her feel his erection on her ass, his clothed body against her naked skin. She was so damn pretty, and he knew that she'd be even more lovely after he spanked her. He knew it from watching Isabelle take control of the striking brunette. Knew it from the club, and knew it from a feeling inside himself.

The first strike of the belt on her skin made her groan. That wasn't what he'd expected. He was deeply aware of how well she'd be able to stay contained within herself. But maybe it was the months of fore-play leading up to this point that gave her the freedom to let loose. He let the belt find the roundest part of her ass, and he watched the berry-coloured mark appear against her pale skin. He let the belt land again, and watched the third stripe line up right under the first two. He was good at this game, never working too long in any one place, heating Jodie thoroughly, and making her toss her hair and buck. A pony. A stallion. Waiting to be saddled and ridden hard.

How many would he give her? Just a taste, he thought, a glimmer of what might happen later. They were both too ready to put off the main event for long. Still, he needed to show her that he was in control, which meant that he striped her ass until her face was flushed, her full lips parted in a seemingly endless sigh, and her eyes glistened with impending tears.

No, he wouldn't go that far. He wouldn't make her cry now. He'd wait and see how long that would take – another time. He would stretch it out until she vibrated with the intensity of the pain. Right now, he needed to have her.

Needed it.

'Roll over and put your hands over your head, baby,' he told her, and she instantly followed his order. The way she moved was hypnotising. Every little gesture tugged at him. He wrapped his belt around her wrists, held on to the free lip of it, and pulled tight. Then he slid inside her and Jodie moaned again. Yes, she was ready for him. The scent of her arousal overwhelmed him as soon as he got right up close to her. He rocked hard, once in, once out, and then drove in just as hard again until they were joined together.

'Oh, God, yes,' Jodie sighed, tilting her head back against the pillow. Her eyes were closed for a moment, as if she were lost completely within herself. Then her eyelashes fluttered and she stared directly at Nick as she spoke again. 'That's it. Just keep doing that.'

'You like that?' he said, taunting her, pushing up on his arms and then sliding back inside her again. He gave her only this little sample of pleasure before withdrawing again. A little pressure on her clit, a tiny thrust and, as soon as she sighed again, he slammed back in. He adored doing it like this; the sensations melding together. Rough and sweet, hard and fast. And he liked how Jodie responded; in tune, perfectly matching each of his actions. She seemed as turned-on as he was, ready for anything. Ready forever.

She arched her body to meet his, and he saw how excited she was by everything they'd done, and by everything that they might do in the future.

'Now give me your ass,' he said, and her eyes locked on his for a moment, but she didn't disobey. Slowly, she moved her body, rolling over again so that her ass was in perfect position for him. As if to further encourage him, she lifted up her hips, pressing against his body. His cock, moistened with her juices, slid easily between the cheeks of her ass. He didn't go slow now. He found what he wanted and plunged inside. Jodie let out a harsh breath at the jolt of the intrusion, and then even that turned into a sigh.

Nick pushed in as deep as he could go, and then withdrew almost as quickly. He adored everything about this position. He could look down at the lines on her ass, caused by his own belt, and when he touched them, just gently stroking his fingers over the slightly roughened skin, Jodie contracted tightly on his rod. Now he was the one to moan, but that didn't stop him from continuing the ride. He used his hands to split her ass cheeks wide apart, gazing down as he worked her. Nick liked to watch, seeing the muscles tense and release in Jodie's back, seeing the way her entire body absorbed each thrust. Her asshole tightened against him, and his breath caught as he felt the climax build.

When he came into her, Jodie closed her body around his, swallowing him up. She turned her face to the side, and he saw in her eyes the way she'd looked the first time he kissed her. Then he saw in the depth of those silvery grey eyes something new. Maybe she would always be changing. Maybe he would never own all of her.

A slippery little thief of hearts right to the end.

'There is one little bit of unfinished business,' Jodie said, looking over at her lover. He had the lazy glow in his eyes that she knew meant he was deeply satisfied. But she could tell from his expression that he would be ready to go for a second round in an instant. All she had to do was arch her back and spread her legs and he'd be on top of her again, plunging hard, holding her wrists together over her head, and whispering to her the exact words that she wanted to hear. But first, they had one thing to clear up.

'Don't talk work now,' Nick sighed, tracing his finger-tips along the valley of her flat belly. His touch was light and probing at the same time.

'No, this is important. We've got to settle this business right now. Before we go any further –'

It was amazing to Nick that she could look so in control of herself after behaving so out of control only moments before. That was class, wasn't it? The way she gave herself completely over to a sensation, and then captured all of her emotions back inside her once again. Jodie was one to watch.

'Can you really go further than that?' he asked, teasing. After what they'd just done, Nick couldn't even imagine what their next session might be like.

'Come on,' Jodie said, 'we really do need to talk.'

'You're right,' he finally agreed. 'What are you going to do now that you've given up Max?'

'That's easy: Jodie Silver, Imports and Exports. Time to go into business for myself, don't you think?'

'But not the jewel-stealing business, right?'

She flashed her eyes at him, then nodded. 'No, I'm

done with that. The ARTone heist was my finest hour, orchestrating the disappearance of both the girls and the jewels. Sure, it was an obvious publicity stunt, but I was thrilled to pull that off. It took Heidi and Isabelle, Cameron and George. ARTone had hired many private dicks, and I made sure that Cameron and George were there in the ranks. They were the ones who emptied the cases while the girls and I stripped down and ran to the limo outside.'

'But Liz knew about it all?'

'Of course. She had to.'

'And you made sure that I was positioned right next to the most famous gem of all.'

'I knew you would be. I had every faith in your ability the whole time. I was as sure that you'd take the ring as I was that you'd find the jewels in the Wolverine Web Design office. You were the only one who'd know where to look. You could make it seem as if the creator behind www.yoursforthetaking.com had deposited them there, and you could clear Isabelle and Heidi by portraying them as innocent victims of Max Sterling's charm. They were part of a publicity stunt, while he had a darker motive entirely.'

'But how did you know that I'd figure everything out?' Nick was sprawled next to her, but he'd made sure that their bodies overlapped in several places. Her leg crossed his. One of his hands held hers. They were intertwined in delicious, pretzel-like ways. 'Come on,' he urged her. 'Tell –'

'I knew. Sometimes, you just know.'

'All right,' he said, 'so now which business is it that you feel we haven't finished?' As he asked the question, he glanced up at her. It was obvious from the way he moved his head that he'd prefer to continue gazing at her body. But he forced himself to lock on to her eyes.

'There's the matter of the bill.'

'Bill.'

'For your services rendered.'

'I don't understand, Jodie.'

She untangled herself from his embrace and walked naked to the desk by the window. She looked amazing without clothes on, her body instantly turning him on again. Nick had to force himself to focus on what she was saying. 'You've put in several months, God, probably ten hours a day. You're a workaholic, which I like. I'm one, too. When I have my mind set on something, I can't think of anything else.' While she spoke, she slid into a fresh set of panties and a pair of lounging pyjamas, then she sat on the edge of her chair facing him.

'But what bill?'

'You got the retainer, which I know held you for a little while. But now there's the balance to discuss.'

Nick, suddenly understanding, still found himself in shock. 'You hired me.'

She nodded.

'You hired me.' This time there was more spacing between each word, as if he were trying to convince himself of the truth.

She nodded again.

'I don't get it. Why would you do that? Why would you want me to know what you were up to? Who would it benefit?'

'I saw you at the club, liked what I saw, so I tried to figure out a way to catch your interest. Real interest. Not just some dallying fancy you might have. Have me and leave me. I understand the thrill in that, but I was tired of it. And I thought you and I might have a chance together. That is, if you gave us one.'

'But how'd you know all that?'

'You don't have to be a private eye to get information on someone, you know. Every time you go online, there's an advertisement for finding out your lover's secrets. Learn your spouse's email code. Find the dirt on old boyfriends – or learn the facts on new ones.'

'Those are mostly scams.'

'Sure, but I did some digging of my own. I know your history. You never stay with anyone too long to get attached. I wanted you to get attached to me.'

Nick started to laugh. 'So you hired me –'

'Are you angry?'

He was still amazed at how cleverly she'd managed to fool him. It took finesse, the way she'd worked. And it took style. Two things that Jodie had in spades. But it also took a laxness on his part. He'd refused to see the things that were right in front of him. Clouded by how interested he was in her. More into her than into the case. After a minute, he tried to think back to all the different clues he'd missed. Right away, he realised that the whole situation with Jodie and Isabelle and Cameron and Lucas was about far more than overlapping lies – it was about overlapping *lives*.

'Start at the beginning,' he said. 'That first phone call.'

'That was me, putting on my most aristocratic voice.' She cleared her throat and then adopted a slight British accent as she continued to explain. 'I got an invite to a special event, and I decided to invite you, as well. It came to me on a whim, as a way to stimulate your interest.'

'You're pretty good,' he said, 'and I was extremely hungover. I didn't even consider that the call wasn't legit. When the money was wired to me, I had all the faith in the employer that I needed.' Now he hesitated, trying to piece the remaining fragments together. There were still plenty of things that didn't make sense to him. 'But that lady – the hostess at the party, she knew me.'

'That was easy. I got information to her that said the pieces were being protected by a private detective. That you were the one who had been hired. She had no reason to doubt the veracity of what I told her. It's simple to convince people of things if you act sure enough yourself. Confidence is the number one factor for getting people to believe a lie.'

Nick nodded. He used that bluffing-style method all the time. 'You're good at poker, aren't you?'

Jodie grinned. 'Try me someday. You'll never win.' Then more seriously, she repeated, 'You're not upset?'

'No. Not at all.' As he spoke the words, he realised that they were true. 'Shows what a back-ass private dick I am. I didn't even think to do any research about my employer. Lost so much time just focusing on what you were doing. Who Max really was. What your plans might be. And you were the one with all the informants. Lucas and George and Isabelle. And that blue-haired chick at Airhead. Do you know someone at Sammy's?'

'I know Sammy.'

'And you told him to let me know you were going to Europe, didn't you?'

She nodded.

Secrets, Nick thought again. He remembered talking to Sammy about Isabelle and Jodie, remembered how Sammy acted so cool, as if he'd never seen either girl before. Now, Nick stood up and walked to his clothes.

'You're not leaving?' For the first time, there was a note of fear in Jodie's voice.

He shook his head. Then he reached into his side pocket and pulled out a slim cream-coloured envelope. 'Open it up.'

With one crimson-red nail, she cracked the seal, then pulled out a stiff piece of cream-coloured stationery. It was the type of old-fashioned monogrammed stationery that men used in the 1940s for important personal letters. On it was Nick's resignation letter. He was bowing out of the case rather than turning Jodie in. She smiled broadly when she read the words.

'I didn't have a physical address. I was going to email the employer today to get it.'

'Better to deliver the news in person.' Jodie smiled.

'You didn't really want that ring anyway, did you?' Nick asked.

She shook her head.

'And you must know that the one on your finger's a replica.'

Now, she was the one to nod. 'You wouldn't be who you are if you'd actually stolen the real piece. I knew that you'd find the jewels, and that you'd figure I switched the real with the fake. So you did a double-switch easily enough. It was fun for a fantasy, though.'

Again he had to ask. 'But how'd you know?'

'Secrets,' she said, 'have legs.'

He grinned at her, recognising his own statement coming back to him. So she really did know Sammy, didn't she? That was the only way those words would have been echoed.

'Once you start talking, they start walking.'

'But *you're* not going anywhere,' Nick said, getting off the bed and grabbing Jodie around the waist. He lifted her in his strong arms and brought her back into the centre of the bed. Then he pulled out the bedside drawer and grabbed her regulation steel handcuffs from within. Her eyes were on him as he locked her wrists into place. So she wasn't the only one with a secret or two up her sleeve, or down her garters.

'And you know about the handcuffs, how?' she teased.

'I'm a private eye, sweetheart,' he said in his best Bogart impression. 'It's my job to know.'

She squinted up at him. 'You were here before.'

'Very good.'

'In my bedroom.'

Now, he was the one to nod.

'Where else were you?'

'Where have you been lately?'

She ticked off the different places with a smile in her voice. 'Isabelle's, Cameron's, Heidi's ... I always like having an audience. It was fun to pretend you were there, to imagine that you might be watching. It would have been a let-down not to have found you if I'd looked.'

He moved up her body, slowly. Jodie could go nowhere captured so securely in his embrace and by the cuffs. Since Jodie was still dressed in the pyjamas, he leaned over and reached into the pocket of his leather jacket for a Swiss army knife and brought out the blade.

'You're a good boy scout at heart, aren't you?'

'I don't know about good.' He sliced through the sheer pyjama top, and spread it open, then made his way to the slim grey pants. He could have simply pulled them down, but that wasn't what the mood called for. Eyes on his work, he destroyed the pyjamas with a single slip of the blade, opening the fabric with one long slice. Jodie trembled as she lay in the remnants of her fancy pjs. Now, she had on only a pair of turquoise blue satin panties trimmed with lace the colour of a robin's egg. These were panties she'd stolen in Europe, but Nick didn't spare them either. They held no sentimentality for him. Slipping the edge of the knife under the waistband, he cut through the delicate material.

Once again, Jodie was entirely naked, surrounded by the colourful fabric scraps, all that remained of her expensive outfit. Nick moved between her legs and began to lick at her pussy. He thrust his tongue between them, tasting her, sweetly at first. Tenderly. Jodie groaned softly and lifted her hips upwards. She was held firmly by the cuffs, but she had a full range of motion and was able to wrap her athletic legs around Nick and gain the contact she craved from his mouth. There was a sexy urgency in her actions. A pulse that beat from her to him.

Nick didn't mind her helping him. The energy from her body, the excitement that she obviously felt, fuelled his own passion. He used his lips to ring her clit and sucked hard. He made his tongue into a point and tapped it lightly where she would feel it the most. Then he moved away and looked up her body.

'So it's true what they say about thieves?'

'What's that?' she asked, her ever-changing eyes already glazed with pleasure as she stared down at him. Her cheeks had grown flushed and her hair tousled by the way she moved on the bed. Nick believed that she'd never looked so lovely before.

'That deep down they want to be caught.'

'I can't speak for all thieves,' she said, and there was a dark note of humour reverberating in her voice.

'But you can speak for yourself. All this time, that's what you wanted, right? That's why you hired me. Why you had Liz at the museum put me on the case. You wanted to be caught.' His voice was husky. Barely even a whisper. 'Right, Jodie?' He had to hear her say it.

'Only by you, Nick,' she sighed, arching upwards again. 'Only by you.'

As she moved in Nick's embrace, the ring on Jodie's finger caught the light. When she turned her head, she saw the pure red fire there, gleaming in the inky blackness.